Alice IN WONDERLAND HIGH

Alice in Wonderland High

RACHEL SHANE

MeritPress | fw

Published by
Merit Press
an imprint of F+W Media, Inc.
10151 Carver Road, Suite 200
Blue Ash, OH 45242. U.S.A.
www.meritpressbooks.com

ISBN 10: 1-4405-8466-4
ISBN 13: 978-1-4405-8466-4
eISBN 10: 1-4405-8467-2
eISBN 13: 978-1-4405-8467-1

Printed in the United States of America.

10 9 8 7 6 5 4 3 2 1

Library of Congress Cataloging-in-Publication Data

Shane, Rachel.
Alice in Wonderland High / Rachel Shane.
pages cm
ISBN 978-1-4405-8466-4 (hc) -- ISBN 1-4405-8466-4 (hc) -- ISBN 978-1-4405-8467-1 (ebook) -- ISBN 1-4405-8467-2 (ebook)
[1. Environmental protection--Fiction. 2. Orphans--Fiction. 3. High schools--Fiction. 4. Schools--Fiction.] I. Title.
PZ7.1.S48Al 2015
[Fic]--dc23
2014039500

This is a work of fiction. Names, characters, corporations, institutions, organizations, events, or locales in this novel are either the product of the author's imagination or, if real, used fictitiously. The resemblance of any character to actual persons (living or dead) is entirely coincidental.

Many of the designations used by manufacturers and sellers to distinguish their products are claimed as trademarks. Where those designations appear in this book and F+W Media, Inc. was aware of a trademark claim, the designations have been printed with initial capital letters.

Cover design by Frank Rivera.
Cover images © iStockphoto.com/digimann/YangYin.

This book is available at quantity discounts for bulk purchases.
For information, please call 1-800-289-0963.

Dedication

To Denise,

For being my first critique partner and for still being the first person I send my drafts to today.

Acknowledgments

Lewis Carroll wrote in *Alice's Adventures in Wonderland*, "Begin at the beginning . . . and go on till you come to the end: then stop." This is excellent advice not only when it comes to writing a novel but also when it comes to writing acknowledgments.

This book's journey started with my parents, Steve and Nina, without whom this book—and I!—would not exist. Thank you for believing in me, supporting me, and encouraging me to follow my dreams. You always pushed me to be the best person I could be, and for that I'm grateful. Thanks also to my sister, Becca, for cheering me on and for always answering my boring contract questions.

Thanks to my wonderful husband, Josh, who has been there every step of the way and inspired me the whole time. You helped me grow my passion by sitting through many young adult television shows and movies with me. I knew you were "the one" when you agreed to attend the midnight release party for the final book in my favorite YA series.

Preemptive thanks to my daughter, Quinn, for not getting mad when you realize I named you after the villain in my book.

Thanks to JoAnne and Richard Preiser, for your unending support. I'm so glad I married into a family with similar literary appreciation and aspirations! And thanks to Dan Preiser, for taking my perfect author photo.

Thanks to Erika, Crista, Chelsey, Amanda, Nikki, and Jeremy, for always being there for me. To all my creative writing professors at Syracuse University, for giving me the tools I needed to create. To my NBC writing group, who helped me wield those tools. To the Fearless Fifteeners, for sharing this journey with me.

Thanks to everyone who read early versions of this manuscript. Melissa Landers, for your critical eye for details and for helping me grow Alice herself (as a character, not via a magic mushroom). Heather Strickland, for your in-depth overall notes. Michelle Hodkin, for pointing out that my perfect first sentence was originally buried somewhere in the middle of Chapter 1. Janet Gurtler, for your awesome suggestions on the first few chapters. Jennifer Hoffine, for your thoughtful critique. Angela Ackerman and Pendred Noyce, for giving me amazing line edits. Sarah LaPolla, for your excellent editorial suggestions. Jessica Love, for holding me accountable with check-in emails. Rachel Simon, for keeping me afloat and for helping me write these acknowledgments. Everyone else at CritiqueCircle.com who read chapters and offered me valuable feedback. And thanks to everyone who supported me along the way, from Twitter to message boards to attending NYC YA book events with me.

Thanks to my critique partners, Denise Jaden, Chandler Baker, and Jen Hayley. Denise, you had the unfortunate privilege of reading all the wrong versions I wrote of *Alice* and helping me find the direction for this right one. Whitney owes her riddles to you. Chandler, our brainstorming sessions make my books stronger and with fewer plot mistakes, plus our daily Gchats fuel me to keep going. Jen, I wrote a large portion of this book while sitting across from you, and now even though you're across an ocean, I still feel like you're with me every step of the way.

Thanks to the entire Merit Press and F+W Media team for putting all their hard work into every aspect of this book. Special thanks to Meredith O'Hayre and MT Cozzola for all their managing editing and copy editing magical powers. Thanks to Frank Rivera for the gorgeous cover.

Thanks to my agent, Jim McCarthy, for swooping in and being a total ninja rock star. I'm so glad to have you in my corner.

Thanks to my amazing editor, Jacquelyn Mitchard, for loving this book as much as I loved writing it and for making my dreams come true. Your editorial insights made the pages sparkle and gave clarity to Alice's nonsensical world.

CHAPTER 1

If there was one thing I'd learned so far in high school, it was this: good girls are just bad girls who don't get caught. I'd avoided detection for almost three years, perfecting my goody-two-shoes image so my classmates—and the law—would forget all about my unconventional hobby, a social killer best kept hidden, like an STD.

And maybe if I'd kept up the façade I wouldn't be faced with words that never used to be in my vocabulary: *expulsion*, *ecotage*, *vigilante*. *Prison*.

But the thing is, if I had to do it all over again? I wouldn't change a thing. (Okay, maybe I'd skip the part where I accidentally wore see-through pajamas in front a boy who was not my boyfriend.) What was a little blemish on my high-school transcript when it might save people? Save my friends? I had to keep reminding myself of that as I waited for the verdict on all my crimes. Or as I liked to refer to them, my missions.

On the day of the first mission, I crouched in the empty school hallway right outside the teachers' lounge, wishing my bones were made of titanium steel to give me a little more reinforcement in the courage department.

"I still can't believe you talked me into this, Alice," my best friend Dinah Tenniel said. She was talking to me but looking at Dru Tweedle, my other . . . friend. The extracurricular activities had let out early and the teachers were all in a "meeting" in the gym, leaving the school open and vulnerable. Rumors had been flying that the meeting was actually a staff party, complete with an open bar and a hypnotist. If only we could hypnotize the teachers permanently.

"And I can't believe, after all my begging, all it took was a promise to be the school mascot with you." I pressed my ear to the door of the lounge and listened for any sounds coming from within. To get them to *finally* agree to help me take action, I hadn't just promised to wear the itchy uniform; I'd sworn to be the tail end. It was a two-part stallion costume, and someone had to be the butt of the joke, so to speak. It was Di's brilliant plan to get close to the football team and have an excuse to talk to them. But hey, wasn't that what friends were for? Having a companion for the embarrassing things. If anyone caught me breaking into the teachers' lounge, stealing the school's supply of letterhead, and donating it to the recycle center alone, my reputation would be as endangered as the rainforests.

"All your other mission suggestions were lame. But this one?" Dru nodded at the teachers' lounge, her rope-colored hair swinging with the movement. "It might even get the attention of—" She met my eyes and snapped her mouth shut. "No one."

"That's right, because no one can know it's us," I said. "Think unsolved mystery." I tried to ignore the ache in my chest at the brief exchange that flitted between Di and Dru. Ever since Di had brought Dru into our duo over the summer, I seemed to be more on the *side* of the in*side* jokes. They'd even started dressing the same, both currently decked out in unfortunate white pants and even more unfortunate hot-pink shirts. I was of the belief that if your school didn't require a uniform, you didn't create one yourself. Hence my nonconformist jeans and white T-shirt.

I pushed myself into a standing position and faced a row of red lockers opposite the door. "I don't hear any noises. I think it's safe."

That would be your cue to open the door, I coached myself even though my arms dangled at my sides like useless pendulums.

"'I think it's safe,'" Dru mocked in a high-pitched voice, complete with a giggle. "That sounds like a line a boy says when he doesn't have a condom." She made no effort to open the door. Di echoed the giggle only a beat too late.

"I'll check it out first." My voice came out steady even though my fingers shook as they wrapped around the cold metal of the doorknob. I stuck out my chest in hopes it might fool my brain into thinking I was brave. As soon as the door opened, the sound of another door slamming made me let out a tiny yelp and stumble inside the room. The girls screamed and pushed the door shut behind me, sealing me inside the lounge alone. My pulse segued from lazy to marathon. I squeezed my eyes closed, waiting to get caught.

When a year of silence passed by, or at least what felt like one, I crept forward. My sneakers squeaked in a desperate attempt to announce my presence. Traitors. Aside from being packed with paper, the room was otherwise empty. Awesome. My imagination went straight from playing by the rules to hearing things. Or maybe the sound had come from the door on the opposite side of the room. Since no one stood in front of the coffee maker ready to bust me, a teacher had probably left the door ajar and the wind from the open window had blown it shut.

I repeated a new mantra in my head: *paranoia is for wimps and potheads.*

I strode back to the door and poked my head outside. The girls huddled in a corner, whispering, and I let out a relieved breath that they hadn't abandoned me completely. "Come on," I waved them forward. "Coast's clear."

I headed to the copy machines along the far wall, next to the phantom-like door. A metal shelf leaned beside them, where about twenty cases of letterhead-paper reams sat like pirate's treasure waiting to be conquered.

Dru rolled her eyes at the cases of paper. "I know what you're thinking, but there's no way we can carry those out." She shook her head. "No how."

Di nodded. "If it was possible, I'd totally help. But it isn't. Otherwise it would already be done. That's logic."

Nonsensical logic. "There's three of us. We can each take a few reams." I injected my voice with a heavy dose of cheerleader pep. Quite a stretch, because perkiness didn't exactly come naturally to me, not when there was so much to be pessimistic about. "Here, get the other end." I slid a case halfway off the shelf.

"I'm not carrying anything." Dru plopped onto one of the round, gray tables in the center of the room.

Di glanced at her, then at me, before dropping into a seat at the table. "Contrariwise, I can probably only lug one of those. I thought you had a plan?"

"Love that word," Dru said. She'd been encouraging Di's obsessive usage of *contrariwise* after they discovered it in English class. I didn't get what was so hilarious about it. "And anyway, Di's right. This is dumb. Recycling all that paper?" Dru lounged on the table like she was on a throne, talking down at her royal subjects. "Let's each grab a ream and use it to exchange notes during class."

Di's face lit up. "Yeah, it'll be like an inside joke."

Oh great. Another one. "Guys, please," I pleaded in a small voice. "I really want to do this. The school's wasting paper by ordering such fancy letterhead instead of buying recycled." I knew my friends were only helping for the thrill of pulling a prank on the school. Teenage rebellion and whatnot. And since sewing a spandex superhero uniform and crusading all night to save innocent trees only worked in comic books, I'd take any help I could get. Especially when I knew my friends were my only hope.

The thought of failing again made my throat tighten. The petition I'd created freshman year to get a farmers' market started had received more snickers than signatures. And my classmates had never forgotten the time my parents got arrested after chaining themselves to a tree in front of the school—wearing only Adam-and-Eve-inspired leaves—and chanting, "Protect Alice, protect all of us," when all they really meant to do was prevent the school's expansion into the forest. Even today, some people still watched me as if waiting for me to strip down to foliage and prove craziness was hereditary. My parents had left behind a legacy of unfinished missions when they died, and if I didn't complete them, no one would. I'd disappointed them so much in their lives; I couldn't do it after their deaths, too.

"Please. This is important to me." My voice cracked. "It may not change anything, but it could get the administrators thinking."

"About how awesome we are." Dru studied her sparkly-pink nail polish.

" 'Bout time they knew," Di added.

"So you're still in?" I jumped up and down in excitement, though I wasn't sure why they'd suddenly had a change of heart. "We'll find something to make it easier to carry this out. Like a rolling chair or something." My eyes roamed over the kitchen area, messy with exploding-lunch residue. Unless we planned to shred twenty cases of paper with the paper cutter, we had to find another way to smuggle them out of the room. I backed up to lean against the wall when something hard stuck into my spine. I turned around to find the other door. "Let me check in here."

As soon as I entered the room, I exhaled sharply. A teacher stood in front of a large, metal shelf, slipping some colored markers into her messenger bag. She snapped her head toward me and the ends of the white scarf that was tied around her head flopped over like bunny ears. Her icy-blue eyes pierced mine just before her lips curled into a smirk, and I realized she wasn't a teacher at all but a fellow classmate. Whitney Lapin, the girl who was never prepared for class was . . . making a grand attempt at change? Perhaps *attempt* wasn't the right word to follow *grand*; more like *larceny*.

"I, uh—" I bit my lip and backed up a step. The amount of sweat that had pooled in my armpits made my white T-shirt illegal according to the school's banned clothing list.

Whitney waved her palm in the air in a *whatever* gesture. She hopped behind the shelf she was perusing and rolled a TV cart from behind it. "I believe this is what you're looking for."

I blinked at her.

"I assume your silence means your lips are sealed about this." She pointed from herself to me.

I coughed to free my wimpy voice. "What are you doing? In here."

"Waiting for you."

I tilted my head, confused.

"To leave," she added after a moment.

"Why?" I strode forward and grabbed the cart.

"Seems sneaking into the teachers' lounge is trending right now."

That second door slam I'd heard. It was Whitney rushing in here to hide. I glanced back at the closed door. "I'll distract them so you can slip out."

"Don't waste time. I can take care of myself." She slid a few graphing calculators into her bag. "Besides, I'm kind of curious to see if you can pull this off."

"That makes two of us." A frantic aching began in my chest, and even though it probably indicated my fear of failure, I straightened with the realization that maybe it was a desperate need for success. I wanted to prove to Whitney, to myself, that I could do this. With my posture a little bit straighter, I inched the cart toward the door. "Thanks, by the way."

She waited until I was almost out the door before she whispered, "Everything's got a moral, if only you can find it."

What the . . .

Back in the main room, the girls stopped chatting when I dragged the cart through the door. They looked up with wide eyes, like they'd just been caught in the act. What act, I didn't know.

I pasted a smile on my face even though gravity tried to weigh down my lips.

"Oh, good call on the cart." Di hopped off her chair, then caught herself and twisted back to Dru. "I mean, if we were going to go through with it and all."

Dru let out a big sigh. "Might as well. But this prank better go viral."

We learned pretty quickly that the cases wouldn't fit within the metal frame of the narrow TV cart. Each tick of the clock increased the tempo of my heart. The meeting a.k.a. teachers-behaving-badly fest wouldn't last much longer. Dru ripped open the cases with a pair of scissors while Di and I stacked the reams of paper in a Jenga-formation on the cart. Each time the wheels rolled forward, the reams jiggled.

When we finished the third case, the cart was only halfway full, but we couldn't risk getting caught. I stood up and clutched one side of the metal frame. "Di, help me push. Dru, get the door."

She moved in slow motion to the door, but at least she obeyed. A rare feat for her. She must have been getting sick.

Despite a rough time keeping the wheels straight, we cleared the doorway on the second try. I'd never even set that kind of stat in gym class. We made it all the way through the short hallway leading from the teachers' lounge when I heard soft footsteps coming from behind. Whitney escaping.

Dru stood in front of us, directing our path like an air-traffic controller. She'd see Whitney any second. Before I could think of a better plan, I shoved the cart forward, desperate to clear the turn coming up so Whitney could escape sight unseen. Because, the thing was, I trusted myself to keep my mouth shut. But my friends? They traded gossip like a hot commodity.

"You're going too fast!" Di shouted just as the cart broke free of our grasp, gaining speed. Too much speed, in fact. I'd only meant to get us closer to the corner, but the cart was sailing straight toward Dru and the opposite wall. There had always been a rumor that the hallways were slanted, but I'd figured it was something the seniors told freshmen to screw with them. Guess uneven teaching wasn't the only thing the school had a problem with.

Dru hopped out of the way just in time for the cart to crash into the opposite wall. Reams flew off the stack and smacked the floor. As if the first crash hadn't been loud enough to alert 911. I spun around to check for Whitney but didn't see her. I let out a relieved sigh. At least I'd done something good. Helped the girl who had mysteriously helped me.

"You pushed it right at me, Alice!" Dru jutted out her lower lip.

"I lost control." I knelt down and scooped up a ream of paper, avoiding her eyes.

"No how. Like I'm supposed to believe that. I have eyes, you know." For extra emphasis, she pointed to them, as if I didn't have them as well. Thank you, Captain Obvious.

"Stop arguing, okay? Someone might hear." Di darted her eyes around the hallway. Faint music thumped from the gym in the next hallway over, where the teachers were probably shaking their booties.

"We need to get this cleaned up." I set the ream of paper on top of what was left of the stack and grabbed another.

The music and a few whooping cheers blasted for a moment, then faded abruptly with the sound of a door slam. Heels clicked along the linoleum, growing louder as they approached our location.

"Go!" I whisper-yelled. "I'll distract them."

The girls didn't hesitate. They broke into a sprint and ducked back down the hallway we'd just escaped from. Principal Dodgson turned the corner, arms already crossed in anticipation.

Gulp.

"Alice?" Her brow knitted. She was probably wondering why someone as blemish-free as me when it came to trouble was kneeling in front of my botched robbery.

"I can explain." My lips wanted to buckle, but I forced a rubber-band smile onto them. A halo to reinforce my innocence. "Just getting in some extra credit, Principal Dodgson."

She pursed her lips. "Why don't we take this to my office? I find students are more . . . cooperative in there."

Cooperative, as defined by the high-school dictionary: *intimidated, compliant, and fucked.*

CHAPTER 2

Inside Principal Dodgson's office, I focused on my lap, hiding my curled fists at my sides, while she popped two Advil and chugged an entire reservoir of water. The longer she stalled, the more time my friends had to escape—and I had to come up with a get-out-of-jail-free excuse.

"I really do have to get back to the, uh, meeting." As if on cue she hiccupped, a contrast from her sleek, brown hair that was pulled back from her scalp so tight, not a single strand escaped. Sometimes I wondered if she'd surgically turned her hair into Ken-doll plastic in order to appear collected at all times.

"I want to start an eco club." I clasped my hands on the table and widened my eyes in the fake-innocent expression I'd perfected on my parents before . . . well, before their car crash turned me into an orphan. "You were in a meeting so I thought it would be okay if I took some paper to create flyers with."

I held my breath as she studied me with her bloodshot eyes. Sweat formed on the back of my neck. Note to self: criminal activities required full-body deodorant or at least a perfume shower.

"Alice, you're. A good. Student." Her words had awkward pauses in the wrong places. "But an eco club?" The giggle that escaped from her mouth didn't do anything to calm my nerves. Neither did the fact that she dropped her water glass en route to her mouth and it splattered all over her papers. She sat up straighter, peeling the papers off her desk and then acting like nothing unusual had happened. She cleared her throat and spoke her next words slowly, clearly trying to make them sound as normal as possible. "You never came to me about starting one, and frankly," she said, looking constipated as she tried to suppress a hiccup that broke free anyway, "I don't know why you would after all the bad press the energy shortage has gotten in Wonderland lately."

"I know that." I decided to play her way. If I didn't see anything unusual, maybe neither did she. "That's why I was afraid to ask without reinforcements—like the flyers," I added because while most towns embraced and even encouraged "Going Green," Wonderland, Illinois, was more in favor of everyone "Going Black." As in, blackout. The township had deemed the closing of the nuclear-power plant the fault of environmental activists—including my parents—and since we were all feeling the effects of limited electricity, most citizens were very vocal against practically anything with the word *green*. All the more reason I had to fix this.

She hiccupped again, and a lopsided smile slid over her face. "Tell you what. You never gave me problems before. You clean up the mess right now and pick up trash on school grounds the rest of the week after class, and I'll let this be a warning."

I nodded eagerly. A good-girl reputation was like the kiss of death in social circles, but with administrators? Backstage pass.

Or it would have been, if the mess had still been there to clean up. When we got back to the crime scene, all that remained was the TV cart, guts removed, TV still perched on top. Someone either had a warped idea of what would be valuable on the black market or a sick sense of humor. Instead of the paper reams on the ground, chalk outlined where they used to be like a dead body at a crime scene.

Did Di and Dru carry this out for me on their own? It didn't seem like them, but the thought made my heart swell. And if they didn't, then why would someone stage the missing paper in such a showy display?

The answer came very clearly the next morning, as soon as I entered school. A large crowd was gathered around a set of lockers. Unless a cute boy was stripping for test answers, it didn't seem worth it to hop up and down, trying to see over people's shoulders. The curse of being less than five feet tall. Whispers were flying in a jumble of clipped phrases, nothing standing out to give me a clue.

I turned back the way I had come and decided to try for another hallway. Principal Dodgson ran past me, yelling into her walkie-talkie. "Analyze the handwriting! I don't care if this isn't *CSI*. It's our best lead." She stopped short when she saw me and dangled the walkie at her side, where it screeched with static. "Quick, tell me." She pointed at me. "Did you have an accomplice?"

"What?" I glanced around for some clue as to what she was talking about. Truthfully, I'd been banking on her being too drunk to even remember our chat.

"The paper. Did anyone help you take it?"

"N—" The word tried to fly out of my lips in a desperate rush, but I caught myself and stared directly into her eyes, slowing my breathing so my voice came out steady. "No. Why?"

She tilted her head at me. "You don't know why?" She pursed her lips at whatever she saw in my face. "Well, I know it wasn't you, and whoever it was won't be at this school much longer."

My throat went dry. What had Di and Dru done?

Principal Dodgson waved me away just as the warning bell rang. I hiked my backpack farther up my shoulders. The hallways were so thick with students lining the walls, I could barely get through the crowd. I elbowed and pushed, using mosh-pit techniques to clear a path to my English classroom.

When I walked through the door, I stopped short, eyes wide. Every desk in the room had been decoupaged with white paper watermarked with the school seal; not a single surface of faux wood remained visible. A patchwork of shellacked white-and-black letterhead text covered every blue chair down to the floor. Even the items normally on the teacher's desk now rested upon a thick coating of stolen paper. The room was blinding white, like a winter morning, only without school being canceled.

"I heard it was a prank against homework handouts," Dru was saying to Quinn Hart, president of every club she could squeeze into her schedule. "Pretty brilliant, if you ask me."

"Or me," Di added.

Quinn flicked her long, red curls out of her face. "Do you know who did it?"

"Di, do we have any idea?" Dru asked.

"I might have some clue." Di stuck her nose in the air and smiled.

I marched over to the powwow. "Quinn, can you give us a sec?"

"It's cool. I've got some gossip to spread!" Quinn rushed off toward some girls a few desks away.

As soon as she was out of earshot, Dru grabbed my arm and tugged me into the corner of the room. Di followed, naturally. "You can thank me later," Dru said.

"Yeah, we saved your butt. I can't believe what you wrote on the desks!"

"What are you talking about?" I tried to peer over her shoulder at the nearest desk, but the whole not-being-tall-enough-to-ride-roller-coasters-at-the-amusement-park thing kind of prohibited that.

"Don't play dumb, Alice." Dru brushed her fingers through her straight hair. "You should have heard what kids were saying before we got involved."

"Contrariwise." Di leaned in and lowered her voice. "If they think it's a prank against homework, maybe this will actually make you legendary and not the laughingstock of school."

"I didn't do this."

"Then who did?" they said in unison. Awesome. Now they weren't just tag-teaming me; they were becoming a backing chorus.

"Who else would care enough about environmentalism to do this?" Di raised her eyebrows at me.

"Who was coached by her parents for years?" Dru took the next line in the verse.

"Who begged her friends nonstop until they got so annoyed they gave in?" Di's voice cracked. "We could have gotten expelled for what we did yesterday!"

Their words dug into my gut and twisted with the point of a knife. "Di, I—" My lower lip trembled. I swallowed. "And Dru. I'm really sorry that I almost got you in trouble, but I didn't tell on you guys." I grabbed Dru's arm since she seemed to be the one I needed to get approval from, and when her eyes widened, I snapped my hand away. I tried to keep the hysteria out of my voice. "Please. You know this means so much more to me than being coached by my parents."

"Alice . . . " Di picked a piece of lint off Dru's shirt. "I've heard it all before. And frankly, I don't agree with you."

"We only agree on this: the Going-Green crap is a bad idea." Dru crossed her arms.

"If you want to finish what your parents started, you can do it without me." Di took a step away from me.

"Or me," Dru added, though that went without saying.

As the girls plopped down into their white thrones, the bell rang.

A lump swelled in my throat. I pulled out the chair gently, as if making even the slightest sound would set me off. The white paper felt scratchy beneath my elbows. My eyes shifted to read the message scrawled in black permanent marker on my desk.

How's this for waste?

"I need everyone to take their seats." Mr. Hargreaves, our teacher, clapped his hands to stop the jabbering. "School will continue as normal. And just think! If you forgot your notebook today, you'll have plenty of paper to take notes with." He snickered at himself. He was fresh out of college and still had that new-car smell.

A loud sound by the window made my classmates suddenly twist their heads. Cashing in my mob-mentality card, I joined them. My mouth dropped as Whitney Lapin shimmied through the window and into the classroom, knee-high boots first.

I was Going Green with envy. This girl had exactly what I needed: guts to be a bad girl where it counted. In public.

Whitney squatted on the radiator. Her long hair fell down her back in curly crinkles, and the fluorescent lights made it look bleached clean of any color. She wore a pleated miniskirt and a black hoodie, as if she couldn't decide between grungy, trendy, or slutty, though the brief glimpse of her hot-pink underwear skewed the scale toward the latter. The pocket watch dangling from her neck swung in time with the swivel of her hips as she spun to face the class.

Mr. Hargreaves's black Chuck Taylors squeaked as he headed toward her. "Was there something wrong with the doorway, Whitney? Should I call maintenance?" He chuckled, then caught himself and cleared his throat.

"You told me if I walked through the door late one more time, you'd give me detention." Whitney wiped her palms together. "So I didn't use the door."

"You're wearing a watch, and yet you're still late." He shook his head, smile still plastered on his face.

"Some mysteries just can't be explained." She hopped to the floor. "Like the new décor, I'm guessing?" She met my eyes and gave me a little smirk. Suddenly, it all clicked into place. She'd stolen the paper and decoupaged the entire school to get her message across. The girl best known for cutting class and shunning extracurricular activities spent her spare time . . . doing environmental activism?

The other students laughed while Di tapped her pen against her notebook and Dru perfected her scowl. Whitney studied her pocket watch, as enraptured with it as I was with her chutzpah.

"Hang on." Mr. Hargreaves held up a palm to Whitney when she took a step toward her desk. "You'll get mud on—"

"You won't find any mud out there." Whitney dropped into the only open seat left. Directly behind me.

I glanced out the window at the faded, brown grass and barren dirt trench from the dried-up creek outlining it. Not exactly picturesque. I imagined the jerky motion of a time lapse–photography sequence capturing rosebuds popping out of the earth, like zombies breaking free of their graves.

"That may be true," Mr. Hargreaves said. "But next time I'm going to lock the windows."

I spun in my seat, wincing at my creaky chair. I'd been used to rebelling in silence. "I have a crowbar I can lend you," I whispered so only Whitney could hear.

She hesitated a moment, studying me. The corners of her lips turned up in an almost-smile. "Don't worry, time is the easiest thing to steal."

What the hell? When I turned back around, Di was staring at me with squinty eyes. Add superhearing to her list of talents that were a total waste for saving Planet Earth but excellent for spreading gossip. At least Dru seemed preoccupied with a note she was writing.

"What was that?" Di asked, eyes darting between my desk and Whitney's.

"Is something wrong, Dinah?" our teacher asked. Dru's head snapped up. Some people had selective hearing for their own name, but it seemed Di and Dru had radar set up for the other's name as well.

"Yeah, uh . . . " Di's face turned a shade closer to the white scarves every other girl seemed to don lately. "I don't understand why it's okay for her to climb through windows."

"That's not fair to the rest of us who actually come in on time," Dru finished. "No how." She twirled in her seat to meet Quinn's eyes.

Di, however, stared at me, probably waiting for my support. I sank lower in my seat and activated my invisibility shield, hoping Whitney wouldn't remember I used to be a tattletale like my friends.

"I have to agree with Whitney on this one," Mr. Hargreaves said. "She found a creative solution to her predicament."

Creative solution. My idea for recycling was predictable and therefore forgettable. No one could ignore what Whitney had done.

She shot Di a triumphant smile, and I felt caught in an imaginary game of tug-o-war: Di and Dru each clutching one of my hands while Whitney yanked on my feet. Through the rest of class, Di and Dru took notes, becoming student robots instead of the kind of student Mr. Hargreaves wanted. I defied expectations by plotting something more important than how to get an A on next week's test. When the bell rang, instead of waiting for my friends like normal, I headed Whitney off at the door.

That thing holding me upright was my spine.

"What?" She tried to move around me.

"I was wondering—" I stopped talking when she lifted her watch to her face. Only soon as I did, she spun on her heels. "Wait! Did you—"

"I'm late." She pushed past me and out the door before I could say another word.

Di and Dru swooped in on me. "What happened in there?" Di asked.

"Why were you talking to *her*?" Dru added. We weaved through the crowded hallway, grunting in annoyance at the slow walkers rubbernecking at the white-covered lockers. How had Whitney managed to accomplish this overnight by herself?

"No reason." I shrugged it off as if it meant nothing instead of everything.

CHAPTER 3

After dinner, I headed to the Garden Center, a place I'd avoided since my parents died. It always reminded me too much of them, but today after the decoupaged environmental message, that was what I wanted. I hoped it might strengthen my resolve.

I marched up and down the aisles as conflicting scents of roses and pine warred in my nostrils. I sniffed a couple of flowers in a desperate attempt to forget the B.O. of the kid who'd sat next to me last period.

"You have to be kidding me," a girl's voice yelled.

I spun around, thinking someone from school had seen me here. Only the dateless hung out with plants instead of friends. Whitney Lapin stood at the end of the aisle, huddled with a boy, his back to me. The green strings tied around his waist and looped around his neck resembled those of the aprons the Garden Center employees wore.

I jerked in surprise, knocking a bag of seeds off the shelf with my elbow. It tumbled to the floor with a loud *plop*, and Whitney and Garden Center Boy turned in my direction. Whitney's icy-blue eyes pierced mine. She pushed the boy backward until the shadow of a column hid them both.

I heaved the seed bag off the floor and placed it on the shelf, pretending to be a good little shopper rather than Whitney's super-nosy classmate and inventor of the stalkerLite brand of loser. Once I was sure they'd forgotten about me, I inched down the aisle to where they were hidden. Their movements projected jittery shadow puppets on the wall that grew larger and larger, signaling their approach. I ducked behind a large potted plant until fern fronds camouflaged me. There were some advantages to your body's being candy-sized.

"Whitney, come on. I don't feel right about this," the boy said.

"Oh, but you're fine and dandy with the"—she lowered her voice to subliminal-message volume, and I had to hold my breath to make out the word—"ecotage?"

Ecotage? My parents had often used that word. Sabotage as a means to save the environment.

Bingo. My lips curled into a smile. All along I'd been trying to get my friends to help when I should have been searching for other environ*mental*ists like me out there.

The boy shoved his fingers into his pockets. His dark hair flopped into his eyes, a few tufts curling behind his ears as if he hadn't bothered to get a haircut in a while. "I've already given you—"

"Do you want my help or not?"

"Yeah, but—"

"Okay then." She put her hands on her hips and waited.

He stepped forward, glancing around the store, his brow sweaty. I recognized him, but mostly because the gossip swirling at the beginning of the school year had kept the students buzzing for weeks. Chester Katz. He used to go to district schools but had spent the last three years at a posh boarding school somewhere in the northeast. Rumors about why he got kicked out stretched from the obvious—cheating—to the extravagant: student-teacher affair, drugs, hazing gone wrong, bomb threats. It didn't matter which one was true because they all said the same thing: he was not the kind of guy you'd parade in front of your mother. Or sister/guardian, in my case.

He pulled something out of his pocket and dropped it into Whitney's open palm. A flash of gold glinted in the light. A key.

She closed her fingers around it. “Thanks. But really you should be saying that to me.” Her heels clicked as she sashayed toward the back of the store, the hood of her sweatshirt bouncing.

Chester raked his hands through his hair, then disappeared into the opposite room. I had a choice: follow one of them. My feet and brain were in sync as they carried me in Whitney’s direction. I had to talk to her about what had happened yesterday, and from her quick escape after class I figured it was the kind of conversation that needed to take place away from the peerparazzi at school. When I reached the next room, I squashed myself into the shadow of a tree as she approached a staff door. She looked both ways again before inserting the key and slipping inside. A few moments later, she came back out, zipping her backpack.

What did she take?

And how could I get in on it?

I expected Whitney to head my way and give Chester back his key, but instead she exited through a back door into the night air. I hurried after her in time to see her ducking through a small hole in the forest surrounding the Garden Center.

Curiouser and curiouser. Without another thought, I charged for the same opening between the trees.

Branches scraped against my shoulders. I battled against them, freeing first one arm, then the other. I shimmied through until my butt cleared the hole. Brushing my hands to remove dirt, I bent under the next branch. A few steps later, my toe snagged on something that sent me stumbling. I glanced back to see a hardcover book propped open on the ground, with a cup and saucer lying next to it. Okay, that was weird. Either someone was really embarrassed about his reading habits or I had to add “litter problem” to Wonderland’s growing list of environmental violations.

When I pushed through the next set of maple trees, I paused in a small clearing, surrounded by large oak trees draped with Spanish moss. I tried to stop panting so I could hear Whitney's footsteps. Silence. I sagged, staring down at the scratches along my arms.

A branch snapped and I whipped my head to the left. The footsteps started up again. "Wait!" I yelled, abandoning stealth. A cool breeze blew my hair all over my face as I rushed in the direction of the sound.

I burst through a set of trees and emerged onto a deserted street. A dilapidated building took shape on the opposite side of the road, so old it probably didn't even remember its better days. Whitney crossed the yellow line to walk in front of it. I shivered, realizing we were in the part of town girls like me usually detoured around.

Usually.

A spark of color came into view, standing out among the dreary blackness of night. Exotic flowers spilled over the exterior of an abandoned warehouse. Tiger lilies poked out of the broken windows. A cluster of impatiens covered a backdrop of graffiti. Leafy potted plants guarded the broken doorway, as if a garden had sprung up in the middle of the projects to bring them back to life. Growing in a place where everything else died.

I hung back, my mouth parted in awe. Ecotage?

"Hey, K!" Whitney said, pausing in front of a beat-up truck and knocking on its window. She glanced back in my direction, squinting into the distance. The trees swayed in the background like her backup dancers. A figure covered in mud emerged from the jungle of flowers closer to the warehouse. The person shifted an empty pot from arm to arm.

"Did you get it?" he yelled. He was dressed in head-to-toe black. Naturally. Though unnaturally, he wore a black beanie secured over his raised hoodie. I guess this guy was taking the extra effort to make sure hats—or head coverings in general—came back in style. The shadows concealed his face so I couldn't identify him.

"Change of plans." Whitney threw her backpack at him. "I'm. Late." She enunciated each word. Like it was a secret code.

The guy glanced around. "Anything I need to take care of?" He cracked his knuckles on his free hand. I didn't move a muscle.

"Take care of the sense, and the sounds will take care of themselves."

I swallowed hard. She wanted this mysterious guy to take care of . . . *me?* Great. Somehow I'd evolved from pathetic to psychotic stalker in a single day. Even Rome couldn't beat that. I shifted into the shadows, preparing to run at the slightest hint this guy had the mind to go from ecotaging a rundown building to sabotaging something crucial. Like my ability to breathe.

Whitney spun on her heels and pushed through a set of willow trees, disappearing around the back of the building. The guy dropped the potted plant and strode in my direction, eyes searching along the perimeter. If I ran now, no doubt he'd see me and catch me before I could make it ten feet. I crouched low to the ground and backed up at a tortoise pace that would earn me a victory against a hare. An empty jar of orange marmalade rested at my feet, so I gripped it in my shaking hands, brandishing it like a weapon. Too bad people never discarded working stun guns.

He stepped closer, only a few feet away now. His eyes roamed to the spot right above where I crouched. My beating heart—usually such a good idea when its only purpose was to keep me alive—now seemed like a hazard, as though it had switched allegiances, making every effort to get me caught as it thundered in my chest.

I braced myself, deciding the best I could do was aim for his sacred boy parts with my new weapon. Hopefully my track record of throwing like a girl ended today.

Before his eyes dropped to my position, a low, humming vibration startled us both. The guy lifted a cell phone out of his pocket and flipped it open. "Crap," he muttered as he pressed it to his ear. "What? I don't have time for . . . " He listened for a moment. "Hold on, you're cutting out." He turned his back to me and headed toward the warehouse at a fast clip. Breath seeped from my mouth. I set the marmalade jar back on the ground.

The guy stood on the front steps of the warehouse, one finger jammed into his open ear. I didn't know how long his conversation would last before he returned. I knew the smart thing to do: go back in the direction I'd come from and return my death wish to the genie. I generally gave myself good advice—though I rarely followed it. Now I felt stupid. Whitney was scared of me—*me!*—and I didn't want her to think I was a threat. I had to put a stop to that nonsense and explain. Before the guy could finish his phone call, I darted across the road toward the tree line. The trees rattled when I brushed past them.

"Who's there?" the guy called behind me.

I kept going, wiping the sweat from my face. I steadied my sprint, following a trail of footsteps through another dense copse of trees. The woods spilled out onto a chipper street with perky houses lining the road. I paused, my heart still raving to its own techno beat. Out of the corner of my eye, I spotted Whitney sauntering up a driveway into the only house that broke from the cookie-cutter model, to put it mildly. Her house was decorated in swirls of tie-dyed paint, as if someone had turned the exterior into a canvas because he ran out of easels. Ceramic bunnies lined the lawn in descending-size order.

Weird. At least her house matched her personality.

I crossed the street as Whitney swung open her front door, revealing another entryway and another door, this one painted yellow. She stepped inside and unearthed a second key from her bag. When she unlocked that one, she stepped into the next entryway and started opening a blue door. Maybe I'd ingested too many pesticide fumes at the Garden Center, because this couldn't be normal. She certainly had a thing for grand entrances. She fiddled around for the next key and repeated the process through two more doors before finally entering her house. She didn't bother to close any of them, which I took, rather liberally, as an invitation.

I strolled to the front door and peered down the long tunnel of entrances. When I tried to step through the first, it slammed in my face. Even opportunity wouldn't let me knock.

Turning back around, my knee bumped into a small, three-legged table made of solid glass, stationed on her front porch. Raindrop remnants dotted its surface. A small, golden key, much like the one Chester had handed over in the Garden Center, rested on top of it. Smiling, I snatched it up and tried it in the first door. Locked.

I jumped down a step at the sound of a car speeding along the street. Had the guy from the warehouse followed me here? I darted behind the largest rabbit statue. Good thing, because an evergreen car wobbled into Whitney's driveway. Rock music blasted from the open windows. I crouched as low as possible and tried to balance. I'd have aching thigh muscles tomorrow, but maybe shapely legs would give me an excuse to go for the superhero spandex.

The driver got out of the car and kicked the door shut with his foot, then doubled back to lock it with a key. Chester Katz. He'd shed his green apron and wore a black-and-white-striped sweater that looked like some kind of weird homage to The Hamburglar. At least it wasn't the guy from the abandoned warehouse.

I expected him to go straight to the front door, but he disappeared around the corner of the house.

Something was definitely going on here. I sprang from my hiding place and followed him. I was getting really good at spying. Not that that was a skill I could put on my college applications.

A door slammed somewhere around the corner. I amped my pace, then came to a halt at the place I would have expected a back entrance to be. Instead, a small, red curtain billowed in the wind by my feet. Chester was nowhere to be seen. I pushed aside the curtain and uncovered a small door about the size of a notebook wedged into the side of the house.

"These people are totally weird," I muttered, thinking about the rabbits, the ecotage, the doors, and now this tiny, red door. I inserted the golden key. It fit perfectly. "Curiouser and curiouser." Well, a door that size was one way to keep out intruders and stalkers. Like me. I was petite but—thankfully—not doll-size. And neither was Chester—where had he disappeared?

I pressed my eye to the tiny peephole. Flowers bloomed in every variety and color, as if Whitney took sole responsibility for protecting the nation's rainforests. It wasn't a basement; it was a greenhouse.

"It's not pot," a deep voice beside me said. Chester slipped outside through a door in the aluminum siding that hadn't existed a moment ago.

I jumped so hard I knocked my head into the wall, causing me to fall butt-first onto the ground. At least hitting my head might explain everything I'd witnessed tonight. Rubbing the spot with my palm, I looked up to see a tower of boy blocking the moon. He carried a clay mug of green liquid. Foam and smoke billowed out of it, reminding me of mad-scientist experiments in movies. A bump was already popping out of my forehead. If I could move the swelling from my face to my chest, I'd really be on to something.

"I—I didn't think—" I rose until I was eye-level with his ribcage.

"You didn't think of a good excuse for your spying?" Chester shut the door behind him, sealing it back into the exterior. Now that I knew what to look for, I spotted faint cracks in the aluminum siding outlining the door. No knob, so it must only open from the inside. "Wow, we just met and I'm already finishing your sentences," he said.

I shot him my most angelic smile. "Then what am I going to say next?"

"You're going to ask my name. It's Chess."

I didn't want to acknowledge I knew more about him than he probably did about me. So I stayed vague. "I go to Wonderland High."

"Alice Liddell, right?" His lips curled into the kind of killer smile orthodontists and girls like me could appreciate. "Your picture's on the honor-roll board. Every time I pass by it . . . " His smile faded, and I immediately mourned the loss. "Never mind."

"What?" I waited, wondering if he could see right through me to my secrets, like maybe transparency was a side effect of courage. Aside from a few kids who still remembered my parents' tree-hugging slip-up or my lame petition fiasco, most people at school only knew about me if they cheated off me. Luckily, teenagers and goldfish had about the same memory span. New gossip erased old mistakes daily, the circle of strife.

"Nothing, it's—" He tilted his head to the side and his voice grew more confident with each word. "It's cheesy. I'm embarrassed I even thought it." He stared into his cup, then peered at me from under his eyelashes. "But you can guess if you want."

"Um . . . " Strange. Why would he want me to guess an answer he was embarrassed about? Maybe he was trying to stall me before the police arrived. I took a step backward. I knew I should probably make a quick excuse and flee, but he studied me with such intensity, as though he was holding his breath for my answer. So I gave him one. "Every time you pass by the honor-roll board . . . you remember a test you haven't studied for? You wish you had a marker to draw devil horns on my head?"

"That's a good one. Let's go with that." He grinned.

His grin was contagious. Yesterday, his reputation would have scared me off. But now? I was intrigued.

CHAPTER 4

"Want some?" Chess held out the foaming, green liquid to me as we stood in front of the strange, red curtain hiding the secret garden.

I stood on my tiptoes and peered over the rim. "What is it?"

"It's what we give intruders," he said. "Less abrasive than tying them up."

I bit my lip. I was hoping he would forget I didn't belong here. "Too bad. Being tied up does sound tempting." My brain caught up with my words. "Wait, that came out wrong."

He let out a raspy laugh. "Wrong is one interpretation. But seriously, it's Whitney's specialty." He waved the drink in front of me, some of the foam spilling over his fingertips. "Organic. Has a bit of a bite, though."

"By 'bite' do you mean 'poison'?" After all, I hadn't seen him sip it himself. "Intruders can't break in if they're immobilized."

"Poison? Well, if you're going down, I am, too." Chess tipped it to his mouth and chugged a good portion of it. He wiped the green mustache off his lips. "You could wait and see if I'm going to keel over, or try it yourself."

"Excellent, waiting sounds better than my pre-calc homework. How long does it take to kick in?" I checked my watch in a dramatic show, mostly to stall. I had no desire to ingest his little concoction. I'd learned the hard way about drinking unknown things: they usually disagreed with you sooner or later. A night of puking and embarrassing pictures of me passed out were my souvenirs for that educational experience. Come to think of it, maybe he was trying to get me drunk. The curious part of me didn't think that would be so bad, getting drunk with a cute guy at the house of the object of my platonic affection. Alcohol might cure my cautious brain.

But I'd already used up my embarrassing-moment quota for the day.

He tilted the mug to the side, waving it back and forth. "*Drink me, drink me*," he sang.

"If only I could remember that tagline they taught us to combat peer pressure in middle school."

Chess snapped his fingers. "Oh! I remember that. I think it was, 'Peer pressure, the best way to make new friends besides bribing them.'"

"Something seems off about that quote, but I can't quite put my finger on it."

"You're right. 'Bribing' isn't right. It was 'kidnapping.'" He smiled. "This stuff's good for you, I promise. Totally harmless. I was only offering to be nice." He pulled the mug back and his mouth stretched into a thin line. "I really didn't mean to pressure you."

I grabbed the mug from Chess's hands and brought it to my nose. I didn't want him to think I was lame, not when he might be one of the only people who cared about the same things I did. Well, I doubted he cared about the thing currently occupying my brain: his lips.

A potpourri scent drifted from the mug. The liquid slid down my throat, thick and syrupy. I coughed to get it all down.

"Told ya it had bite."

The drink tasted like opportunity. And also like a mixture of cherry Pop-Tarts, ice cream, pineapple, roast turkey, hot chocolate, and buttered toast. Things that wouldn't normally go together but somehow did.

"You have a warped idea of how to carry out orders, Chess."

I shifted to see Whitney leaning against the side of the house, blowing her hair out of her face with a battery-operated fan. *So she wanted me gone*. I tried to keep the disappointment off my face.

"I was getting to that." He turned to me. "You shouldn't be here." His smile didn't intimidate me like Whitney's icy blue-eyed glare.

"I'm sorry," I said. "I didn't mean to scare you, I—"

"Scare me?" She laughed. "So, what, do you have some sort of girl-crush on me or something? Because just so you know, I'm taken."

I focused on Chess, suddenly understanding, but he gave her a quizzical look. "By who?" he asked.

"Note to self," she said. "Next time, do not make Chess head of security. He sucks."

Chess ducked his head under his elbow and gave me a shy smile.

"What you did at school. With the paper and the message. And the warehouse? I think it's awesome."

"That wasn't me." Whitney crossed her arms.

"You were probably seeing things," Chess added unnecessarily. "We had nothing to do with the school."

We. Well, at least that explained how Whitney had managed to do all that alone in one night. She hadn't done it alone.

"Besides, recycling the paper wouldn't have done anything," Whitney said. "This did."

"I know." I nodded. "I want to help." My eyes decided to go big and puppy-dog-like. Probably not the best facial expression for trying to convince people I wanted to do mischief. I forced my eyelids to close in an intimidating squint. Or at least I hoped it looked like that and not sleep-deprived. "I won't say anything."

"No, you will say something." Chess nodded at me. "Blackmail's the best way to get ahead."

They were being nonsensical.

Whitney strode forward, her white-blonde hair swinging behind her. "I'm not worried. It's blackfail when you don't have proof."

"Your garden," I said in a desperate voice, jutting my chin toward the red curtain. "Why did you leave me the key?"

"I didn't leave it for you."

Oh. As if to confirm, Chess held out his hand. I didn't want to part with it, but I dropped it into his palm, my fingers brushing against his skin for a beat too long. "Why . . . " I blinked to clear the fog in my brain. Boys: the leading cause of temporary amnesia. "Why are you growing something like that if you're not using the plants for . . . ?" I met her eyes. "Ecotage."

She smirked. "Pot . . . tentially I could tell you." On the first syllable, her lips popped. I mouthed the words, trying to sound it out. She sighed and added, "Weedn't want you to find out."

"Marijuana?"

"Or maybe some delicious oregano. An Italian blend. Coveted by restaurants and girls who like their food seasoned."

"Whitney . . . " Chess shook his head at her.

I eyed him. "But Chess said it wasn't . . . " *Was that what was in the drink?* Pot was organic, wasn't it?

Oh God, I better not be high. Wait, that was a paranoid statement. Crap. I darted my eyes back and forth between them.

At the same time, they each pointed to the other. He said, "She's lying," while she said, "He's lying."

"Whitney . . . " Chess hissed. I stumbled backward from the sharpness in his voice. "She's already snooping," he continued.

"It's a test, Chess." She pointed the fan at me. "Since she's so good at them in school. She calls the cops, we have our answer."

Answer to what question?

They exchanged meaningful glances and nodded, then turned to me like I was supposed to whip out my cell and call for backup right there.

"There wasn't . . . marijuana in that drink?" I asked.

Whitney burst out laughing. Chess held up his hands in a police surrender. "Correct me if I'm wrong, but I don't think you're usually supposed to *drink* pot."

I decided to believe them. "What did that message you wrote on the desks mean?"

"That's confidential. Right now, you don't even make the short list." Whitney blew her white-blonde hair out of her eyes. "The riddles were handouts. You want info, you have to earn it—and not by tailing me."

My face flushed.

Whitney checked her watch. "We're. Late." She emphasized the phrase again. "Kingston's waiting. Alice, nice to have you stalking me, but I'm afraid it ends here." She started to walk away.

"Wait," I said. Whitney turned around. "My friends, they don't get it. No one else cares that I have things—missions I need to accomplish. If I don't do it, no one will." My voice cracked. "I can't forgive myself if I fail."

She stepped forward, her electric-blue eyes piercing mine with a look that could turn me to stone. Then her lips curved in the slightest of smiles.

"Damn," she said. "Once the floodgates open, things will grow."

"What does that mean?" I wore desperation like a scarlet letter.

"It means I may have some openings. If you know how to open them." Whitney spun around and proceeded toward the back of the house.

That didn't really help with the clarity issue. Openings . . . in a group that might or might not be doing things that might or might not be illegal? "Is this a secret society?" I asked, imagining hazing rituals and initiations and a translation book for Whitney's cryptic riddles.

Chess laughed. "Something like that." He glanced back and forth between Whitney and me. "I'll drive Alice home."

The mug in my hands was definitely looking half full.

Whitney stopped in place. "Kingston's going to be pissed. Wait by the car. I'm coming with you guys."

Kingston. They'd mentioned him before. Was he the guy at the warehouse? I should have realized. The beanie hat wasn't as showy as some of his other . . . well, the only real word was costumes, but maybe he was having an off night. Kingston Hatter was another kid with a bad reputation, like Chess. Except, gossip and rumors about him included solid evidence, such as the mug shot that had invaded email inboxes as spam: *Student Arrested! Must Read.* There was also the small fact that Kingston was strange. Stranger than Whitney's house, if that was possible. These were the types of students I expected to be spending their nights driving home drunk from parties, not converting dead warehouses into environmental meccas.

Chess gestured toward his car, as if I could miss it. "Your carriage awaits." He bowed for good measure.

"How long have you worked at the Garden Center?" I ran my finger over the silver metal poking through the evergreen paint.

He snapped his head toward me. "I don't work there."

I squinted at him. "Oh, I spotted you and Whitney there. Before I followed her. You were wearing a Garden Center apron."

"Well, don't spread that around, okay?"

"Why? I think it's great."

He set his brown eyes on me. "It gives off the wrong image."

"So instead you want people to think you're a . . . " There were many words I could finish with based on rumors—badass, candidate for juvie, nonconformist—but now, talking to him, I knew these didn't quite fit. "I'm just curious."

"There's enough gossip about me. I don't need to go around debunking it." He flashed me one of his trademark smiles. "Alice, why are *you* really here?"

I could tell him about my quest to start a farmers' market in this ever-disappearing, rural town—the very project my parents had been striving toward before it died with them. But it didn't seem like an appropriate time to spill my sob story. So I just said, "Answers."

His breath caught. "To what questions?" He leaned against the car, arms crossed, attempting to look casual even though his face betrayed his interest. When I didn't clarify, he said, "Better question. Are you sure this is the best place to find them?" Chess raised an eyebrow. "Whitney doesn't seem like your type of friend."

"And you don't seem like the type of person who would work at the Garden Center." I swept my hair behind my ear. "Besides, I told you. No one else gets it."

He opened the back door for me. "Look, Whitney has a hard time trusting people, and you didn't exactly make yourself seem trustworthy."

"I didn't tattle on her about the paper." I climbed onto the back seat, and he leaned over me, door still open. I felt like a little kid waiting for her mommy to strap her into the car seat. "I really didn't mean to freak her out."

"I know that. Do something that will get her attention. Impress her," he said. "If you want to, that is. I personally think it's in your best interest to stay away."

"A few minutes ago you stood up for me. Now you're contradicting yourself."

Chess shrugged. "Sometimes both paths are right."

"Why should I stay away?"

He pursed his lips. "What we do—sometimes it's not really . . . stuff we can brag about. You could get in trouble. I don't want that."

"I already figured that out. What with Principal Dodgson threatening expulsion."

"That's not the kind of trouble I meant." Before he could clarify, Whitney scampered toward the car. Chess slammed the door on me and moved to the driver's seat. Whitney plopped into the passenger seat.

"What did Kingston say?" Chess asked.

"I said I'm coming," a new male voice yelled. "Out, Whitney. I called shotty."

He yanked open the passenger door and tugged on Whitney's arm to pull her out. He wore the same all-black ensemble as the guy from the warehouse, mud dotting the surface. Had he arrived to complete whatever order Whitney had given him by the warehouse? My fingers curled around the back-door handle just in case.

She stuck out her tongue at him. "You can't control-alt-command me." She pointed a finger-gun at Chess. "Start the engine."

Kingston glanced at his watch, then brushed his hands over his beanie, pulling it off and taking the hoodie with it. A short crewcut remained. It looked more like a five-o'clock shadow on the pallor of his unnaturally pale olive skin. He slammed the front door and wrenched open the back one. After plopping down next to me, he set his eyes on me, lashes so thick it looked like he was wearing guyliner. If he could turn the stare from death to flirty, he might be cute. He'd probably have to get rid of the scowl, though.

"What are you looking at?" he asked me.

"Kingston, you can't ask that when you're the one staring," Whitney said.

He leaned closer. "No, she's up to something. I can tell." He narrowed his eyes. "If you're trying to crack the mysteries of the universe, don't bother. I've hidden them in a seed and buried them in the ground."

He seemed to be waiting for an answer. "I—I'll keep that in mind if I ever get the urge to try," I said.

He scoffed. "What did I just tell you? You can't try." He thrust his hand out to me and I flinched, but he only pointed. "You a narc?"

My throat was so dry I couldn't even get out my *no.*

"No one uses that word anymore." Whitney readjusted her seat, pushing it too far into his knees.

"I'm bringing it back. You can resurrect words, not people, though I'm working on a solution for that." He turned his wrist so he could undo his watch. It flopped in the air like a whip as he shook it.

I inched closer to the window, wondering if I'd made the right choice after all.

"You didn't answer my question," Kingston said, bringing the watch to his ear.

"Alice and I had a heart-to-heart." Chess met my eyes in the rearview mirror. "She's not going to spread any rumors."

I squeezed my thumb and index finger together and drew them across my lips.

"Whitney tells me you're smart. I hope that's true. For your sake."

"Kingston, God, you could be a little nicer."

"What? You gonna tattle to Mom and Dad?" He struggled to get the watch back on his wrist.

"They're stepbrother and sister," Chess clarified for me.

"Ah," I said. Aside from their reputations and apparent love for plants, I didn't think they had anything in common. While the radical house seemed to fit Whitney, I pictured Kingston living in something more . . . secure. Like a Transylvanian castle with a moat. Or a prison.

"And what are you doing with your watch, King?" Whitney asked.

"I'm *trying*"—he got so fed up, he threw the watch on the floor—"to turn back the time so this little girl never fucked up our evening."

"It doesn't quite work like that." Whitney's tone was serious but contained a hint of sarcasm.

"Obviously." He rolled his eyes. "The battery's dead."

Note to self: getting in cars with classmates could be just as precarious as getting in cars with strangers.

Chess pulled out of the driveway and the car wobbled onto the street. Through the rest of the car ride, no one discussed anything related to the warehouse, the paper prank, or whatever secret these three had. Was anyone else in on it? Kingston kept glaring at me. Chess countered Kingston's glares with sympathetic checks in the rearview.

We neared the main road. I leaned forward and placed my palm on Chess's seat. "Turn left here."

But he swerved the car in the opposite direction.

"Oh no. I live back that way."

"I know."

Goosebumps pebbled my skin. I'd never given him my address.

"Good," Kingston said. "I think they're surveilling the main road."

"Who is?" I blurted, before I could stop myself.

"Them," Kingston snapped in an irritated tone.

Oh right, the ever-illustrious *them.*

Chess stayed straight for a while, then turned down a few more streets, utilizing back roads before approaching my house from a side street. I sat in my seat, stunned. His route avoided annoying traffic lights and saved a good five minutes.

"Nice garden." Kingston burst out laughing.

Heat swarmed into my cheeks. This garden was a last resort, a desperate attempt to start a farmers' market myself by growing the produce and peddling it at a weekend lemonade-type stall. Too bad none of my fruits and veggies had popped out of the ground. The only thing standing was the white rosebush I'd planted with my mom in a prime spot below my bedroom window, long before my pathetic farming-lite failure. I had a better chance of growing boobs.

"You're being too rigid with it, aligning everything in such neat rows." Whitney patted the air in a line. "Plants don't like that. They don't like to be confined."

"And keep your mouth shut," Kingston added, though the threat was unnecessary.

"Ignore him," Whitney told me. "He thinks he's a girl and has the right to PMS."

Kingston kicked her seat hard and she let out an *oof.*

"And just for that we're listening to pop music on the way home." Whitney fiddled with the dial until she found cheery singing on top of a catchy beat.

"Oh no. That punishes me, too!" Chess tried to turn the dial, but she slapped his hand away.

I forced myself to push open the door.

Chess rolled down his window. "You're going to want to lie down. That green concoction? It sometimes causes dizziness."

"I thought you said—Should you be driving then?"

"I'm a rebel." He winked at me.

I turned toward my house and released the smile I'd been harboring. I didn't know what they were up to or what Chess had meant by doing things they couldn't "brag about," but I didn't care. I just wanted to be part of it.

CHAPTER 5

Once inside my room, I pressed myself against the height-measuring strip on my wall. Some girls obsessively weighed themselves. I'd been tracking my height since I started—or rather, halted—my growth spurt. I planted my feet flat, standing rigid like a soldier in a lineup. Instead of a one-handed salute to my officer, I lifted my right hand and held it level with my head.

I marked my height, squeezed my eyes shut, and stepped away to see the result. One eye popped open.

Four feet nine and three-quarter inches.

I . . . shrank? How was that possible? The green liquid was making me hallucinate; that was the only plausible explanation. And in fact, I didn't feel quite like myself. The giggles that were escaping my throat belonged to someone like Quinn, not me. I pressed my fingers to my temples and sank onto my bed. My eyes shifted to my French textbook, lying open, to my homework. I tugged it toward me and tried to concentrate on my lessons, translating the provided poem from English into French. *Comment va le petit crocodile.*

I slammed the notebook shut. No, that wasn't right at all. The word *crocodile* wasn't even in the original English sentence. What was wrong with me? Had the green liquid turned me into someone else, someone not very bright? Like Quinn?

That idea made about as much sense as Kingston wanting to turn back time by winding his watch. Whatever. I had to focus on my goal: finding a way into Whitney's group by doing something to impress her.

But what? I didn't exactly have a year's supply of paper lying around.

The door slammed downstairs. My sister, Lorina. I wandered into the hallway, wobbling, and clutched the banister to keep my balance as I descended the stairs. My head felt light, as if it might float away from my neck at any moment. That drink was definitely strange. Might even win the award over Kingston for oddness.

"Alice?" Lorina stuck her head into the living room. "I got petit fours on my way home."

Maybe food would help. Besides, I had a weakness for tiny desserts. Because as much as I hated to admit it, I adored anything that came in a small package. Like I shared some sort of solidarity with the travel-size toiletries sold in the neglected section of the drug store.

Lorina gestured for me to follow her into the kitchen. She eased the lights to full blast, then lit a few candles so we could actually see each other. Ever since the nuclear-power plant had shut down a few years earlier, the ambience of most homes and buildings was permanently set to *romantic* to conserve energy.

Now I could see the dark bags under her lower eyelids. Her black suit covered her body, baggy because it had belonged to our mother. Unlike me, she could fit in clothes that didn't come from the children's section. Her sunshine-blonde hair cascaded around her face, casting an angelic glow. My own hair, plucked from the same golden harp, concealed me in a similar disguise. Lorina opened a white box tied with a red-and-white-striped baker's ribbon and slid it across the table toward me.

Miniature replicas of bigger cakes waited inside the box, each one covered with pastel fondant and white frosting that spelled out *Eat me!*

"Why'd you splurge on the cakes?" I reached in and took the light-blue one. It fit my mood.

"I have something to celebrate." Lorina's finger hovered over the cakes, dangling back and forth as she tried to decide which one to choose.

I smiled. My lips seemed slippery, like they might slide right off my face. "Oooh. What?"

"Are you okay? You look a little weird."

"Pretty tired." I hated to lie, but I had no idea how to explain the green liquid, not without getting in trouble or hiring a chemist. "So what are we celebrating?"

She reached over and stroked my knuckles. "Alice, you don't have to keep things from me. I'm here for you. If you're sick, I want to take care of you." Her words made me feel shittier than the manure Whitney probably used to make her plants grow.

Of course Lorina would drop everything to take care of me. That was what she did. My twenty-one-year-old sister had put most of the inheritance we'd received into a college fund for me, trading her own education for the role of pseudo-mom. She wouldn't let me get a job, claiming she wanted me to enjoy my childhood like she had done, before she had to abandon it to raise me.

"Really, I'm fine. Tell me about your news." I sat up straighter even though my head felt fuzzy, too stuffed with cotton to operate regularly. "Cute guy?"

She blushed. "No, nothing like that." She wiped her fingers over her brow in a dismissive gesture that clearly showed she wished it were *exactly* like that. "It's work stuff." Lorina administrated the crap out of her administrative-assistant position at the Department of Public Health and Safety for the town. In fact, I sometimes suspected she did all her boss's work on top of hers. "Apparently Wonderland isn't so wonderful lately."

"That's an understatement." We lived in Wonderland, Illinois, a suburb of Chicago where they tore out trees and then named streets after them. Everything pretty and picturesque, like the rolling hills and cornfields my school bus used to pass by in elementary school, had melted into a haze of gray, like someone had zapped all the color with a Photoshop ray gun. Monstrous warehouses squatted on the now-barren lots, and it was only a matter of time before gas masks became fashionable to combat the exhaust fumes being spit out from clogged highways.

"There've been some shady eco-demonstrations going on."

The blood drained from my face. Did this have anything to do with Whitney's group and whatever was going on at the warehouse or the message at school? I shook that thought away. They seemed to be doing good things, not bad. Planting a garden in an unused space was the kind of project elementary schools would force their students to do during an agriculture lesson. Of course, they never did this under the cover of night in absolute secrecy.

"Like what Mom and Dad used to do? With the farmers' market?"

"No, what they did was all in the public eye. This isn't. It's illegal." She chomped down on a tiny cake.

"Illegal how?" My breath waited in my throat. Is this what Chess meant about getting in trouble? With the *law*? I was hoping he meant in trouble with, you know, thorny rosebush stems.

"A lot of vandalism. Nothing dangerous yet, but it's only a matter of time."

The word *ecotage* flashed like a neon light in my mind.

"My boss is getting a committee together to investigate." Her entire face lit up, erasing the dark circles.

"Not the police?"

She shrugged. "My boss was adamant against it. Guess they want to keep it in the department for now. I thought that was a little weird, but—"

"Wait, so are you on it?" I couldn't keep the caution out of my voice.

"My boss is letting me spearhead it. This is my chance to show them I can handle more responsibility. Bigger cases." Usually she investigated claims from citizens about rusty water fountains or garbage men slacking on their trash-removal duties.

I stopped chewing. "Bigger how?"

She pursed her lips. "You don't seem excited."

I studied my clasped hands in my lap. "It reminds me too much of Mom and Dad." It wasn't a lie, but Lorina didn't need to know I thought that was a good thing. Though I made every effort to finish what they started in the privacy of my own room, Lorina had vowed to let their dreams rest with them. If she found out about Whitney's group, she'd try to stop me from joining just like my parents would have if they were still around. They had believed protests should lead to change, not vandalism.

"That's exactly why I want to do this." She bussed her plate to the kitchen.

"Why? If they were still alive, you'd be on opposite sides. You'd be the one trying to investigate them!"

I thought back to a few days before they died, when Mom had barged into my bedroom in the middle of the night. I was in a deep sleep, and I remember thinking for a moment that I was being attacked by ghosts. Mom sank onto my bed and brushed the hair from my face until I sat up. "Alice, I need you to promise me something."

"This better not be about waiting until marriage to have sex." I wasn't even a teenager yet but I loved getting a reaction out of my parents. It made the good things I did seem even more angelic.

"If Dad and I . . . " She tilted her head toward my wall. "If we go away for a while, will you continue for us? With the protests. We need someone we can trust and—"

"No!"

The word ripped through the house, but it didn't come from my lips. Lorina wrenched open the door to my room, arms crossed, the blue streak she used to wear in her hair striking against her light locks. Dad rushed in behind her. She angled her body to speak to both of them. "There's no way I'm helping. If you get arrested again—that's it. It has to stop." She slammed the door on the way out, drowning out my whispered, "I promise," to my mom.

Back in the kitchen, Lorina spun the faucet fast and thrust her hands under the water. She looked so different, so grown up, without the blue streak in her hair. "Alice, it's not like that. They never did stuff that hurt people."

I hopped from my seat. "How is this hurting people?"

She scrubbed her hands vigorously. "It hasn't yet. But trust me, it will. My boss showed us studies. What's happening here started the same way as what happened in Neverland, and several people lost their lives during those stunts. If this continues—" Something clanged against the metal of the sink. Her high school–class ring slipped off her finger from the soapy water and skidded down the drain.

"Damn it!" she cried. I moved to help her, bending underneath the sink to stop the water flow. After I turned the valve, my fingers froze. *Damn it.* Running water.

I thought of Whitney's words to me, the riddle I didn't understand. "*Damn. Once the floodgates open, things will grow.*"

Did she mean *dam*?

And suddenly I knew what I had to do to impress her. Too bad it might make me the prime suspect in Lorina's investigation.

My head stopped buzzing from the weird green liquid about an hour after dinner a.k.a. dessert—one of the advantages of having a twenty-one-year-old for a guardian. When the clock blinked a set of numbers I usually only saw during the school day, I paused at the doorway, listening. The silence was eerie at night, each tiny creak of the house settling magnified, ominous enough for a horror movie. I tiptoed down the hallway so quietly, even ghosts would be envious.

It took forever to get down the stairs, and I readied an excuse just in case. *I was still hungry from my lack of dinner*. That would play into her guilt. But of course it wouldn't explain going through her workbag.

The zipper sounded louder than my morning alarm. I cringed, shaky fingers hovering over the contents.

I dragged all the documents out of the bag and placed them flat on the entryway table. They were reports but not the kind that appear in the newspaper police blotter. These were photocopied versions that had originally been written longhand on ruled paper. Antiquated in the technology age, but that was probably the point. Paper trails could be destroyed with a quick flip of a lighter or a trip to the paper shredder. Computer files were backed up and archived, making it difficult to get rid of all traces.

I flipped through the pages, skimming the headlines. Several documents had similar headings like *Warehouse vandalized* or *Parking lot vandalized*. But then there were others: *Grocery store robbed*, *Supermarket defaced*, *Water tainted*. There was a giant, stapled packet labeled *Greenhouse incident* that seemed important.

I went back to the document about the warehouse. I figured that would be the easiest way to check if Lorina was investigating Whitney and Chess.

Warehouse covered with plants and flowers . . .

The metronome of my pulse shifted from whole to eighth notes. I had to set the paper down because it suddenly became too heavy to hold.

A few deep breaths gave me the courage to try again. Who needed pep talks when you were committing robbery?

The parking-lot incidents were nearly identical. I shuffled those pages to the back and pulled up the grocery-store stuff. This one looked different, only because it contained a single sentence.

Reports of missing produce inventory—no connection yet, but keep eye out.

I flipped the page . . . *all Shoptown food chains in a twenty-mile radius were covered with feathers.*

A giggle burst out of my mouth, betraying my oath of silence. I clapped a cold palm over my face, accidentally knocking the papers off the table in the process. They fluttered to the ground.

The curse word I wanted to say waited in my throat ineffectively. I squatted down and shuffled the papers into a pile in random order.

Lorina's door creaked open.

I froze, body rigid, and then survival mode kicked in. The papers were all turned every which way; I couldn't put them in her bag like this. I slapped the edge of the pile against the table a few times until the pages settled into a single direction just as the footsteps started in the upstairs hallway. I didn't have time to zip the bag, so I left it and dashed with the grace of an elephant into the kitchen.

I thrust open the fridge right as Lorina appeared in the doorway, squinting. "I thought I heard something."

I pointed to the undeniable evidence of the fridge. "I got hungry."

She nodded. "Me too."

My brain was too busy trying to sort out what I'd read to make idle conversation, so I stuffed a cake in my mouth followed immediately by another one before I'd even finished chewing. Lorina grabbed a few cookies from the cabinet and walked with me back upstairs, forcing me to leave her open bag and unread files behind. Besides, I'd come to a decision and the other files probably wouldn't sway me anyway.

I wanted to be part of Whitney's group, whatever it entailed. Committing to this, I nudged my laptop awake on my desk. A few keystrokes later, a new email window popped open. I rifled through the school address book until I found her email address.

My fingers paused on the keys. I was about to type a long explanation of my plans, but something felt off about that. Like maybe I shouldn't leave behind such an obvious trail of evidence.

Whitney embraced spontaneity and mystery; I would, too. *Tomorrow*, was all I wrote. I hit send before I could second-guess myself. Buffalo stampeded into my stomach. I had to do this. No time for planning, no backing out.

CHAPTER 6

The next morning, I left for school before the sun started its daily routine. I wore ugly, yellow rain boots and the jeans I'd accidentally changed the color of from blue to spotted brown with my klutziness—seriously, drinking and driving should be illegal with all beverages, including coffee. Only an oversized men's flannel shirt could make my outfit sexier.

Behind the school, the air smelled like wet towel, and my hair frizzed in a direct betrayal of my blow dryer. I amped my pace, determined to get this part over with before any teachers arrived. My yellow boots and terrible fashion sense wouldn't keep me incognito for long.

And the only thing I could be sure of about Whitney's group was that they operated in secret.

The creek ran parallel to the back of the school, only a few feet separating them. The creek held only about an inch of murky, brown water instead of the five-or-so feet it had the capacity for. A vast field of dead grass stretched beyond it, sucked dry without water. The weather seemed to be conspiring with the township to keep our town from producing crops. Rain at this time of year was rare, and when it showed up, it was underwhelming. Today's forecast called for disappointment and sporadic mist.

Hoisting the backpack over my shoulder, I followed the creek in the direction of the lake that sat a few hundred feet away. My flashlight beamed a circle of light along my path, and the heavy flirting of crickets kept me company.

A snapped branch in the woods drew my attention. I squinted into the distance but only spotted trees swaying in the growing wind. I shook my head and forced myself to keep going. *Stop being paranoid.*

Several hundred feet along the creek, the sound of rushing water made my ears perk up. Large rocks, piled higher than my head, blocked the flow of the water. But that was no surprise; there were some dollhouses taller than me. Twigs and dead leaves stuck out between the rocks, water seeping through the crevasses. It looked massive, but I hoped I could redirect at least a trickle of water back to the field.

After I set my bag down, I stepped into the creek and braced one hand on the dam. The rocks wobbled beneath my fingers. I smiled. "Easy peasy, mac and cheesy."

One by one, I lifted the rocks and heaved them into the forest. Birds fluttered their wings in response. I wiped sweat from my brow, probably leaving a giant streak of dirt behind. Excellent. I'd neglected to put on makeup this morning and the dirt really completed my outfit.

If only my parents could see me now. They might even be proud.

Rain dripped from fat, gray clouds—sporadic at first, but then coming faster and more fervently. My windshield-wiper eyelids couldn't clear my vision fast enough, but it was too late to stop now. The meteorologists had a warped sense of humor if they classified this as *mist.* I lugged rock after rock, each one growing heavier in my tired arms. Mild chatter from the students hanging out near the side of the school marked an hourglass of time running out.

I slid my shaky fingers beneath another average-size rock and couldn't budge it. My hands felt useless, like decorative bathroom soap, there only for show. Tears broke through and streamed down my face. I sagged, breathing hard.

This was stupid. Crying wouldn't move the rocks, and giving up definitely wouldn't. Picturing Chess's impressed smile if I completed their test, I lunged for another rock. My muscles screamed, and the ache triggered another stream of tears. I yanked with all my strength, freeing the rock. Several more teetered. I hopped back farther into the creek right before all the rocks tumbled to the ground in a desperate escape from their tight-knit clique. I sympathized with their bid for freedom from the status quo.

The water shot out at me, and I lost my balance, falling on my butt into the mud. I didn't have time to react—the water pulled me under and covered my head. *Goodbye, feet,* I thought when the water swallowed them. My first instinct wasn't survival—it was embarrassment.

How lame would it be to drown in a five-foot creek?

My head burst through the surface and my lungs gulped oxygen. I grabbed a nearby branch, but the current protested, pushing against me. One finger slipped, then another. I gave in, flipping onto my back and floating down the creek, in control now that I wasn't panicking.

The scenery blurred by, trees becoming streaks of green. Then I saw the school rushing at me like a car accident I couldn't swerve away from. The water had overflowed the banks and was rising up the side of the building. Something liquid this way comes.

"Oh my God! Someone fell in!" a voice yelled.

"Anyone a lifeguard?"

I reached for the edge of the creek and tried to pull myself up, but the current was too strong. I kept slipping. So I raised my arms in the air and did my best drowning-victim impression.

"Move over, lametards." Whitney sloshed through the flooded grass to reach me.

Her hand gripped my wrist. The water pooled around her ankles. She tugged so hard, I thought she might take my arm and leave the rest of my body. That would certainly put an end to my environmental endeavors. And my homework, except for French oral pronunciation.

Soon both of us crashed into the shallow water covering the grass, panting.

Yet, I couldn't help smiling. The grass was wet, wasn't it?

"Nice outfit," Whitney said, releasing my wrist and hopping to her feet. Her black leggings hid the water stains.

"Thanks." I stood up and crossed one ankle over the other, concealing my boots as best I could to prevent them from drawing any more attention. "I mean, for saving me."

I wiped water away from my eyes and scanned around for my bag. Crap. I'd have to double back to the dam once the commotion was over. A crowd of students watched us, umbrellas shielding them. Thank God I'd left the boring white T-shirt at home and opted for something colorful. "This is not a museum attraction." Whitney gave the crowd a dirty look.

Most scattered, heading for the entrance, while a few lingered, pulling out cell phones and turning into amateur paparazzi.

"So, what? Figured it was a good time to practice your crawl stroke?" Whitney forked her fingers through her straggly hair.

"No, I was auditioning to become a lifeguard. I think I failed." My teeth chattered and goosebumps embossed my skin. I rubbed my shoulders.

"Really, because I think you had a different agenda," a male voice said. I turned around to find Kingston stepping toward me, the forest behind him as though he'd come from the opposite direction of the school. He carried an umbrella, but his jeans were soaked through, like he'd been standing outside for a while. His bright-yellow rain hat matched my boots. Well, if Di had an outfit twin, I guess I could have one, too. "Wasn't necessary with the weather forecast, huh?"

"Perfect cover?" I tried.

"Maybe if you didn't almost get caught."

"I'll get better next time, I promise." I directed my words at Whitney.

"There won't be a next time." For emphasis, Kingston tapped on his watch. "It's broken, remember? No time but right now."

"Let me just observe or something." Beggars couldn't be choosers, but they could still be beggars. "Or send me on another mission! I don't care what or where—"

"If you don't care where, then it doesn't matter which way you go." Kingston kicked his leg, spraying water at me. "And my advice is to go whichever way we're not." He pointed in one direction with one arm and the other direction with the other arm, then switched them so his arms folded awkwardly. "What are you waiting for? You're sure to get somewhere if you walk long enough."

"I want to go with you guys," I said in a small voice.

Whitney studied me for a moment. "The keeper of secrets will never leave the trail."

"No, Whit." Kingston shook his head.

"What does that mean?" I asked Whitney, knowing she wouldn't actually tell me.

"It means a few things." She left it at that.

Kingston's head shaking grew more frantic. "It's a terrible idea."

"What is?" I eyed Kingston. Whitney might not tell me, but I hadn't yet tested him.

"*It*," he replied with an eye roll. "You do know what *it* means?"

"I wouldn't be asking if I did."

"What, did you cheat your way through English class?"

Oh, he meant that *it*, as in the pronoun. Well, at least I cleared up *that* confusion. "I wish I could just prove my—"

Kingston reached into his pocket and tossed a handful of pennies at me. They ricocheted off my wet clothes. "Here, wish on them. Find a penny, fuck a penny. Because wishes are useless. Just like you."

"What's going on here?" Our principal sludged through the mud, clapping her hands in warning. Her eyes turned to the new moat surrounding the school. "Which one of you fell in?"

"Alice did." Whitney stood up. "The rain must have caused the creek to overflow. I rescued her."

I nodded to corroborate her story, grateful that at least we were in this together. Sort of.

"This is the second time you're on the front lines of a recent incident." Principal Dodgson studied me with squinted eyes. She seemed sober now. Too bad.

Kingston snickered and backed away from our little powwow.

Mr. Hargreaves came running out, his pants dripping water onto the ground. "The English wing is flooding!"

"Get the students away from it. Send them home!" Principal Dodgson turned to me. "Alice, you go to the nurse and wait there for me."

"But I . . . " needed to go back to the creek. My eyes pleaded with Whitney, but unfortunately my gesture was as difficult to decipher as her riddles.

Principal Dodgson grabbed my hand. "We don't want you tripping again, now do we?" I stifled a cringe. Just what I needed after my embarrassing fall, to be seen engaging in a public display of affection with my principal.

My foot slipped on a muddy area, and Principal Dodgson tightened her grip. When I stood on solid concrete, she let go and watched me take a few teetering steps. After a minute, she rushed off toward the English wing.

I turned back toward the creek to call out to Whitney, but she and Kingston were already gone.

In the nurse's office, I shivered under a cotton blanket and tried to coax my body temperature back up. As each second passed on the clock

I grew more and more antsy, practically ripping the paper covering the exam table into shreds with my shifting. Principal Dodgson came back about a half-hour later. Her wet pantsuit clung to her in a way that would never pass the school dress code. "You're not dry yet."

"We have that in common."

"Nothing gets you drier than a dry confession." She shook her finger at me. "You don't normally hang out behind the school." She said the words *behind the school* like they included a one-way ticket to detention. "And this is twice now you've been connected to school vandalism."

"I swear. Last time I was just trying to make flyers and—"

"I know you couldn't have stolen the paper because you were with me at the time."

I nodded. "And this time, I went out there because I heard the commotion and slipped on the mud." I made my eyes wide and innocent. "I was trying to help."

She pursed her lips. "Well, that does seem like something you would do." She balled her hands into fists. "That's it, I don't care how much energy it uses up, I'm turning the security cameras back on. We could have caught them by—never mind." She waved her hand away. "Did you see anything suspicious?"

A blast of air conditioning made me shiver. "Suspicious?"

"Anyone else out around the creek before you got there?" Principal Dodgson undid her bun and wrung the water out of her short, brown locks. "Come to think of it, how did Whitney rescue you? Was she already there?"

"No, of course not," I said. Her question sounded like an accusation, and the last thing I needed was Whitney taking the fall for my mistake. "She came afterward. Why?"

"The English wing is flooded. We can't hold a school day if the students need life vests to swim to their classes. And I don't believe it's the rain. Someone tried to get school canceled the other day with the vandalism. And I bet that same someone was fooling around with the dam today. Probably to get classes shut down."

"Nonsense. Have you checked the dam?" I held my breath.

"That's my next order of business." Mascara ran down her face, making her look more like a sweaty circus clown than a school principal. "Well, this isn't your problem. Whoever did this will be punished. But I am keeping my eye on you."

My skin prickled. I could only hope the rain and the overflowing creek had washed away my backpack with my neatly-typed homework inside, the telltale evidence linking me to the crime.

CHAPTER 7

It took three days for the utility department to declare the school arid and no longer prime for surfing thanks to my little stunt. Students dusted off their alarm clocks and treaded into the halls, whispering that Mother Nature hadn't caused the flood.

My eyes darted from classmate to classmate, desperate to catch any indication that anyone suspected my involvement in the act of environmental-social suicide. I hoped no one would notice my missing trademark backpack or the lame excuse that I'd forgotten my textbooks at home. I tried to wear the Model Student skin suit, but it didn't fit as snugly as it used to.

I wasn't sure whether to be grateful or not that Di and Dru ignored the fight we had in English and acted like nothing—including helping me out with my environmental goal—had happened. Selective memory loss comes in handy when you're unpopular. I'd failed with Whitney, and unless I wanted to eat lunch alone in a bathroom stall, I had no choice but to keep up the same pretense.

The gym locker-room door burst open and smacked into the wall. "I know who did it!" Quinn Hart rushed toward the girls still lingering by the lockers. Anything to get people to listen to her and stretch out her fifteen minutes of high-school notoriety.

She did have a great sense of rumor.

I dropped the sneaker I'd been holding, fingers going from still to earthquake before Quinn even finished speaking. *Please let her be talking about two people having sex in the janitor's closet or something.*

"Did what?" Dru piped up before anyone else could play the "Who's there?" role to Quinn's knock-knock joke.

Di's eyes flitted toward Dru, then Quinn. "Yeah, I want to know!" Quinn wasn't speaking specifically to us, so I eyed Di sidelong.

Quinn flicked her long, red curls out of her face. "The creek, silly! They found evidence."

She rushed over to her eager audience of Di, Dru, and me. The girls across the way inched closer.

"Wh . . . who was it?" I managed to get out of my dry throat. I thought of my abandoned backpack.

"Whitney Lapin, right?" Di asked, turning pure speculation into the hottest rumor. Her tone was competitive, like she could one-up me with a better question.

Dru nodded. "She complained about the dry grass in English the other day."

"She didn't!" I blurted. It sounded like a counterattack, but I had no desire to win the role of Quinn Hart's new minion.

"I don't get why you keep sticking up for her." Dru brushed her sandy hair into a quick ponytail.

"Contrariwise, why you keep talking to her." Di used her fingers to pull her loose strands into an almost identical hairstyle.

"I don't." Not by choice.

"Whitney Lapin?" Quinn's brows knitted together. "As in Kingston Hatter's sister?"

How did everyone else know that info but me?

"Yeah. She pulled Alice out of the creek," Dru said. "Seemed like a forced alibi."

"Which, by the way, is so weird that you were out there." Di shook her head at me.

"Oh, well, it wasn't her," Quinn said. I let out a breath. "But speaking of her, I heard Kingston went to jail!" Quinn's eyes widened like camera lenses as she turned to me.

I tugged on ratty gym pants. "He does seem like the jail type."

"For the creek?" Dru asked. "No how."

"Contrariwise," Di said. "That would make sense."

"No, not the creek!" Quinn playfully slapped at the air directly in front of Di. "It was a prank pulled on us by Neverland High. Some Homecoming-rivalry bullshit or something."

"That's great!" I resisted the urge to do a victory dance, mostly because I couldn't dance.

"I know. Now we have an excuse to get them back!" Quinn yanked open her locker and removed a red gym shirt embroidered with little hearts. My faded, gray hand-me-down wasn't nearly as cute . . . or peppy.

"Wait . . . how do you know it was a prank?" I jammed my foot into the sneaker.

"Some graffiti and streamers and stuff stuck to a rock. So lame. We can do much better."

I fidgeted with my shoelaces. Whitney obviously had gone to a lot of trouble to cover for me. No wonder she wasn't interested in my help. And, ugh, did I just start a war with a rival school?

Dru cracked a smile directed at Quinn. "Are you planning something? To get them back?"

"Oh, I don't think that's a good idea," I said with more force than I'd meant.

"Contrariwise—I do!" Di hopped in place with excitement.

Quinn turned her back to me and focused on Dru and Di. "I'm moving tomorrow, so I kind of have to focus on that first, but we'll talk about it in a few days, 'kay?" Her voice was practically giddy with mischief.

The smile that spread over Di's face was like a punch in the gut. Even though we weren't on the same page anymore, it sucked to know your best friend preferred others over you. Dru had stampeded into our friendship over the summer, grabbed the reins, and steered Di away from me. Directing her right into Quinn's path. Though I guess you could make the same argument about Whitney taking the reins over me.

Di tilted her head to me. "So are you in?" She pleaded with her eyes. I got the message loud and clear: I better agree and shut up about my *ho pas*.

"Um, sure."

I'd lost my chance with Whitney; I couldn't carry out anything myself without it resulting in disaster. And yet . . . my old life fit me about as well as an outgrown pair of pants that squeezed my flesh and cut off my circulation.

I knew I'd have to work harder. Either at finding a way into Whitney's group or at forgetting they existed.

Our gym teacher blew his whistle to start class. "We're running laps today, people." Apparently a student had gotten injured earlier in the day on the flood-warped gym floors, so the teachers were forced to switch the curriculum to the Presidential Fitness test we usually did in the spring. "If you have to walk, that's fine for today. But do your best. It's a caucus race. No winner, no beginning, no end, just running."

The athletes didn't waste any time, charging for the track and competing against each other. I jogged at a comfortable pace with Dru and Di. And Quinn.

"So are you moving out of town?" Dru asked Quinn.

"Nope." There was a hop in her step. Odd. Most people didn't get excited about staying *in* Wonderland. I was curious what she had to say, but then Chess swept past me in a quick run, his hair as messy as ever. No one ran beside him. "My parents are building—"

I may have failed with Whitney, but maybe there was still hope with Chess. "Be right back."

I launched into an Olympic-speed run to catch up with him. Something rattled in my pocket, but I ignored it. My heart woke up from a nap and rammed against my chest. Since my legs were so short, I had to run a lot faster, but I had extra motivation now. I sped past other students, who watched me like I was crazy for participating in class with such enthusiasm.

Maybe they were on to something.

By the time I caught up with him three-quarters of the way around the track, my breath came in punching gasps and my blonde hair stuck to my neck. I wished I'd had the foresight to bring a ponytail holder. Or my game.

His feet slapped against the ground, and I'm not ashamed to admit I checked out his butt while I evened my breath. At least I wore a smile when I approached him. "Hey," I said. It was all I could get out between gasps. My lungs were rebelling, but then again, so was I.

"Oh, hey." He slowed his pace and jogged beside me. "Nice stunt. With the no school, I mean."

"Yeah, I didn't actually mean to do that." I wiped sweat from my brow. "Quick question and then I'll leave you alone."

"No, stay."

Even though my leg muscles throbbed from the torture I'd just put them through, it felt like they were dancing. "Is that what Whitney meant? With her 'Open the floodgates' riddle?"

"She thought you were spying on us. This was her way of making sure you're on our side. But you weren't exactly stealthy."

I squinted into the bright sun. "I can be."

His feet came to a dead stop. “Why are you doing this?”

I stumbled as I stopped short. “I want to help.”

“Yeah, but what’s in it for you?”

You. The word hovered in my mind, but I kept it there, unsaid. Still, I knew that was only a small part of it.

A few students jogged past us, tilting their heads at our association. Chess didn’t seem to notice.

“You guys are making a difference. Right?” Suddenly I realized I had no idea. Maybe I *wanted* to think they were doing good things.

“Yeah, we are. Sort of. In our own way.” He started a slow jog.

In our own way. Chess had told me the group did stuff they couldn’t exactly brag about, and the “pledge” task they’d given me could’ve gotten me expelled. Which made me wonder . . . “Does what you’re doing with Whitney have anything to do with why you got expelled from boarding school?”

We jogged a quarter of the track before he finally answered. “I’m sure you’ve heard the rumors.”

“I want the truth.”

“You can’t always get what you want.” His smile ignited bad thoughts in my mind. Thoughts of how I could make it even wider.

I focused on the red track beneath my feet, anything to avoid swooning over his lips. “Oh no. Not you too with the riddles.”

He laughed. “That’s not a riddle. That’s the Stones.”

“Oh.”

“Which rumor was your favorite?”

Odd question. “I don’t know.” I recalled the ones about murder. I wasn’t sure how far they would go with everything. Or even what their agenda was. The environmental stuff could just be a cover for something more sinister.

“Pick one.”

Since it was all I could think of, I said, "I'm hoping the murder one is false."

Two students passed by us, and Chess waited until they were out of earshot. "Well, I promise you I haven't murdered anyone. Songs, yes. I murder those a lot. Time, too. But Whitney murders that more than I do."

My step lightened. "That's good. Murder would be the only thing to dissuade me."

He clenched his jaw and suddenly got very quiet. After a while he said, "Whitney, Kingston, and me . . . we have reasons for what we do. You don't."

I stumbled mid-stride. "So you don't want me to join your . . . secret society?"

"No, it's not that. I want— It's—" He raked his hand through his shaggy hair as a couple more students ran by us, checking us out. "Never mind."

"What?" I cocked my head to look at him. A hole was unraveling on the shoulder of his T-shirt. Since I was shorter, it was right in my line of vision and I couldn't stop staring at it.

"It's just, trust me. I would have noticed sooner if you were into this kind of stuff."

"I'm not the same girl I was last week," I said. "So how could you possibly have noticed?"

"I feel like I know who you are." Chess met my eyes, and I stumbled again.

"You're going by rumors. And we both know rumors might be false." I held his gaze even though all the rumors about me had been accurate until last week.

He jerked away from me. "Point taken. There's a lot we don't know about each other."

My feet slammed onto the rubbery asphalt with too much force. He pumped his arms with equal aggression. Silence wasn't my preferred form of communication, but we were mastering the dialect.

I eased my pace. "But you did know my address the other day . . . "

He cupped the back of his neck. "Um . . . that was a lucky guess?" The end of his sentence rose in pitch like a question.

"Really lucky. Care to try again with the lottery?"

He chuckled. "Actually, I memorized the school directory."

I squinted at him. "Who does that?"

"It was either that or study for a test." He eyed me sidelong, like he was waiting to see if I'd buy it.

I hoped the real reason he knew my address and wouldn't tell me was good, like an endearing crush on me, and not something I should be afraid of, like a favorite pastime of watching girls get changed, through binoculars.

I wiped a line of sweat from the back of my neck. "Good call there. You know what they say. You can't spell *studying* without *dying*."

"Yeah, see, knowing your address saved lives."

"You're a real hero," I said. The sun beat down, casting him in an angelic glow. "See, I know you're not a bad person. So why do you let everyone think you are?"

"That's what I've been trying to tell you." He stopped to tie his already-tied laces, forcing me to bend over to hear him. "I do bad things. That doesn't mean I can't make up for it sometimes."

"Like how?"

"Like . . . " He rose to a standing position, towering over me and casting me in shadow. "What are you doing tonight?"

A surge of hope rushed through me, bursting through a smile on my lips. "Nothing."

"How about this. I'll pick you up, say, around eight?" His voice trickled with temptation. "And we'll talk about this in . . . private."

Private sounded dangerous, even if it meant making out and not ecotage. I straightened my shoulders. "It's a date." My cheeks flamed at the realization of what I'd said. He raised one eyebrow. "I mean, sounds good." I fidgeted with my hands, clasping and unclasping them while he watched me. I had to distract him somehow. Remembering the rattling from my pants, I pulled out a pack of mints from my pocket. I offered one to him.

"Is this a riddle? Are you trying to tell me something about my breath?" He grinned as he took one from the pack.

The teacher blew the whistle to signal the end of class. The students raced back toward the school, running faster than they ever did on the track. One stopped when he saw my open pack. "Hey, can I get one?"

I tossed him the pack so he would go away and I could keep talking to Chess. The boy took one and passed the pack off to his friend, who wanted one, and so on and so forth until the last student returned an empty pack to me. I shook it to be sure, then fake-pouted.

"Awww, don't be sad. Here." Chess stuck his hands in his pockets. "Maybe I can give you something to cheer you up."

"You don't have to," I said. He pulled out one hand and massaged his jaw, so I rushed in with a joke in case I'd offended him. "The moral of that was: don't be generous."

"Well, I passed that lesson. Because I plan on being chivalrous, not generous. As coincidental as it is, I think I have some mints on me." But instead he pulled out a . . . razor. His cheeks turned a shade of red Quinn would be envious of.

"Do you always keep toiletries in your gym clothes?"

"It's a weapon." He swiped it through the air like a sword. "Self-defense. Since pocket knives are banned at school."

"Ah, weapon. Yes, that's what my mints were, too. Someone has to fight the good fight against halitosis." Or in my case, coffee breath. My mother always told me to remember two things: Wear clean underwear in case you get into a car accident. And always carry mints in case you talk to a cute boy. I was glad the mint advice was the only one I'd needed so far.

"Well, I beg your acceptance of this elegant razor." He bowed and held it out to me. "Since I did promise and all."

"Thanks, but I'd rather have your number." I said, then caught myself. "In case anything comes up before tonight."

"Oh." He rubbed the back of his neck with his palm. "I'd rather you didn't."

The smile disappeared from my lips.

He must have seen the disappointment on my face because he quickly added, "I don't have a cell phone. It, uh, got confiscated. I was using it to cheat on a test, so . . . I won't get it back for a while."

"That explains your rebel comment in your car. What about your landline?"

"My dad's really strict, no phone calls. So eight o'clock?"

I nodded, cheeks unable to contain my smile.

"By the way. Your question before? You were right about part of it. All those rumors are false." He took a step backward. "But you're wrong about why I don't go to boarding school anymore." He gave me a sharp wave, then turned around and headed for the locker room.

I stood there in the wake of his abrupt departure, watching him run away. Okay, I admit it, I liked watching him from behind.

A shadow darkened in my peripheral vision. "Well, you certainly have a talent for being annoying."

I looked up to see Kingston wearing sweatpants and a "No one cares about your blog" T-shirt. A trucker hat crested his head. "Where did you come from?"

"Gym, like you."

"You did not." I took a step away from him. I'd spent about ten minutes total with him so far in my life, and I could never get those back. My fleeing was preemptive.

"A knot!" Kingston craned his neck, searching. "Where is it? I'll undo it. Though as a general rule, I prefer tying things up over letting them loose." He fell into step beside me. "And FYI, I was sitting in the bleachers the whole time, watching your pathetic flirting attempt. Not my fault if you're incredibly oblivious."

"What class did you cut? Since you obviously weren't participating."

He gathered a wad of sweatpants fabric in his hand. "Do these look like my normal clothes? This hat isn't even mine!" So either he stole it or he was delusional. Tough choice. "I forged a doctor's note." He lifted his palm to his mouth and fake-coughed. "I'm so sick."

"Yeah, you look like you're about to keel over."

"That's not funny," he said in a serious voice that almost made me follow it with a "sorry." But then I remembered my level of sympathy for Kingston wouldn't even register on a normal thermometer.

"You must be sick because you're not acting like yourself. Talking to me like a normal person instead of threatening me." Or, you know, trying to solve the mystery of time travel via a broken watch and some determination.

"I haven't gotten to that part yet." He leaned into me, so close his warm breath coated my face. "And I'm not going to threaten you. It's too early for that." He checked his watch. As long as he went by his stalled watch, it would never be time for threats. Though I did wonder what time he thought would be appropriate. "I'll tell you what I know and you can do what you want with that information, as long as it's the right thing."

His riddles weren't nearly as cryptic as Whitney's. He might as well have spelled "stay away" in skywriting. My throat went dry. As much as I could pretend he didn't intimidate me, I'd be lying to myself. "What do you know?"

"I know what you're up to. You want us to get caught. I saw you talking to that girl." He pointed back at the empty track as though that might clarify whom he meant. "The one with the red hair? She's like president of a bazillion clubs."

"Quinn Hart? I don't think—"

"Then you shouldn't speak." He let out an exaggerated sigh.

"What about her?" I asked. A full minute passed by, with him fiddling with his watch and ignoring me. I knew how to get his attention: mention the only thing that could hold it. "It's *time* you told me about her."

"Him. Time is a him. Clearly you haven't spoken to him or you'd know that."

"We haven't really had a chance to get acquainted."

He lifted his head and studied me. Particularly, he studied my chest. "I can tell."

Oh my God! Was that a jab at my needs-a-magnifying-glass boobs not having had a chance to grow? I crossed my arms to shield his view. "What about Quinn?"

"She's always snooping on my conversations, like she might get extra credit for unearthing something."

I pursed my lips. Quinn did that? Maybe that was how she gathered her gossip ammo: she sniffed it out of people.

I rolled my eyes. "You don't know anything."

"Chess may be blindsided, but I'm not. I know you're bad news, and I'm not going to sit by and let you ruin everything."

"I'm not going to ruin—"

"And I know for a fact Chess is not what he seems. So I hope you're just using him as an in to the group and not because you like him. Because when you learn more about him, you won't."

Kingston might be off his rocker and off in his interpretation of everything else he'd told me, but this was one area where he held the crowning expertise.

CHAPTER 8

The more I thought about it, the more it seemed like something was strange about the things Chess knew about me. He knew my address without ever having spoken to me before or being in one of my classes. He knew I was on honor roll. He claimed he would have known if I was into "this kind of stuff," which meant he believed he knew me. He seemed almost excited to see me when he caught me spying, like it was a reunion and not a bust.

So where did he know me from?

Later that day, brushing my hair in my room, I kept going back to how he'd known the way to my house. It was like common knowledge to him, like he'd *been* there before. Too bad we didn't take attendance from everyone who ever entered the premises. And the closest thing we had to a security camera were the photo albums gathering dust in my—

Wait . . .

I dropped the hairbrush back on my dresser and headed to the hallway closet where we stowed the things we wanted to forget, like evidence of bad haircuts and the discarded violin carcass from the five seconds I'd attempted to learn. The only kind of instrument *I* should ever have played was the radio.

I yanked out a bunch of albums and set them on the taupe carpet. This might have been a long shot, but it was my best shot. I balanced the top album on my cross-legged knees and flipped it open. My mind was focused on haystack needles, so seeing my parents' smiling faces caught me off-guard. My throat tightened. I slammed the cover shut, as if to shut out my emotions.

The image stayed in my brain like a carbon etching, and my lower lip trembled. I sucked in desperate breaths that couldn't clear the lump. I hadn't looked at these photos since . . . before. It was hard to remember them as happy, as alive. It was hard to remember *them*.

Taking another deep breath, I opened the book. My parents stood in front of a crowd, arms latched around a few other adults I didn't recognize. A protest sign dangled from my mom's hands: *Gone Fission = Going Green*. I turned the page to find documentation of another mission. Only one other guy appeared in every photo with my parents. I traced my finger across the slick plastic film, envying them. The lump in my throat dissolved and renewed determination took its place.

Maybe one day I'd come back and study their methods, but for now, this book wasn't what I was looking for. I grabbed the next one on the stack and found a pic of Di and me sunbathing during a family barbecue where we thought we were so sexy because we were finally allowed to wear bikinis. I remember thinking I might one day fill out the cups in the bikini. Oh, how naïve I once was.

I almost passed right over the page when I glimpsed a photo at the bottom and my mouth opened. There, at the same barbecue where Di and I had stripped down to jailbait-wear, was a photo of a younger Chess. He sat on a bench in the background of my past. His hair was shorter, and he was obviously scooting away from a man who'd tried to put his arm around him.

I didn't remember Chess at all. Di and I had been too busy trying to get the attention of one of Lorina's guy friends who we had a *huge* crush on while he probably thought we hadn't yet graduated to solid foods.

The guy next to Chess looked familiar, but not because I knew him—

—Because I had just flipped through hundreds of pictures of him in the album with my parents. Chess's dad had been involved in all my parents' environmental protests.

It seemed like Chess was deliberately trying to keep the info that our parents knew each other a secret. If I'd had his phone number, I would have canceled the date. But then I had a better idea: use the date to get answers. And yeah, I hoped the answers would be the kind I could get behind, like he wanted me to like him for him and not because my parents had liked him.

I changed my outfit a bazillion times before settling on something boring because I didn't have anything more exciting. Jeans and a plain, white T-shirt. I was a walking Gap advertisement.

I sidled down the stairs. Lorina lounged in an armchair, her feet planted on the ground instead of dangling off the side like mine did. She watched the TV in a trance, which was odd. The last few days, the TV had remained off while Lorina studied maps and pored over notes filled with her loopy handwriting.

I was about to open my mouth to say something when I caught my reflection in the mirrored china cabinet. An unruly lock of hair had escaped its flock. I patted it down.

"Do you have a date?"

Leave it to Lorina to notice the moment I indulged in narcissism. "I'm going out with a friend." My cheeks betrayed me, blooming a rosy pink.

She shut off the TV. "It's a school night."

"Yeah . . . School project."

Lorina stood up. "Not the way you're blushing."

Of course, that made me blush all over again.

She placed her palms on my shoulders, a giddy smile on her face. "Who is he?"

I couldn't tell her. Not when she might be investigating him. So I did the next best thing: distracted her. "Any new developments in the investigation?"

She let go of me and swung her arms at her sides. "Not anymore. My boss axed the project. Apparently things have died down."

"They have?" My own frown matched Lorina's. I wondered if Whitney had ceased operations after my flooding fiasco.

"Yeah." She twisted the class ring on her finger. "Nothing's happened in a while. My boss is thrilled. Thinks we scared them. But I don't know. I think they're lying low."

The sad part was we both hoped for the same thing, but for very different reasons.

"Well, good job then." I headed into the kitchen and swiped the box of leftover petit fours. They were getting stale, so they might not go to Chess's heart—by way of his stomach—but at least they wouldn't go to my hips. "You should celebrate the victory, maybe go out and get ice cr—"

"Oh no." She lifted a finger at me. "You're not getting away that easily. Alice, dating on a school night isn't allowed."

"I won't be home late." I cringed at my lame plea. "And my homework's done."

She stretched the skin of her face with her fingertips. "I understand, Alice, I really do. Hey, I'd kill to go on a date tonight."

I wavered in place, not knowing what to say or do. Part of me wanted to trudge upstairs and stop putting her through all this extra pressure. Give up what I wanted, like she had done for me.

"If I was only your sister, I'm sure I'd be helping you sneak out." She let out a strained laugh. "But I have to be more than that. I have to be—"

"No." I straightened my shoulders. I knew where this was going. Not just tonight, but for the next few years. She'd stay home to set a good example, but we'd both lose. I crossed my fingers behind my back, knowing there was only one way to prevent this and hating myself for what I was about to do. "You're not my mom."

I wrenched open the door and slammed it shut, then leaned against it, my eyes closed and my breath ragged. Oh God. I was such a wretched girl. I considered opening the door and apologizing. I half-expected her to come outside and yell, but she didn't, which made the knot in my stomach grow bigger.

Bright headlights swung into my driveway a few minutes later. I pushed my hair behind my ears and strutted toward the car, praying the brave appearance would seep into my psyche. Chess leaned over and popped the door open for me. Seventies rock music drowned out the neighbor's barking dog. As he twisted the radio dial to a new station, I sank into the passenger seat. "I have a present for you." I settled the box on my lap.

"That's kind of weird because I have one for you."

I clasped my hands in a prayer position. "Please let it be a razor, please let it be a razor."

He laughed. "This one's courtesy of Whitney." He pointed to the back seat where my backpack rested on the cushions.

"Oh." I closed my eyes. "Thanks." If Whitney had given it to Chess, it meant there would be no future opportunity for her to give it to me herself.

"What's yours?"

I lifted the lid to show him.

"Wow, you bought those for me?" The grin made me wish I had.

"Wait until you taste them." *Because you won't be as excited then.*

He reached over to grab one, but I shut the box, suddenly regretting my idea of salvaging cakes from a life of mold by pawning them off on a guy I liked. "They're for dessert! Which makes me wonder . . . where are we going?"

He abruptly swerved the car to the shoulder of the road and put it in park. Suburban houses outlined the street, an odd background for . . . parking? Didn't the guy usually bring the girl to some scenic overlook if he wanted to make out? My clammy hands slid apart. I might be on a direct path to shedding my good-girl image, but not like this!

He twisted off the radio he had worked so hard to set, and stared out into the moonlight. "Alice, I have a confession to make."

I held my breath, stupidly wishing he might confess his feelings for me.

"I haven't decided where I'm bringing you yet."

"What are the options?"

"We could get coffee or something. Sit and talk." He tapped his fingers against the steering wheel before pinning me with his intense gaze. "Or we could go to Whitney's."

"Do you want me to choose?"

He leaned his head back against the seat. "I want you to stay out of this stuff. If you get hurt because of me . . . us . . . well, I'd feel awful."

His words sent a cold sensation racing up my spine. "Hurt?"

His mouth hung open for a second. "In trouble."

"I know what I'm doing."

"Are you sure? Because I don't think you do."

I turned toward the window. "I'm a big girl." I laughed at the irony.

"Hey," his voice softened. "I didn't mean to upset you. It's just—I heard about your parents."

I faced him again. "And I heard about yours. Well, your dad, anyway."

He shifted in his seat, forehead creased. After a beat, he said almost cautiously, “What do you know?”

“I know my parents and your dad used to do protests together. I found pictures. Including one of you at my house.”

“And?” He clasped his hands in his lap.

“And in gym you said I didn’t have a reason for doing this stuff. But I do.”

He met my eyes. “You know? I thought you didn’t.”

I squinted at him. “Wait—know what?”

He studied me for several seconds. “What our parents were doing.”

“You mean the protests? I know they got the nuclear-power plant shut down. And they were trying to get a farmers’ market started.”

His face relaxed. “Yeah.”

“That’s exactly why I want to do this. I feel like I owe it to them to make it happen.”

He was already shaking his head before I even finished. “Bad idea. Too public. It would draw too much attention to us.”

“But—” Words died in my throat. I’d thought for sure they would help me if I could get in good with them.

“Option A?” He raised his eyebrows at me.

I couldn’t maneuver my lips into a *yes*. I had too many questions. “Does your dad still do this stuff? What happened to your mom?”

“Mom died when I was four. Cancer, the aggressive kind. And my dad stopped a while ago. Everyone did, which is why I started.” He chuckled. “And for the record, *that’s* the reason for all the rumors. Whitney started them to get suspicion off me because of my connection to my dad.”

I relaxed. “So the rebel comment was a lie? I feel so betrayed!” I slapped a palm against my chest and scoffed. “Why did you really get kicked out of boarding school?”

He nudged me with his shoulder. "I never said I got kicked out." He sighed. "My dad lost his job, so we couldn't afford it anymore. Simple as that."

"Oh." I reached out to touch his hand. "I'm sorry. And I'm sorry about your mom."

"We're dealing." He shrugged. "It's fine."

We sat in silence for a moment, hands connected. His mouth curved into a quarter-smile, only a portion given away. Just like his answers.

"What did you mean when you said you would have noticed if I was interested in this stuff? Because of my parents?"

Chess curled one hand around my shoulder, meeting my eyes with a new intensity. "It's because I kind of . . . staked you out. Not, like, in a creepy way."

"So you weren't the guy sneaking into my window to watch me sleep? Crap, I thought I'd solved that."

He laughed. "When I came back to school, I wanted to find you. I thought you might join up with me. But it seemed like you—I don't know—you didn't care like your parents had, so I left you alone."

"That's because I hid it from everyone until recently. I kind of made a fool out of myself freshman year, and I didn't want to do it alone the next time."

He flipped the car into drive. "Okay, I'll take you to Whitney's."

"How'd you hook up with her anyway? I mean—" As soon as the words *hook up* came out of my mouth, my mind supplied a mental image except with me in the starring role. My brain should be rated R. Thank God the darkness hid the blush spreading across my cheeks. "Meet! Didn't you just move back here?"

"About six months ago. Sort of. I didn't actually live in Wonderland all summer, but when I came back, I caught Whitney stealing some seeds at the Garden Center. I let her off the hook in exchange for her help."

Lines indented my forehead. "What kind of help?"

He looked away. "Whitney will kill me if I tell you. Keeping the group's secrets is, like, the one rule we have. Well, besides 'don't get caught.'"

"Does that mean I'm not in? Even if we're going to Whitney's?"

He sighed. "I like Whitney and Kingston and all, but you . . . you're different. Wholesome." He didn't see it, but I cringed. "I was kind of hoping we could be . . . " He glanced at me. "Friends or whatever. Just the two of us."

My heart raced. I hoped *whatever* was a synonym for *making out*. But as much as I wanted to explore that kind of friendship, I couldn't shut off my curiosity about Whitney and her missions. "It doesn't have to be that extreme. We could still be . . . friends, and I can still join your group."

His eyes held mine. "I like a girl who can read my mind."

He said something else, but I couldn't hear him. I was still stuck on the word *like.*

CHAPTER 9

"You brought her, I see." Whitney leaned against the conglomerate of open doors forming a pastel tunnel into her house. Her arms shook as if the doors would spring closed any moment and knock her over.

"Nothing gets by you." Chess relieved her of doorman duty and held them open with more ease.

She gave him a dirty look, then turned to me. "Think of this like a verbal contract. You enter, you keep your mouth shut."

Taking that vow, I stepped through the doors, then paused at the décor inside. Hats—ranging from formal top hats to the artistic creations usually found on the Queen of England—dangled from a chandelier. I spotted the trucker hat Kingston had been wearing in gym perched delicately on one of the hooks. White polka dots covered a purple wall in front of me. Curvy stripes of varying widths alternated in teal and subdued candy-apple red on a different wall. The mirror in front of me distorted my body like a fun house.

Whitney must have seen me staring because she said, "My mom's an installation artist."

"What does that mean?"

"It's art you have to go see. Experience." She gestured at the five-door concoction. "It's really a pain sometimes, everything in the house has been remodeled into something else—something far more annoying."

We followed her into the kitchen. Large, metal spikes poked out of the refrigerator door instead of a torture-chamber wall where they belonged.

I pointed to it. "New diet regimen?"

She flicked her eyes toward the fridge. "Obstacles for our basic survival needs."

"It's a bitch to open that thing," Chess said. "You have to hold your arm at the right angle or you might end up in the hospital explaining you weren't trying to slit your wrists."

"That sounds like a case for Child Protective Services."

She shrugged. "I keep essentials in the basement fridge. That one I haven't let her revise."

"Your house is like a museum." I set the box of days-old cakes on her counter.

"Yep. Look, but don't touch."

"If you charged for tickets," Chess said, "that would cover some funds."

"But then what would Kingston be good for?" Whitney chuckled to herself and stopped in front of the kitchen counter. Bending underneath, she pulled a blender out of the cabinet.

Chess reached above her and retrieved cups off a tall shelf. They were repurposed from various found objects. A shellacked paper-towel roll had become a highball glass. Layers of buttons were welded together in a closed formation. He even set a conch shell wrapped in tightly coiled wire on the counter.

Whitney slid a cutting board and knife over to me. "Chop this." She tossed me an array of herbs.

I spotted lavender and basil among a bunch I didn't recognize. They smelled flowery and a little musky, too. "What are these?" I pointed to several unfamiliar herbs of various shapes and textures.

"The special ingredient."

"Where's Kingston?" Chess asked, shaking some spices into the blender.

"Finishing up a sale."

"Does he work at the Garden Center, too?"

Whitney snorted. "No. He'll be here in a sec. Then we'll have a little huddle."

I chopped the herbs until Whitney snatched them away and added them to the blender. Chess angled his body over the fridge and pulled out some kind of murky liquid without submitting himself to a bloodletting ritual. He boiled the liquid on the stove and added some other ingredients that looked like cherries and coffee beans. Then Whitney dumped the contents of the blender into the pot. I watched in awe, trying to figure out this odd recipe.

Kingston arrived fifteen minutes later, wearing a cowboy hat. Whitney poured the foamy substance from the stove into the four glasses. They each grabbed one and left the last, shaped like a perfume bottle, stopper and all, on the counter with no further instructions. I clutched the delicate glass in my hands, unstopped it, and brought it to my lips.

Definitely the same stuff from the other day. Healthy but dangerous at the same time. Like them.

"Here's the deal, Alice," Whitney leaned against the counter. "You kept your mouth shut. Noted."

"But you still fucked everything up." Kingston watched me like he was trying to dissect me with his eyes. I diverted my gaze.

Whitney shot him a look. "Language." She turned back to me. "We like to be a little more incognito than that."

"I know. I didn't know what I was supposed to do. I mean—"

"You think we have instructions?" Whitney scoffed. "That's not how this works."

I snapped my mouth shut.

"I checked with the plants. They're against her." Kingston plopped into a chair and put his shoes up on the kitchen table. He talked to plants. Why was I not surprised? "For the record, my vote's still no."

Chess met my eyes. "Well, mine's still yes."

"I feel like I always have to do everything around here." Whitney stomped over to Kingston. There were only three seats around the table—a musical-chairs art installation?—so she scooted in beside her stepbrother and gestured at the empty seats.

"Really, I won't mess things up anymore." I plopped into one. "I respect what you're doing. You're making a difference."

Kingston pointed a finger-gun at me. "You have no idea what we're doing. You just assume you do."

Chess kept telling me the same thing. Maybe I really *was* only seeing what I wanted to see.

"We each have a purpose." Whitney tipped the cup to her mouth and took a long drink, spilling a drop on Kingston's lap. He pushed her off his seat and more liquid sloshed over the rim. "I create the missions and provide supplies. Kingston is our security guard, and he funds our projects." Whitney hopped onto the table. "And Chess—"

"Is the muscle?" He twisted his hands around his mug. "The brains?"

"I was going to say *motivation*." She shifted her vision to me. "Anyway, Alice, we—"

"How does Kingston provide the funds?" I asked, only because I saw where Whitney was going: they had all the bases covered, so they didn't need me. I needed to distract them until I could think of something I could offer that they didn't already have.

Kingston coughed several times in succession. "There's no way I trust you with that information."

What did that mean? I pressed my lips together as I thought back to Chess's earlier comment about catching Whitney pilfering seeds. I could easily see this group justifying stealing from corporations to fund their projects.

"Whit, we discussed giving her another chance," Chess said.

"Did you tell them about my parents?" I asked him. Kingston rolled his eyes, like I was about to tell them this was my way of rebelling over their restrictions against having a boy in my room or something equally lame.

Whitney squinted at Chess. "No. Is there something I should know?"

"I didn't think it was relevant." Chess shrugged.

"It is!" I slapped the table in my excitement.

"So you do know the meaning of *it*. That proves it." Kingston pointed at me. "She's a liar. She lied before."

I ignored him. "This isn't some fluke thing for me. Chess's dad and my parents used to have a group like yours. I can prove it. I found a photo album with evidence."

Whitney leaned forward. "I'm listening."

I opened my mouth and shut it again. "But that's it. I just meant that it's . . . in my genes to be part of your group." I held my breath and tried to keep my face steady instead of shattering from anticipation.

"No, about the photo album. I'd like to see it. And anything else you can find about the stuff your parents organized." She pursed her lips. "Chess, you should have told me this."

I shifted in my chair. "Um, okay, but . . . why?"

"All questions can't have answers. Or at least ones I want to share."

"Can I exchange the album for . . . membership?"

Kingston bolted from his chair, banging his mug down on the table. My teeth clattered together. "That's it? You're going to let her in because she may have some information? We already tried with Mr. Katz and got nowhere, which is exactly where this will get us."

I contorted my eyes and lips into an expression that would best crown me as an angel, halo and all.

"This is the wrong path," Kingston continued. "The right one's not even visible. It's covered with leaves and twigs."

"You do realize we're inside, right?" Whitney kicked him with her foot.

"Only temporarily."

Whitney nodded as if that made sense. "Well, it's not just the information. There are some bigger things we've wanted to do that we could use an extra hand on. Like that parking lot that used to be the nuclear-power plant?"

I expected Kingston to whine about that with some lame excuse, but he sighed melodramatically like a little kid who didn't get his way. What could have possibly made him give in all of a sudden?

"All right, Alice." Whitney drummed her fingers on the table. "We're going to do something tonight. We could use you, but we can't get caught and we can't mess up."

I swallowed hard. Perfection and I weren't exactly cohorts in our endeavors. Usually I lagged behind someone else's lead. Second in the class. Third wheel in friendships. Fourth in their group.

"You get info on a need-to-know basis." Kingston shot me a smile that revealed a thin, blue line above his gums. He coughed again and took a sip of green liquid.

"It's a probationary period," Whitney clarified.

I chugged my foamy, green drink, hoping it would give me some kind of liquid courage, like spinach for Popeye. I knew *something* interesting was sure to happen if I drank this liquid. "I'm in."

Whitney pushed herself off the table. "I have to get some supplies upstairs. Want to start loading the car, guys?"

"Send Alice to get the supplies." Kingston flicked his wrist at me.

Whitney swirled her mug along the glass table, leaving behind streaks of green. "Yeah, it's probably good if you're out of the way for a few minutes."

"Whatever you need."

"Fetch me my gardening gloves. There's also a fan somewhere; get that, too. Then wait there until we're ready."

"Where are they?" I stood up.

Whitney shrugged. "I can organize missions, not myself."

The three of them led me to the foyer and disappeared around the bend without another word. Upstairs, several closed doors lined the hallway. A picture of a skull and crossbones hung from the first door. How unoriginal. Must be Kingston's; he didn't strike me as a burgeoning well of creativity. I opened the only unpainted door in the hallway, the one going against the status quo.

A floral, earthy scent attacked my nose. Palm trees shielded Whitney's bed in a canopy. Flowers sprung from open drawers, nestled into soil instead of clothes. Above her bed, an enlarged architectural drawing took up the length of one entire blue-painted wall. A blown-up blueprint. Pushpins of varying colors stuck out in specific spots with tiny, almost-illegible handwriting scrawled beneath. Symbols that looked like crude hieroglyphics marked info I couldn't decipher beside each pushpin.

Curiouser and curiouser. A secret code for a secret society.

I climbed onto the bed. Each of the pushpins identified a target. I recognized some of the red ones from Lorina's information file. Large blocks of black marker censored whatever information Whitney had written under the location titles. My finger traced from the red pin by the school creek to the green one marking the school itself. Paragraphs of text remained visible and untainted.

Ideas to cut off power supply: flood school so water damages wire. Maybe with creek?

My skin tingled. These words had been crossed out with a single pen stroke. So the creek mission had nothing to do with irrigating the land? If so, why did that seem to be checked off with a red pushpin?

New plan. Cut wires? How to do w/out getting fried or caught? No access in teachers' lounge. K checking other areas.

That was why she'd snuck into the lounge that day? Not to steal supplies but to look for a power source?

Outside, a car door slammed, and I jumped. Last thing I needed was to get caught snooping. I headed over to her messy desk and rifled through some of her papers. My fingers traced over math problems and AP chemistry lab reports. Underneath one stack, I found the battery-operated fan Whitney'd been using the other day, like the kind I used on hot summer days outside in the garden. Fan down, gloves to go.

The sounds of hushed voices, a car trunk opening, and a few sharp thuds provided guidance to the others' progress. My hands dangled at my sides as I looked around, trying to think like Whitney. Finally, I spotted a pair of mud-encased gloves hanging from the back of her door as footsteps stomped on the stairs.

"Here, put this on." Whitney tossed me a black hoodie with a white-flowering vine crawling up the back. "It'll conceal your hair."

I lifted the hood over my head. As we walked toward the car, I snuck a glance at the foyer mirror. No longer would I be mistaken for a goody-goody. I looked like I belonged with Whitney and her friends.

As I slipped into the back seat of Kingston's truck, I caught a glimpse of the clock and immediately tried to forget what I'd just seen. I told myself I was already in enough trouble with Lorina; a little more wouldn't make much of a difference. Kingston caught me looking. "Now who's angry with time?"

"It's later than I thought."

"Of course it is." He tapped the digital numbers. "This clock is precisely two days late."

Chess filed in beside me. I scooted an inch toward him. "What are we doing?"

"We like to call it reforestation. Opposite of deforestation."

"Clever. Another drive-by planting at an abandoned warehouse?"

"Something like that," Whitney said from the passenger seat. "Not a warehouse this time."

"I love what you're doing. Taking all these dead and lifeless places and giving them new life."

"That's not the point of this." Chess shrugged in an offhand way.

"If only it were," Kingston said. "Then maybe I'd wake up."

My knee rested against Chess's denim-covered leg. So casual, he probably didn't even notice, but somehow it felt close. It took all my willpower not to press my knee harder into his and see if he registered it.

We passed by LEGO building after LEGO building in the sprawling landscape of Wonderland, pressed so close together they were almost attached. The farms that had once existed here were now fairy-tale myths. The site of the old nuclear-power plant Whitney had mentioned was now just vast pavement, littered with a few stray cars. As we drove to our destination, my knee bounced up and down. This high was greater than any triple-espresso shot. "Thanks for letting me come."

"You might think differently if the police show up." Whitney tugged the cords of her hoodie tighter to conceal her hair.

"Jail? Not fun." Kingston gunned the engine. "All those jokes about not dropping the soap bar? I didn't even get a freaking soap bar."

I swallowed. I had been hoping his mug shot was Photoshopped. "Why'd you go to jail?"

"Botched mission," Whitney said.

"I took one for the team." His voice contained more pep than a can of Red Bull. "Maybe next time you'll be the one who has to sacrifice."

Was that why they had let me in? Chess nudged his leg against mine to stop it from shaking.

"Kingston, stop trying to scare her," he warned. But it was too late. My heart raced and my throat felt tight. I was officially terrified.

CHAPTER 10

I had expected the mission to take place in a dilapidated part of town. Warehouses with broken windows, and asbestos seeping into the air. Some dead place we could bring to life. It had never occurred to me this mission might be the opposite. Some newborn place we would destroy.

We parked in front of a set of brand-new houses, each with construction stickers plastered in the windows. "Sold" signs sprouted out of the manicured lawns. This particular cul-de-sac was a replica of several others we had driven by. A virginal development, not yet broken in by the living.

"What's wrong with this place?" Even my feet hitting the pavement couldn't disguise the panic in my voice. "I mean, I was happy when they built it."

Three sets of eyes narrowed at me.

"Because of the solar panels on the roofs?" My head volleyed back and forth between them. "It's environmentally friendly!"

This was Wonderland's answer to the energy problem. Citizens fed up with living like vampires in their houses were snatching up the new properties in less time than it took to build them. Since housing prices in the rest of Wonderland had dropped so low, I'd heard rumors that a lot of young, fresh-out-of-college families were bidding as soon as they went on the market. The social class was always greener on the other side.

"Not even six months ago, this place," Whitney stabbed her finger toward the houses, "used to be a farm."

"A fucking great farm with a lot of land that provided crops to several cities in the area." Kingston unloaded a plant from the back of the truck and set it on the ground.

"The last farm in a hundred-mile radius, actually," Chess added.

"But now it's a housing complex," I whispered, understanding.

"It's a devastating loss." Whitney tossed a metal shovel onto the ground with a tinny *thud*. "You know how much land the farm has left?"

I squeezed my eyes shut, afraid of the answer.

"None," Chess said. "The township confiscated it all, kept changing zoning laws and permit regulations and raising taxes until the farm owners couldn't fight anymore."

"What happened to the farmers?"

Chess lifted a leafy plant from the trunk that obscured his face in shadow. "They fled the area. Couldn't afford to live here anymore." He paused. "We think," he added as an afterthought.

"So what are we going to do?"

"Not what I want to do. Which is destroy this place. That would really get the message across." Kingston brandished a pair of gardening shears like a weapon.

"We're making a statement. Showing the town what they lost, what this used to be," Chess said.

"What it still could be if they tear down the houses and turn it back into a farm." With her gloves on, Whitney picked up one of the potted plants and a bag of soil and carried them over to the front of the house.

I chose a tray of purple azaleas and headed after her. "You're just like your mother," I teased.

Whitney rolled her eyes.

"You are *revising*, aren't you?"

She set the plant down on the front steps and pulled a screwdriver from her pocket. She jimmied the front lock until it popped open. "Chaining yourself to a tree is cliché and you'll get arrested. This will get noticed. It has to. There's a family moving in tomorrow." Keeping the door propped open with her foot, she reached for the potted plant.

I transferred my weight from foot to foot. Maybe I'd been wrong to want to be involved. This family would probably be super excited to come to their new home tomorrow, only to find it vandalized when they got there? That wasn't doing good for the environment; that was breaking and entering.

She poked her head out the door. "You're not second-guessing yourself, are you?"

"No." I picked up the azaleas and followed Whitney inside.

"I know what you're thinking," she said. "But it's not a random family. It's the owners of this new development. And we're not going to mess things up. The family will still move in; they'll just have to bypass a few plants to do it." She headed to the kitchen where she opened the bag of soil and dumped one quarter of its contents into the sink. "Think of it more like . . . decoration than destruction." She removed the pink flower from its pot and replanted it into the soil. After patting it down, she ran the faucet and looked up at me. "There are more sinks and bathtubs."

I lugged the flowers to the bathroom. After I finished the sink there, I hustled back to the car for more supplies. A lizard scurried across my path. I yelped, jumping back a step. Kingston snickered at me. I squared my shoulders and kept going. Chess unloaded large planks of plywood from the trunk and carried them toward the house, one by one.

"What are those for?" I asked, passing him on my way back to Whitney.

“Planting flowers in sinks is annoying, but its not going to make anyone stop building stuff over farms.” Chess grinned in a way no emoji could replicate. “We’re barricading the door.”

My stomach practiced for an Olympic-gymnastics tryout. This was getting harder to condone, but still, what they were doing wasn’t *too* damaging. I kept reminding myself of that.

Kingston bent down and inspected one of the flowerpots. “Not much, sir,” he said, saluting it. He glanced back, squinting at us, then leaned into the flower conspiratorially. “Your secret’s safe, don’t worry.” He patted the petals and straightened up, getting back to work as if nothing odd had occurred.

After Whitney and I finished inside the house, we deposited two large pots on the porch guarding the door. She secured them down with some kind of sticky substance she glopped on the bottom. Using the battery-operated fan, she lay on her stomach and blew air into the small crease where the pot met the porch. A few minutes passed and she tested the strength of the bond by yanking the pot this way and that. Satisfied that even a tornado couldn’t budge it, she moved on to the next plant.

“Krazy Glue?”

She capped the bottle. “That’s for amateurs. This one’s my own concoction.”

I thought back to the AP chemistry notes I’d found in her room. In eighth grade, she took first prize at the science fair for her chemistry experiment but had never entered another competition. Maybe she hadn’t quit after all, just stopped advertising her talents, stopped drawing attention.

Meanwhile, Chess and Kingston looped ropes through the holes at either end of the planks and secured them with Boy-Scout knots onto the drainpipes. The planks stretched across the front of the house like window-washing lifts. They loaded them with plants, slapping on the same glue Whitney had used on the porch.

Kingston stopped every now and then, bracing his hands on his knees and gasping for breath. I wanted to tease him because he had teased me, but I wasn't that sadistic. Whitney, however, didn't share the same philosophy. "What? Do the planks weigh more than five pounds? Maybe you should practice with soup cans."

"Shut up. I'm still sore from when you both abandoned me and made me do that warehouse all by myself."

"Wimp. That was forever ago," Whitney said.

"I don't see you lifting these heavy planks." Kingston stretched his arms skyward and forced himself to keep going. His pace slowed, like he was trying to trudge through quicksand.

Stepping back, my breath caught in my throat. Long assembly lines of plants covered the entire bottom half of the house in four neat rows, blocking the door so the family couldn't get inside without removing them. A vertical forest. We weren't destroying the house, but our statement couldn't be ignored. A smile curled on my face as I watched my new friends in awe.

"Hey, where's the ladder?" Chess asked Whitney when we had finished filling the last of the planks already attached to the house. The top third of the house remained uncovered.

"See, this is why bringing her was a bad idea." Kingston gestured to me with his chin. Beads of sweat outlined his forehead. His skin looked pale, flu-like. "We couldn't bring the ladder with her in the back seat."

I pulled the strings of my hoodie tight, trying to disappear.

"Why didn't you put it with the plywood in the back of the truck?" Whitney asked.

Kingston held up his hands. "Hey, don't go blaming me. This wouldn't have been a problem if it had stayed where it was."

"I guess we could call it a night," Whitney said. "Save some supplies."

No one made a move for the truck.

I'd carried out every task they'd given me tonight, but I'd still managed to be more of a burden than a benefactor. I wilted against a large oak tree perched in front of the house, its branches covering most of the windows.

"No way. What we did isn't *big* enough. Let's burn the place down." Kingston pulled a lighter out of his pocket and whipped it in the air.

"Hey, let's not get crazy." Whitney held up a five-finger stop sign.

"Too late for that, Whit. We have to do something!" Kingston bent down and picked up a rock off the ground, clutching it in his fist. He wound his arm and launched the rock at the house. His home-run aim smashed a window on contact, right through the construction sticker.

"Stop!" The panic in Whitney's voice set me on high alert. I straightened, bumping my head on one of the lower branches.

Kingston searched the area for another rock. I peered up at the branch above me.

"Wait!" I lifted my leg onto the lowest branch. I reached for the one above me and pulled myself up, leaves rustling. My muscles strained until my feet found purchase on the next branch up.

Kingston paused, arm frozen in mid-throw.

"What are you doing?" Chess rushed over and grabbed my leg.

I kicked his hand free. "If I climb this, I can get into a higher position. Go up to the roof and put plants up there." I climbed onto another branch. "No need to smash windows."

"No." His fingers encircled my leg again, and his warm hands burned through my pants. "I'm not letting you do that. It's not safe."

"It could be kind of cool." Whitney approached us. "We've never done that before. And it would be a bitch for them to take down. Or . . . " She smiled wickedly. "They could leave them up and our statement stays like a warning beacon." She hopped up and down at this idea.

Kingston dropped the rock and clapped his hands once. "I'm all for watching the monkey climb."

"This is a really bad idea," Chess said.

"Please," I whispered so only he could hear. "Let me show them I can be useful."

Chess's jaw shifted. "Fine. Get me some rope. Alice, don't climb yet."

While Whitney dashed off to get the rope, Kingston crawled onto the hood of the trunk and leaned back, his arms crossed behind his head, watching my show.

Chess climbed to my spot on the second branch, the tree shaking in protest. "I know most of what we did today is kind of insane, but you don't need to win the competition."

I pressed my lips together. He was snarking up the wrong tree.

He wrapped his arm around my waist. I loathed the extra fabric the hoodie concealed me in. "Now if you fall, I can catch you."

"You'll fall, too," I pointed out, even though I folded into his touch.

He brought his lips close to my ear. "Alice, you don't have to do this. You're in, okay?" His warm breath sent chills down my spine and tingled in my ear. I closed my eyes and savored the sensation.

"I want to." Gripping the branch above for support, I twisted around to meet his eyes. "I'm tired of holding everyone back. Holding myself back."

"Does that mean you're going to try still? With the farmers' market?" His chest stilled as he waited for my answer.

I bit my lip. I didn't want to lie to him. He seemed to be the only person I didn't have to pretend with. "I get why you guys don't want me to do that yet. So I'll postpone it." Until I could figure out a way to do it publicly, without drawing attention to them if they wouldn't help. "I understand how it would mess up what you're trying to do. But this isn't just about the farmers' market. You know that."

"Right, you're sticking around because of Kingston." He raised his eyebrows a few times.

"He and I have *so* much in common, it's like we were separated at birth." I chuckled. "But no, the other reason I'm sticking around is . . . " I took a deep breath. "In this tree." I couldn't believe I had said that! My cheeks burned. Whitney grunted as she rummaged through the car. Kingston hopped off the trunk to help her. "I'm really attracted to the plants."

He laughed. "Yeah, that's what I'm attracted to, too." He pulled on the zipper of his hoodie.

A door slammed. Whitney headed our way, rope swinging in her hand. Chess spoke in a rushed whisper. "Alice . . . you should know. We didn't tell you everything tonight. Our goal, our purpose or whatever. You only got half the story. The other half?" He sighed and looked away. "It would probably scare you off."

My skin prickled. I didn't want to ask this yet, not until they trusted me. But this was the perfect opening. "I saw something in Whitney's room. About trying to cut the school's power supply?"

"It's not what you think."

"I don't even know *what* to think."

Whitney hopped below us. "The rope you ordered."

Chess and I both pulled away, but I stole one last glance at him. I didn't know what to think about the power-supply stuff I'd found, but I knew what I wanted to believe. That I had been right all along; this group *was* doing good things, just in a roundabout way.

Otherwise, I wouldn't be able to justify my involvement.

"We tying up Alice?" Kingston shouted from the car. "Using her for ransom?"

Whitney clucked her tongue. "Don't worry. I plan on having a little chat with him tonight. Right now, I'm more worried about *him* giving us away than you."

The corners of my lips twitched until they formed a smile. She finally believed I was trustworthy! They couldn't be bad guys.

Right?

Chess twirled the rope around his hand like a lasso and looped it around a thick branch toward the top. He then tied both ends around my waist with sailor knots. There," he said. "Now you won't splatter to the ground if you fall."

"It would make for a killer art installation." I lifted myself onto a higher level and then another one.

Panting, I paused, my arm muscles working overtime. I had some tree-climbing experience, but it was the ten-foot one in my garden, not this fifty-foot monstrosity. This was climb and punishment.

"I'm starting to get wrinkles," Kingston hissed from below.

I ignored him and pressed on anyway. From the way Chess cheered me on below—"Steady now, you're doing great"—I expected him to be fully decked out in a miniskirt and pompoms.

When I reached the top, another rope came flying up at me and I managed to catch it without falling out of the tree. Miracles do happen.

"Hold on," Chess yelled, "we're tying a pot to the other end."

The rope tightened until it was ruler-straight from the weight of the plant. Trusting Chess's harness would hold me, I pulled the rope until the pot made its way through the branches.

With the pot in hand, I swiveled to focus on the roof. Two feet of empty space separated the shingles from the branch I balanced on. In order to get across, I would have to stretch my body like a bridge. It had looked much closer to the house from below. Cause of death: depth perception.

Suddenly, something soft hit my back. I wobbled for a moment but managed to regain my balance as another soft thing hit my arm. It was sticky and left a streak of . . . frosting? "Stop throwing things at me!" I yelled. "Are you trying to make me fall?"

"What? That's crazy! I thought you needed a push forward," Kingston said from below. "You froze. And it's not like I'm throwing rocks." He jiggled the petit-four box in his hands. Clearly, he didn't know how stale they were.

"Hey." Chess snatched the box out of Kingston's hands. "She brought those for me."

Kingston laughed. "She must not like you then because I tried one and—" He stuck his finger down his throat and made loud simulated-barfing noises.

I bit my lip. "I don't know what he's talking about."

"No one ever does," Kingston said.

I turned back to the roof, trying to find my resolve again.

"If you're scared, I can get some more rocks," Kingston so kindly offered.

That fueled me forward. I took several calming breaths, then tightrope-walked toward the edge of the branch. I tossed the plant onto the roof. It landed sideways and rolled down the shingles. My teeth ground together. But the pot snagged on the gutter and rested there.

I blew my hair out of my face.

I surfer-balanced on the wooden arm and lowered myself inch by inch onto the teetering branch. By the time I lay on my stomach, I wasn't sure which was shakier, my limbs or the tree's.

I made the mistake of looking down. Adrenaline surged in my body, pumping hot blood into my ears. My pulse raced, my muscles strained . . . and I loved it. I'd never been this high before, never seen the tops of my friends' heads. I was tall up here.

Smiling, I glanced up at the tip of the branch only to spot a lizard crawling along the storm drain. Heights I could handle. Reptiles, not so much. I didn't dare breathe, just tried to aim telepathic commands toward it. When it crawled closer anyway, I opted for actual words. "Shoo! Go away!"

"You okay up there?"

I forced the word "Yeah" out of my mouth instead of what I wanted to say: a rant about the lizard defending the house from alien invaders like me.

I hugged the tree limb, finally earning myself the nickname most go-green-haters liked to shout: tree-hugger. The lizard paused in front of my fingers before deciding my arms were a bridge. It crawled onto my forearms, its tiny feet tickling me. *Ignore the sensation. There is no lizard. Lizards are imaginary creatures, like unicorns.* It continued down the rest of my body. A ticklish sensation radiated over my legs. My nose twitched. When the lizard reached my ankles, it danced back and forth. I lost it. My mouth opened up in a fit of giggles.

The branch sagged from my spastic movements, bending closer to the roof. I curled my fingers as tightly as I could around the limb and shook my leg to try to get the lizard off me, not realizing the motion would throw me off balance. My weight shifted and my torso mimicked a headfirst bungee jumper.

My scream was worthy of a horror movie.

The lizard fell off my leg and tumbled to the ground below. But I couldn't think about that.

"You murdered Bill!" Kingston yelled. "Poor guy."

"Bill?" Whitney said.

"You don't like the name Bill?" He pressed a finger to his lip. "What about Artie? Nah." Kingston's voice turned thoughtful. "He seemed like he'd have a one-syllable name."

I clenched my teeth and tried my best to stay . . . alive. Gripping my ankles around the branch, I swung my arm above me, searching. My fingers clasped something cold and smooth. The rain gutter. With one final trapeze move that would surely have won me maximum points in the Presidential Fitness pull-up test, I tugged my entire upper body onto the safety of the roof, then swung my lower half up to match.

Pausing there, I resisted the urge to kiss the solid surface.

"Wow, good job," Whitney called, already picking up a plant and tying a rope around it. All the fear of my near-death experience evaporated.

"You mean, God job," Kingston said. "Since she seems to be playing God. Murdering innocent animals."

Chess placed his hand on Kingston's shoulder. "Hey, lay off. It was self-defense."

"Karma's not that forgiving. I should know."

"Oh, but karma's totally on your side about throwing cakes at me?" I yelled while Whitney used a makeshift rope-over-branch pulley system to send plants up to me.

"I said I should know." For once, Kingston made sense.

While I placed plants on the roof based on Whitney's directions, Chess climbed up to the top of the tree with a scrap piece of plank wood. He fastened it across several branches using ropes and nails. I preferred my descent method to my grand ascent.

"What did I tell you?" He took my hand and helped me onto the same branch he stood on. "Oh, right, that it was a terrible idea to go climbing this tree."

"Should I remind you that I succeeded?" I couldn't keep the proud smile off my face.

"Should I remind you that you almost didn't?"

I had a lot of almosts in my life. Things I wanted to do but didn't. There was an *almost* standing with me on this branch.

I leaned forward, invading his personal space until my lips rested against his. Turned out a near-death experience made you aggressive.

His lips moved against mine, fierce and hungry. My arms wrapped around him, a makeshift harness. My mind was full of exclamation points.

I broke away from the kiss. "That shut you up."

He grinned with a smile I wanted to devour. "Wait, I'm still talking. I don't think it worked yet. You should try to shut me up again."

I accepted that RSVPlea and kissed him again. Every atom in my body danced with excitement.

"Great," Kingston said, and Chess and I broke apart. "We're coupling off now. Whitney?"

She gave him a dirty look. Chess and I climbed down the rest of the tree, and every time he placed his hand on my waist to steady me, my skin tingled. We reached the others at the bottom where they had finished loading the car.

Even though I stood on solid ground, I felt like I was floating.

"I hope you didn't find that climb *too* difficult." Whitney grabbed the rope from my hands. "Because the missions only get more dangerous from here. Can you handle that?"

My smile threatened to drop, but I had good reflexes. Still, I couldn't get out a confident *yes.*

"What?" Kingston smirked at me. "Katz got your tongue?"

The heat sweeping through my cheeks was a good match for the sweat crowning my forehead at Whitney's reference to future missions. And then her words caught up to me. There *would* be future missions. I was in the group! It took all my stored willpower and a few aching muscles to keep from doing a victory dance. "I'm ready for anything."

I'd procrastinate on worrying about the dangerous future missions tomorrow. Today, I had great next-pectations.

CHAPTER 11

The next day in gym, I didn't get a chance to share more than a smile and a wave—that Kingston intercepted—with Chess because the teachers conspired against us and separated our classes into different Presidential Fitness tasks. I desperately wanted to hear about the mission. Did the family move in? Were the police onto us? I'd have to try to pry info out of Lorina after work.

If she ever talked to me again, that is. She hadn't waited up for me when I got home, which only made me feel as icky as the dirt encrusting my hands from the reforesting. I wanted to take that as a good sign—after all, if she didn't wait up, she couldn't punish me—but I was never good at reading the signs or anything else that didn't come from a textbook.

Before lunch, I stopped at my locker and found a note inside. *Follow the creek into the center of the forest at afternoon tea time.*

A thrill shuddered through me. My next mission?

A quick Google search on my phone during lunch led to learning English tea time was held between three and five P.M. I decided to split the difference and go with four. I practically danced in my seat during my last class, my eyes flirting with the clock's hands. The smile stayed plastered on my face, like I had some silly secret I could barely keep to myself. Di kept eyeing me but didn't press it any further. She and Dru were too busy mourning Quinn's temporary absence from class.

After I double-checked the area to make sure no one could see me, I slipped out the back of the school and traced the contour of the creek.

A few paces into the woods I came across the ruined dam, now covered with spray paint. “Neverland rules!” and “Homecoming. It’s on.”

Fifteen minutes later, a sharp, burnt-herb scent filtered toward me, unnatural for the forest. As I kept walking, the scent grew stronger, and then a shape came into focus. My stomach dropped when the shape started to resemble Kingston, complete with a fedora concealing his shaved head.

I slowed my pace, craning my neck looking for Chess or Whitney. I tried not to make my movements too sudden, but his head snapped up anyway. A slow, Grinch-like smile spread over his face.

Had he left me the note or were the others coming later, late as usual? Hoping for the latter, I squared my shoulders, lifted my chin, and plowed toward him. Even if this was Kingston’s doing, I was a little curious about why he’d gone through so much trouble to set up this private meeting.

He sat cross-legged on a large rock, a green, blown-glass tube in front of him. The tube spread out into a bulbous sphere at the base, with a stopper extending in the opposite direction from the tube. Keeping his eyes on me, he dipped his head and pressed his lips around the mouth of the tube. He flicked his lighter onto the stopper. Bubbles boiled inside the base. His chest contracted, staying concave for a few moments. Then he blew out a puff of smoke in my face.

I coughed, recalling the first riddle Whitney had given me. Marijuana. It certainly didn’t smell like cigarette smoke.

“Who are *you?*” Kingston’s eyelids drooped over his red-rimmed eyes. “What do you want from us?”

I blinked at him. *This* was why he had made me come out here? “What am I doing here?” I crossed my arms.

“You’re gonna give me some answers.”

My blood stilled. We were alone, in the middle of the woods, and no one knew where I was. But I couldn't let Kingston see that fear and use it against me. He would be counting on that. So I forced myself to act like Whitney: aloof and unafraid. I lifted my chin. "I don't think you're very good at seeing the future."

"I see the present fine, though." He curled his legs beneath him. "In fact, I see you don't really have a good reason to join up with us. Well, except for your little crush, but I hope you're not that pathetic."

A million reasons why I wanted to join bottled up in my throat. Each one pegged me as desperate. If Whitney were faced with the same problem, she'd spit a riddle in his face, her confidence unaffected. I stole a page from her playbook.

"That's nonsense. Nothing's what it is, because everything is what it isn't. And contrariwise"—Ugh, hopefully it would never get back to Di and Dru that I'd stolen their favorite word—"what it is, it can't be. And what it can't be, it could. So there." Okay, maybe I needed to leave the riddles to Whitney.

He blinked at me.

I sighed and added, "Whitney and Chess seem to accept me anyway. I think I've proven I'm not going to rat you out."

"Doesn't matter. I don't trust you."

"Then why are you smoking pot in front of me?" I rested one hand on my hip. "We both know this isn't about trust. Perhaps *you* should explain yourself."

He shrugged. "I have my reasons."

With Kingston, I couldn't be sure his reasons were logical. I shook my head. "Whatever." Clearly he was trying to intimidate me and make me uncomfortable by smoking pot in my face. "I don't have time for this." I turned around and started back the way I had come.

He slithered off the rock and cut me off. "That's where you're wrong." He grabbed my shoulder. "You have all the time in the world." His nails dug into my skin as he shook his watch in front of my face with his other arm.

I froze in place. Would he really hurt me? Out here with no one to rescue me?

"You can't leave yet!" he said. "You're gonna hear me out. It's important." He let go of my shoulder, and I stumbled backward. A twig snapped beneath my foot.

I rubbed my shoulder and stifled a sob.

"Overreact much? Chill out and keep your temper."

"You're one to talk." I waited for him to continue, but nothing else came. "Is that all?" My fists were clenched at my sides. I wanted to disobey rules, not follow them, and I especially didn't want to follow Kingston's.

"No." Kingston walked back to the rock and inserted the tube into his mouth.

He blew out another puff of smoke, lifting his lower lip above his upper lip. "Want some?" He held the bong out to me.

"No, thanks, I'm good."

His lips curled into a half-smile. "See? You proved my point."

"That I don't do drugs? Submit to peer pressure? Share with strangers? Take your pick."

"You're not ready for the dangerous stuff," he said. "You think we only go around decorating buildings with flowers?"

"No," I admitted. I already knew some of the other stuff they did or were planning. Blacking out the entire school wasn't exactly a minor infraction. And I knew the township wouldn't have gone through the trouble of putting together a committee to stop people who went around giving out free landscaping.

"I don't know why we're even bothering anymore. All these flowers." He waved his hand at the forest surrounding us. "They're just going to be destroyed. Wither and die. We can't keep impossibilities alive."

"That's very poetic of you."

"This isn't about poetry. It's about reality. Ever wonder why we don't want you going in that basement? How we fund our missions?" He tapped the bong.

I groaned. So they *were* growing pot. And selling it. Or at least Kingston was. I had to hope the others weren't involved, because Whitney had defined Kingston's job as providing the funds. "Why are you telling me this?"

"Do you approve? 'Cause you really don't have a choice." He broke into a coughing fit, which I thought was from the pot, but he hadn't taken a drag in a while. He pulled a clear bag out of his pocket filled with what looked like dried mushrooms. He popped one in his mouth and closed his eyes, chewing. Great, now he was shrooming, too. At least being high might explain his usual psychobabble.

"Why are you telling me this?" I repeated. "If you don't trust me."

Kingston set the bag of mushrooms down and rummaged through the pockets of his leather jacket. "I trust you with this because if word spreads, these photos get emailed to the whole school." He pulled a piece of paper out of his pocket and thrust it at me.

I held the paper with shaky hands. Two photos were printed on it: one of me on the roof last night, the other of me wrecking the dam in the creek. I'd told Whitney when I would carry out the mission, and she'd been first on the scene to pull me out of the creek. But maybe Kingston—and Chess?—had stayed behind to cover it all up, watching me through the shadow of the trees. Kingston *had* come from the direction of the woods when he'd joined me after Whitney's rescue.

"So I'm not worried you'll tell anyone about this." He tapped the bong with his fingernail. "There are other secrets I want to protect more." As if suddenly remembering something, he let out a small gasp, snatched the mushrooms up, and stuffed them back in his pocket. "Which brings me to my next demand." His dark eyes held mine. "Stay away from us. *All* of us. That includes your whipped boy toy. Or my finger might accidentally hit send."

My throat got tight. All the doors in front of me slammed shut. The look on Kingston's face was so menacing, I inched backward, ready to run away and give in to his demands. He watched me, so still, like he didn't dare breathe. And in that stare, I saw opportunity. "You think I'm a threat," I whispered, testing out the words. Then, I repeated them louder, more confidently.

"You are to me," he said. Not as forceful or demanding as before.

I eyed him. "Why?"

We stared at each other for a long time. He broke away first.

"You're not like us."

The words sounded false, like an excuse, covering the real truth of why I threatened him. "You don't know anything about me."

"That reminds me. Who are you?"

"A member of your group." I grinned at him.

"No. See, that's the thing. We were much better off before you got involved." He used the pipe to point at me. "We never had to cover up a mission before your flood."

"But your friends still let me in. Do they know about this meeting?"

"They'll thank me later. They only see the big picture, but I see everything else, the stuff they're overlooking. I have sources they don't have."

"The plants?"

His face paled. “Why? What did they say?” I jutted a hand on my hip, so he continued, “And don’t try to get your little friends to defend you. If I hear about this from them . . . ” I had no idea if he meant Whitney and Chess or plants. He twirled his finger in the air and sang, “*You’ve got mail.*”

“Okay,” I said, my voice quavering and desperate. “Maybe you’ll realize I’m not a threat if I explain.” I swallowed. “My parents used to—”

“Blah blah. I don’t care. You’re doing this because you’re rebelling or some other stupid reason. Not because you have to.” He rose from the rock, snatched the bong, and left me standing in the middle of the forest, wondering what obligated the others to do this besides desire.

“That’s the thing, though,” I whispered to the empty woods. “I *do* have to.”

But I didn’t know how to continue, with his blackmail hanging over my head.

CHAPTER 12

At home, I knew Lorina must be mad, so I resorted to bribery. Win her over with a good meal, despite my lack of culinary talent. I had dumped frozen raviolis into boiling water when the door opened. I thrust my hands under the faucet.

"Do we have any pasta sauce?"

"You're cooking dinner? This isn't going to work, Alice. You can't just—" Lorina entered the kitchen and set her purse on one of the chairs, stopping short when she saw the table set like a four-star restaurant. "You used Mom's good china?" Her face didn't look surprised as much as . . . scared.

My smile fell. "We can't be afraid to use her things. She wouldn't want it stuffed forever in a box. Besides . . . " I turned off the faucet and wiped my hands on a paper towel. "Aren't you hungry?"

"Starved, but—"

"You've been working so hard, I wanted to do something nice for you. I even made lemonade." Her favorite. I pointed to the pitcher on the table. I hoped it tasted okay; the lemons we had looked a little suspect. "Plus, I feel bad your investigation was canceled." Hint hint, give me information.

"It's back on," she said with a casual wave of her hand as she grabbed a jar of sauce from the back of the cabinet. I handed her a pot and she poured the sauce inside. "But Alice, we need to talk about last night."

"I'm sorry for the way I left. When you said you had to be the parent, it made me miss Mom and Dad. I had to get out of there before I got too upset." This was good practice, in case I ever had to lie to the police.

"I'm sorry, too, then." Her lashes fluttered against her eyelids. "But I need you to cooperate. This is hard on me, too, and I . . . "

She didn't finish, but she didn't have to. Her message came across loud and clear. Raising me had been hard enough without my rebellion. I felt like a golf ball was lodged in my throat.

"I'm not letting you off easy, but I want to trust you. Okay?"

"I'll be good, I promise." I crossed my fingers behind my back. "So the investigation is back on? What happened?" I lifted one shoulder in hopes it would appear casual and not calculated.

"There was another incident last night. I was right. They were lying low." She smiled to herself. "I had to go on site today to investigate."

"What kind of incident?" I turned my back to the simmering pots to conceal my eagerness for information.

She pursed her lips. "I shouldn't talk about it."

"Who am I going to tell?" A strained laugh escaped my lips. I clanked a fork against the side of the pot to cover it up.

"I trust you. I just don't want to get you upset."

"I want to know. In a weird way, it's like I'm learning more about Mom and Dad, what they might have done." Even though my heart squeezed, I pressed on. "Makes me feel closer to them."

"All right." Lorina proceeded to tell me how the family had arrived and had to spend hours with the police and Lorina's team from the Department of Public Health and Safety. The fire department removed most of the plants but couldn't budge the ones on the front porch. The movers tried to go through the garage instead, but there were a few large items, like couches and tables, that couldn't fit.

As her story went on, my appetite faded and a stomachache subbed in.

"Do you have any idea who's doing this?" I asked when she was finished, getting the words out before holding my breath.

She wiped her brow. "So far all leads have been dead ends. We checked out all the people who'd been part of . . . you know."

"Mom and Dad's protests." The words were like encoded messages: encrypted to prevent tampering with.

She nodded. "Most of them don't even live in Wonderland anymore."

"And the ones who do?" I thought of Chess's jobless dad.

"The police dismissed them. They either had watertight alibis or not enough evidence to connect them to the crimes. My gut says we're looking in the wrong place."

"Wh—Where do you think the right place is?"

"I don't know. These crimes are more organized." She tapped her fingers on the table. "Maybe I need to figure out who would have the resources to pull this off. Someone must be supplying all those plants." She rose from her seat and headed to her purse.

"What are you doing?" The panic in my voice could have convicted me right there.

"Calling the Garden Center."

"No!"

She squinted at me.

"I mean, that place is tiny. There's no way they could continually supply that many plants. They grow the stuff themselves and have plenty of customers." I shut off the stove. "Besides, dinner's ready."

She gnawed on her lower lip. "Yeah, you're right."

"You need to try wholesale flowers or something. Maybe someone is ordering online?" I scooped the raviolis into bowls. They looked like they needed another few minutes, but luckily my terrible cooking skills might not make this suspicious. The sauce helped hide the evidence further.

She sank back into her chair.

"Were all the activist stunts like this one?" I carried the bowl over and set it in front of her before she could reconsider the Garden Center.

"This was the first one at a housing complex, if that's what you mean. Warehouses and parking lots have also been vandalized."

"That's all?"

"Let me think." She scooped a ravioli into her mouth and chewed. And chewed and chewed. Guess they were really chewy. "They recently glued all the locks of Town Hall shut, which was odd considering they broke a few of the windows." Had to be Kingston. And Whitney's glue. "If the alarm hadn't gone off, I don't know what would have happened. They'd already damaged so much."

"Because of the windows?"

"No, they must have done that last, since it triggered the alarm. Before that, they tacked a makeshift greenhouse on the back entrance. There was graffiti, too. That was why we started the investigation."

This must be the *Greenhouse incident* I saw in her files. "What did it say?"

She poured lemonade in both glasses. "'*This land has been re-zoned. Sucks, doesn't it?*'"

That reminded me of what Chess had said about the township changing zoning laws and eradicating the farm because of it. "What else did they do?"

She tilted her head to the side. "Why are you so curious?"

I dropped the fork into my bowl, flinching. It sounded louder than a car accident. "Um . . . because you are." I studied her, really studied her. Sure, creases extended from her tired eyes, and her hair stuck out from her bun at odd angles. But her skin glowed. Freckles that had long been hibernating appeared proudly on her nose. Even her clothes fit her better, no longer hanging off her skinny frame like a sheet over a ghost. She'd tied a belt around her T-shirt in a way that looked almost fashion-conscious.

"What?" She glanced down at her clothes, tugging at the belt.

"You look . . . like a grownup."

"Oh?" She shifted her weight to lean on one hip. "So you think I'm old?"

I grinned as I took a sip of lemonade. "You're Grandfather William!" I teased, referring to our grandfather who hadn't aged well and looked eighty years old even in photos of Mom as a baby. "The light makes your hair look white." I giggled.

"You think *I'm* old? In high school, I never made dinner or spent my free time recycling. You're the one that needs the cane." She stabbed at another ravioli.

"Right, you spent your time dating boys. Remember those creatures? They're not myths." My smile was so wide, it could rival Chess's.

She chomped on her pasta but didn't retort with a snappy comeback. Suddenly, the lighthearted fun in the room went down the drain with the water.

"I'm sorry," I said.

"It's fine." Lorina swiped her palm across her brow. "You know, maybe you're right."

"That's what my teachers always say."

"I'm sorry, too. For the way I acted yesterday. I'd like to meet this guy you like. As a sister, I mean."

My smile wavered. I wanted Lorina to take part in my life, to love the things I loved . . . well, not in the same way, but I couldn't lead her right to him. He was the culprit she was looking for.

And then a realization hit me like a stun gun. I didn't have a guy. Because if I did, Kingston would set me up to take the fall for all the activism like he had threatened. Which meant I had to stay away from him. My eyelashes fluttered. "I don't think that guy and I are . . . happening anymore."

"Oh, Alice." She placed a comforting hand on my shoulder. When she removed it, she made me sit down while she cleaned up and took care of me—something I hadn't realized how much I actually needed.

My shiny, new driver's license waited patiently in my wallet, but that didn't mean I had access to the car I shared with my sister. She only gave me free reign when she could find another ride through her work carpool, which was rare and usually only when I begged. Asking Di for a ride to school was a last resort. I needed a distraction. For Kingston, not me. Let him see me with Di and think I'd cowered. Scratch that, let him see me with Di and Dru since they came as a pair nowadays. Scratch that, they came as a trio. A trio that didn't include me.

Since Di and Dru had some important meeting with Quinn the next morning that I apparently wasn't invited to, it meant we left for school when Kingston still lay snuggled in his bed, totally defeating the purpose of my request. But I couldn't back out now. I slid into Di's back seat.

"So she's trying to get to the bottom of this?" Di reversed out of my driveway.

"Shh," Dru hissed. Her eyes flicked to me.

I flicked mine right back. "I'm sorry my presence is preventing you two from plotting a revenge prank."

"That's not what this is about. We would never do that. No how." Dru raised the volume of the radio.

"Contrariwise, we're helping Quinn investigate who vandalized her—"

"Shut. Up!" Dru nudged Di as she turned onto the main road, making the car swerve.

"Wait." Gears shifted into place in my mind. Quinn saying she was moving. That her parents were building something. Her being absent yesterday. Whitney saying they were targeting the owners of the new solar-powered development. My temples pounded. "*Quinn's* house was the one that was refor—uh, targeted by ecoterrorists?" I cringed at the word, but I needed answers here.

Dru spun around in her seat, hair swinging into her face. "How do *you* know about that?"

"My sister told me." I prayed a silent thank you for quick thinking. "She's investigating the incident."

"Oh." Dru's face softened. "What else did she say? Does she know anything?"

"Why is your sister investigating that?" Di's face was scrunched up in an impressive display of wrinkles. "I thought she checked on small claims, like making sure restaurant bathrooms had washing-hands signs." Oops. I never did tell her about Lorina's promotion.

I rattled off a quick explanation of her new job. My pulse pounded a mile a minute. I'd never been so eager to get to school. Kingston had sent me a secret message yesterday; I would do the same today to Whitney, but I had to do it before Kingston could spot me slipping it into her locker. I had no idea when he would arrive to spy on me, so I had to do it ASAP.

As soon as we pulled into the empty parking lot, I thanked Di for the ride and rushed off, but not before I caught them exchanging a glance behind my back.

I sprinted toward Whitney's locker, racing down the empty hallways. I scribbled off a hasty note asking if she'd known it was Quinn's house. Once that was done, I hopped in place for a few minutes, too antsy to sit still. I decided to use my newfound energy for productivity. And okay, also a distraction. I headed toward the gym locker room to deposit a clean change of gym clothes.

I rounded the corner to turn into the girls' locker room when a shadowy movement caught my eye. Curiosity weighed down the Libra decision-making scale, and my head swiveled as if on robotic remote control. The dark shadow morphed into the shape of Chess's body.

I strode toward him, my mouth twisted in a smile. But when he froze in place and his face fell, I stopped, too. He seemed the opposite of happy to see me, something I couldn't make sense of during our statue reenactment.

"What are you doing here so early?" He tried to relax his face into a smile, but his body stayed rigid, on high alert.

"I rode with Di and Dru. Speaking of which, did you know the house—" I cocked my head. "Is your hair wet?" His dark hair glinted in the light like it was made out of plastic.

He touched his hair. "Oh, um, I got caught in the rain." He wiped his now-wet hands on his thighs.

My eyes shifted behind him to the window, confirming what I already knew. Skies the color of raspberry ices with buttery-yellow rays sliced through the pinks. "What rain?"

He rotated around to check the window. "It was raining when I left my house."

It wasn't raining in Wonderland at all today. "Do you live far?"

"Um . . . " His hand cupped the back of his neck. "Yeah."

I hadn't expected that. "Oh, cool." I stepped toward him with fantasies playing in my mind of wrapping myself around him, breathing in his wet-hair scent, and learning more about this new information. "So anyway, did you know the house yesterday was Quinn's?"

Chess craned his neck left and right as if checking for eavesdroppers. My stomach dropped. I hadn't seen Kingston snapping photos of me outside the dam. He could be lurking in the shadows now, too. "Don't be mad, but yeah. Her parents own the whole development. It was the only thing that would get notice."

"She's trying to figure out who did it!" I took a step backward. "I should go. Maybe try to do some damage control."

"If we can fool the township, we can fool her. No worries." He grinned, and the smile melted me. I wasn't mad at him. I'd direct all my anger toward the person who deserved it: Kingston. "What are you doing later?" he asked. "I think we should—"

Kiss? *No, don't think that.*

"—talk."

"I can't." The word was barely a whisper.

He paused for another moment, then gave me a single nod. "Okay, then."

A lump lodged in my throat as he brushed past me. I swallowed thickly, wanting to crumble into a fit of girly tears. But it was better this way. If he thought I was angry with him, it would keep Kingston in check, and it might make Chess get over me. Besides, I wasn't sure if I could trust him anymore.

Because I'd caught Chess in a lie.

If he lived far enough away to get caught in a rainstorm before school . . . his hair would have been dry by the time he got here.

CHAPTER 13

Kingston's blackmailing left me on high alert, so when Whitney hovered over my desk in English after I'd avoided her for two days, I was prepared.

"Hey," she said, more question than statement.

"Hi." I stared straight ahead in a stupid game of peekaboo, as though closing my eyes would keep her from seeing me. Another thing Kingston had robbed me of: my logic.

"You never responded to my note," Whitney said.

She'd written a cryptic explanation and slipped it in my locker. I could barely decipher it, but I already had the answers. "I didn't know what to say."

"How about 'yes.' Because you have plans tonight."

"Too much homework." I slid my notebook into my backpack.

Di and Dru exchanged subtle smiles. Whitney yanked the portion of my notebook that was still sticking out of my bag. She scribbled a quick message on the back cover, then cupped her hand over it, shielding it from the girls' view.

We both know you'd rather hang out with us.

As soon as I met her eyes, she scribbled it out.

I forced the words out. "I can't anymore."

"I need you, Alice." She sounded like she meant it.

And I needed to hear that. I closed my eyes and repeated my mantra of *I can't anymore.* It felt more like a death sentence than a backing out of potential plans.

I gave Whitney a shrug of one shoulder and followed Di and Dru out of the room, which led me straight into Quinn's waiting arms. I let my eyelids flutter closed for a few seconds before I pasted a too-big smile on my face. It scared me how easy it was to feign interest in things I didn't care about, like a stupid plot to get revenge on Neverland High or figure out who was behind the damage to Quinn's house. I supplied her with as many conspiracy theories as I could, doing my best to keep Whitney and Chess off their radars. I kept reminding myself I was protecting them and biding my time until Kingston stopped keeping tabs on me.

Too bad I'd become his new favorite pastime. He seemed to pop up everywhere: waiting outside my classrooms, rattling down my street in his truck at unexpected times, sitting outside in the school parking lot like a volunteer security guard. Either he was really stepping up his intimidation efforts or he'd been reading a lot of spy novels. Several times, he tried to speak to me, mouth forming the shape of my name. I turned around and ignored his laser-beam eyes singeing a hole in my back.

In gym, Chess and I avoided each other like we had some unspoken agreement. Kingston practically glowed with triumph. It took exhausting effort to refrain from stealing glances in Chess's direction. I had to forget him, not pine after him.

So when a shadow darkened my locker at the end of the day about a week after I'd rejected Whitney, I hoped for one dumb second it might be him. I had gotten so used to nonsensical things happening that it seemed kind of boring and stupid for life to go back to normal.

"What do you know?" the shadow asked. Girl's voice.

I twisted around to find Whitney leaning against the adjacent locker, sizing me up. I scanned the area for Kingston. I didn't see him, but that didn't mean he wasn't lurking, cell phone in hand. "Is that a riddle?"

"No, I'm the one trying to decipher what the hell is going on with you. It's not as fun on the other side."

I commanded my feet to step in the direction of the school parking lot, but they refused to listen. I threatened them with amputation.

"So a hint would be nice," she said. "About why you're avoiding everyone."

"This . . . isn't for me after all."

"Because of Chess?" She raised her eyebrows.

I clutched my book to my chest. "What do you mean?"

"I mean you've been acting weird ever since you saw Chess the morning after your PDA freak show, and I don't believe you're that upset about Miss Queen Beeswax's house."

"Did Chess say something? Does he miss me?" I clamped my hand over my mouth. Someone must have snuck into my room and performed a brain-to-cardboard transplant. "I mean, not that I care or anything."

"Okay, I get it now." She peeled herself from the locker. "Well, Chess will be happy."

Her words shot through my body like a bullet aimed at the heart. "Why? Because I don't care?"

I shifted from foot to foot, trying to jumpstart her mouth through telekinesis. The guy waiting for the locker below mine joined my foot-tapping dance.

"Listen, I'm going to have a private meeting with myself. But not here." Whitney eyed the guy who used the locker below mine. "It would be nice if you followed. Especially because I know what's going on with you."

Did that mean she knew about the blackmail?

Whitney headed down the hallway in the opposite direction of the parking lot as students hopped out of her path. She walked with the kind of determination that let you know she'd plow right on into you if you didn't move. I squared my shoulders and tried to walk with the same stomping gait instead of my fluttery, girlish one.

As we glided past the French classrooms, she stabbed at the keys of her cell phone.

"What are you doing?" I gasped out, then covered my mouth.

"Telling the boys to wait in the car." She threw her cell back in the front pocket of her messenger bag.

Knowing Kingston was nowhere near gave me courage to walk beside her. We turned into the drama wing and entered the room where the school stored old set pieces and costumes.

Inside, Whitney picked up an old cuckoo clock and tilted it in the light before setting it back down on the shelf. Her fingers roamed over dresses of every style and century, hanging from a wobbly rack. I stood in the center of the room watching her, my hands trying to squeeze my notebook into a flatter plane. When she picked up a pair of coral earrings from a jewelry box, she pocketed it.

"I don't think you're supposed to take anything."

She swiped another piece of jewelry from the box. "There are a lot of things I'm not supposed to do."

Sailors practiced knots in my stomach.

"Sit down or help shop. You're making me antsy."

The nearest prop was an oversized bird's nest from last year's poorly reimagined version of Aesop's fables. Whoever thought morals would make exciting pop musical numbers had clearly overestimated the average student's willingness to attend school activities. I rested in the scratchy weave of branches.

"Why is Chess happy that I'm . . . " The word hid in my throat but I coaxed it out anyway. "Quitting?"

"That's not why." Whitney knelt in front of a basket of hats, rummaging through them.

"Dumb it down for me."

"He thought you were mad at him. But I kept telling him you weren't." She grabbed a handful of ornate pins and stuffed them into her bag. "So then he thought it was because you found out about him and that's why you didn't want to be in the group."

"Because he had wet hair? Why was that, by the way?"

"So, clearly you don't know and therefore something else changed your mind." She opened a drawer from a nearby bureau, peered inside, then slammed it shut again. "And Kingston was in a great mood all week. We both know that's rare."

My heart beat faster. She'd figured it out. "You can't let him know you know!"

"*I'm* not scared of him." She flung another drawer shut.

"But you're not the one he threatened," I whispered. "He said if I told you—"

"Let me guess, he'd make sure you took the fall?" She rolled her eyes. "He's so predictable."

The door swung open, and I jumped out of the nest. Whitney continued rifling through another rack of clothes, completely relaxed as both Chess and Kingston entered. Chess took one look at me and paused in the doorway. His fingers indented the soda can he clutched in one hand. Kingston glared at me under the shadow of his newsboy cap. The smile I was supposed to wear for Chess spread slowly over Kingston's lips as he extracted his cell phone.

He punched in keys, gawking giddily at the screen like he'd uncovered a website with free porn.

"Don't." Whitney tossed a pillow at him, knocking the phone out of his palm. The cell skidded across the floor and under a bureau.

"You said you told them to stay in the car!" I blurted.

"I lied." Whitney shrugged. "I thought that was obvious."

Chess backed into a corner of the room, not meeting my eye. He perched on the top of the bureau, his elbows propped up by his knees. He stared into the soda can like it held all the answers to his finals.

"What exactly did you threaten her with?" Whitney asked Kingston.

"I did you a favor. She's a serpent, a fucking snake in the grass."

"Who uses the word *serpent* anyway?" Whitney resumed her shopping spree.

"I like it," Kingston said. "It sounds evil."

"I think I've proven I'm trustworthy." I stole a glance in Chess's direction and gave him a quick, forbidden smile. If the smile's recipient didn't see it, was it like a tree falling in the woods?

"I thought we had an understanding, Alice?" Kingston drew his finger across his lips.

"She didn't tell me, King. It wasn't that hard to figure out. You were practically gloating about it." Whitney tossed a blue Victorian dress at Chess. It hit him in the face and draped over his head. He reached up and pulled it off, messing up his hair. "And Chess, stop moping. That's why she was acting all weird. Not because of you."

"Really?" He lifted his eyes to meet mine. I shot him the best nod I could muster. His shoulders relaxed, and he rose from the bureau. He walked over to me while the others watched, dropping the soda into a trashcan on his way.

Kingston retrieved the mopey expression Chess had discarded and fastened it to his face. "You better not start making out here," he threatened in a voice that could make a baby cry. Or maybe it was more like a voice that sounded like a whiny baby.

"Or what?" Whitney asked. "What were the terms?"

I stood and grabbed Chess's hand. "He said I had to stay away from you. From the group."

Chess twisted me around and pulled me onto his lap on the nest. His hands encircled my waist, squeezing like a harness, like he couldn't bear to let me go. He smelled so good, a mixture of soda and boy. I crumpled into him, trying to get as close as possible while still being PG.

"Enjoy it." Kingston crossed the room to the bureau and bent to reach beneath it. "As far as I'm concerned, she broke the deal. She's a fucking snake-in-the-grass spy. She acts all innocent, like a *little girl,* and then—bam! The truth comes out, and we're all screwed."

"Don't be ridiculous," Chess said, resting his chin on the top of my head. "She hasn't told anyone."

"Yet." Kingston swept his arm beneath the bureau and retrieved the cell. "Little birdies always sing."

"Kingston, if you even think about hitting send, you'll regret it." Whitney slammed down the receiver on a rotary phone she'd been inspecting. "I'll be forced to extend the same courtesy to you. I know plenty of things you don't want revealed."

"I'm not hitting send." He strode over to Whitney and lifted the cell phone to show her something. "See that girl next to Alice? The other blonde? That's her sister."

Chess tried to leap off the nest, but my body weighed him down. "Now you're threatening her family, too?"

But of course, that wasn't what Kingston was doing.

"Want to know where she works?" Kingston pulled the cell phone back so he could see it and pressed more buttons. "Health and Safety." He clicked again. "The assholes who are investigating us. Do you recognize that, Whit?" His voice was schoolgirl giddy.

She squinted at the screen. "Is this true, Alice?"

Kingston walked over and graciously showed Chess and me the three photos. One of Lorina and me walking to her car outside the grocery store. Another of Lorina entering Town Hall. And the last, of her with clipboard in hand at the scene of the house reforestation.

I didn't like Kingston, but I hoped he'd grow up to be a private investigator.

"Her sister is leading the investigation. Alice is a snaky spy." He leaned against the wall and pointed the cell phone at me, a satisfied smile punctuating the gesture.

"Is Kingston right? Are you spying on us?" The air conditioner drowned out Whitney's whispered words. I blamed my goosebumps on the blast of cold air.

I twisted in Chess's lap to face him. He kept his arms tightly secured around me, but his eyes swam back and forth as he studied me.

"I'm not working for my sister as a spy." I tried to keep my voice steady, so it would sound as truthful as it actually was. "But she *is* investigating you. I'm on your side, though." My voice cracked. "I would never betray you."

Chess squeezed me tightly. I hoped that meant he believed me.

"If that's true, prove it." Kingston crossed his arms.

"How?"

"Steal your sister's keys to Town Hall and let us in so we can look at their files."

My stomach settled into the floor. "That's . . . insane."

Chess waved his hands in the air. "No way. Too big a crime if we get caught."

"Everything has a boundary," Whitney said.

"Well, then I don't trust her. She needs to prove she's with us, not her sister. This is the only way to do it."

My pulse beat at the base of my neck. "I don't feel comfortable breaking and entering."

"I'll do it." Kingston reached into his pocket and extracted the bag of mushrooms. "Just get the keys." He popped one in his mouth.

"Are you getting high at school?" I blurted before I could stop myself.

He burst out laughing. Everyone stared at him. "Sorry," he said while chewing. "Joke. You had to be there."

I didn't point out the obvious: we *were* there.

"Okay." Whitney zipped up her messenger bag and retreated into a rocking chair. "I think there's only one course of action here. I'm sorry, Chess, but we need to disband the group."

"What?" Kingston ripped himself off the wall and stomped into the middle of the room. He spit the half-chewed mushroom on the ground. "How will that solve anything?"

"It's too dangerous now, King. Too many people know too many things. If you found out about Alice's sister, it's only a matter of time before she finds out about us. I don't see how we can continue. I'm really sorry, Chess."

I felt like a brick tied to his ankle, dragging him to the bottom of the ocean. I rubbed his hand as an apology, but I knew it didn't really solve anything.

Chess sighed. "Yeah, I understand."

"Fuck that." Kingston picked up a garbage can and threw it at the wall. Papers flew everywhere, and Chess's soda can sprayed like a geyser all over the dresses. "All this time I've been patient, waiting for my turn. Chess isn't the only one being screwed over by this."

"I know," Whitney said.

Guilt took residence in my stomach. I'd messed things up for everyone. Even Kingston, who, it seemed in an ironic twist, had put Chess before his own needs.

"No." Kingston kicked the wall with his foot. "My problem might not be as time sensitive as Chess's, but it's still a problem. It still needs to be fixed! Whitney, come on." Sweat dripped down his forehead. "You promised."

The tension was so thick it pushed against my lungs. No one said anything, not even Whitney. She could have made more promises to calm him down, but she didn't. Kingston swiveled to face me. "Alice." There was something in his eyes that I might have described as *pleading* if I weren't talking about Kingston. "You have to know. One side will get you closer, the other side will get you farther." He bent down in front of me. "You understand?"

"One side of *what?*" I glanced over Kingston's shoulder at Whitney. She shrugged.

"The mushroom." Kingston waved the bag in my face. "What do you think I mean? The group! Obviously. They're giving up. I'm not. I'll get you closer."

Blood gushed in my ears. Chess's breath was heavy against my neck—and oh, it felt good. Everyone waited for me to speak, to choose. There wasn't a choice, even with the group disbanded. Even with Whitney probably hating me. "I'm staying with them, Kingston."

He straightened. "Fine. I don't need you. Or your keys." He stalked toward the door and perched his hand on the lock. He'd already had the last word, but apparently that wasn't enough. "I'll fix this myself."

He slammed the door. Silence boomed for several beats.

"Well." Whitney sat up, breaking the tension. Chess let out a breath. "That fixes one problem," she said. "But there's one more." She set her eyes on me.

Whitney may have been a master of riddles, but I didn't need to be a CIA code cracker to decipher the obvious message: Whitney didn't want me here. I slid off Chess's lap, a lump swelling in my throat. I hoped I could make it outside before I choked on it.

"Where do you think you're going?" Chess tugged the bottom of my shirt.

I pivoted to address them both. "I'm sorry I messed up whatever you were trying to do. I wish I could have helped."

"Then consider me a genie," Whitney said.

Chess chuckled at whatever he saw in my expression. "Whitney . . . " He gave her an exasperated look.

"Fine. We're done with Kingston. Not you."

CHAPTER 14

"But why keep me over Kingston?" I divided my gaze between Whitney and Chess.

Whitney pulled herself out of the rocking chair and dusted off her pants. "He's not seeing straight."

"He's too focused on revenge," Chess translated, rising from the bird's nest. "Not just on you, on everything that's hurt him. He's sabotaging us with his blackmail and surveillance stuff instead of concentrating on what's important."

"Important. Ah, yes, doing drugs at school is vital to saving the planet," I joked.

"Those aren't magic mushrooms. They're shiitakes. He's obsessed. I'd say it's weird but . . . it's Kingston."

I chuckled as I followed them to the door. "How do you know you can trust me?" I paused. "Wait. That came out wrong. I mean—"

"Alice, I'm not blind." Whitney held the door for me. "I've known about your sister for a while."

"I wish you'd told me," Chess shook his head at me in a reassuring, I'm-not-mad-at-you gesture.

"There's a lot of things Alice could have told us." Whitney pulled the door shut behind her. "Like what she knew."

I paused in the hallway while they continued down it. When they realized I wasn't following, they both turned back to me. "I want to make one thing clear. I won't spy on my sister," I said. "Just like I won't feed information to her."

"Worth a shot." Whitney padded back down the hallway. Chess held out his hand for me to take. A smile broke out on my face as I wrapped my fingers in his.

"Where are we going?" I asked.

"I'm going home," Whitney said over her shoulder. "I don't want to be around for whatever Chess has planned."

Redness spread over his cheeks. "Well, I want to have that . . . talk soon. But I really do have to get to work."

I knew he meant we would do anything *but* talk, and that scared me as much as it excited me. Now new, concrete questions pounded in my brain. Chess was clearly keeping something from me based on the wet hair (showering at school? Why?), not to mention the mission of the group. If he was going to let me into his . . . well, let's go with heart, just like he let me into the group, I had to trust him. And he had to trust me. They'd chosen me over Kingston, and that meant I should be privy to the info. All the info.

"Oh, right. I forgot you took an extra shift." Whitney turned to me. "Alice, if you want I can help you get your garden in shape."

"You don't want to face Kingston!" Chess teased.

"I'm not scared of him, but that doesn't mean I have to put myself in his war path."

Chess dropped us off at my house. Digging her fingers underneath the soil, Whitney uprooted almost everything I'd worked so hard to position. She replanted them in a chaotic matrix. In some spots, flowers crowded while she left others so sparse, a forest of animals could make their nests in the empty space. She allowed my thriving white rosebush to remain in place, towering over the other flowers. Whitney told me one of the reasons my plants weren't growing was because I'd mixed friends and enemies together, planting my asparagus too close to the onions in my vegetable garden. She also suggested I buy oyster shells and soak them in the plant water, because it removed acidity.

After she finished, I went inside and brought out my parents' photo album, the one she'd been eager to see when I first tried to join the group.

"Oh cool, I almost forgot about this."

I held it out of arm's reach. "Only if you tell me what your agenda is."

"You have to talk to Chess."

"He told me the same thing about you a while ago."

"That was just an excuse for him. It's not *my* place to tell." One thing about Whitney I both admired and despised: she fiercely kept everyone else's secrets, including mine.

"He's going to play the same game of monkey-in-the-middle." I handed over the album, only because I wanted to watch what she focused on. It might give me some clue.

She flew through the pages, barely even pausing at any of the pictures. When she came to the end, she pursed her lips. "This wasn't as helpful as I hoped."

"What were you looking for?"

"Doesn't matter. It wasn't here."

I snatched the book back up. "It matters to me."

"Fine, I was looking for photos of people I don't know, so I could try to find out who they were. I recognize everyone here."

"Why?"

"Because I'm trying to identify everyone who might have been involved in this stuff." She pushed herself off the ground and wiped off her hands. "To warn them." A question formed on my lips, but before I could get it out, she said, "Those are the only answers I can give you."

"If I'm going to help you do illegal things, I need to know why."

"I know. I think it's time. And if I think it's time, it must be late."

During gym the next day, I let Di, Dru, and Quinn go ahead of me to the track while I lingered behind, waiting for Chess to come out of the boys' locker room.

"Hey," I said when Chess emerged from the gym, trailing behind his teacher. Kingston followed, hands jammed in pockets, baseball cap on his head. Neither acknowledged the other, but both glanced in my direction.

"Need an escort to class?" Chess propped out his elbow for me to take.

The students marched in a funeral procession toward the track, obviously trying to use up as much time as they could before the teachers put them to work. The teachers ushered the students inside the track gates, blowing whistles like prison guards.

"Yeah, I probably should be going to class." I looped my arm in the crook of his elbow. It was silly, we were just going to gym, not Homecoming or anything, but I couldn't keep the giddiness out of my step.

"Well, if it were up to me, we would all be sleeping, but the teachers don't seem to agree." He steered me past a few girls sneaking peeks at their cell phones.

"Right. See, you get it. There are more important things than gym." Like kissing him. Or finding out why he had two people doing his bidding. I shivered from the crisp fall air. Chess drew me closer to his body, sharing his body heat with mine. "And I consider this walk of great importance."

"Great importance?" Kingston said from behind us. "You consider the genocide of innocent blades of grass important? You're trampling all over them!" I twisted around to see him cupping the side of his mouth and whispering to the grass. "You owe me." He glanced up and met my eyes, then said in a louder voice, "You're pathetic."

This from the guy who lost all his friends because of paranoia. Guess that really was a side effect of pot.

The two students in front of us checked over their shoulders, one meeting my eyes, before darting for the parking lot straight ahead. Away from the track. I eyed the teachers on the track; they had no clue. The students near us kept walking, mouths shut, desensitized to cutting class and other forms of rebellion.

I leaned toward Chess's ear. "Did you see that?"

"I did." His tone was curious.

"Remember how I said I probably *should* go to class?" The breeze blew my hair around my face as I waited for him to nod. "I was lying." I tugged on his elbow.

"Good idea. Now there'll be some proof to all the rumors Whitney started." He let me lead him toward the parking lot.

Kingston rolled his eyes as we passed. "Keep on corrupting her."

When we reached his car, Chess ducked. "I don't usually keep my keys in my gym shorts, only razors, but," he pulled out a metallic object that glinted in the sun, "I do keep a spare here." He grinned.

As he fit the key in the lock, my nerves crumbled. He opened the door and stood there, shifting his weight. Maybe he was as nervous as me? His arm traced an arc in front of the door, welcoming me. It took a lot of effort to lift one foot and then the other, but eventually I coaxed them onto the back seat. I slid over to make room for Chess.

Once inside the car, we both sat there for a moment, staring straight ahead. Then we turned to each other and laughed.

"You make me do bad things," he said.

"Payback."

A foot of space separated us because I'd slid over too far and he hadn't moved in close enough. Now he inched forward and lifted one hand as though he was going to put it around my shoulder. Except he didn't, he held it there in midair. I turned to look at the hand, wondering what he was going to do with it, and his lips connected with my ear.

Oops.

He sprang back. My heart beat so fast I worried it might scare him. I leaned forward. He took my cue but bent his head in the same direction as I did. Our noses crushed together. This time, I pulled away, giggling.

"At least this isn't awkward," I joked.

"That would be embarrassing." He cupped my chin in his palms and brought his lips to mine, slow and cautious. I sank into the moment, savoring what I'd missed. The kiss intensified and so did the warmth spreading over my skin. I wrapped my arms around him, desperate to pull him closer. I couldn't get enough of him, and my heart swelled at the prospect of trying. My fingers grazed the short hairs at the back of his neck, rigid in some places and smooth in others, like he'd taken a razor there and hoped for the best.

"Wait," I said against his lips, when I finally mustered the willpower. I inched back away from him, scolding myself inside for stopping the kiss. I tilted my head to the side to thwart temptation. "I need to know—everything."

"What do you mean?" He snuck in another kiss. Sneaky bastard.

I had a lot of questions for him, but my brain refused to sift through them. It was too focused on the blinking neon lights that spelled out KISSING! "The missions and stuff. Why?"

"Alice, let's talk about this later."

"Okay." My lips met his again, and this time the kiss revved up faster than a Lamborghini. He leaned into me, pressing my back against the door. It took several pep chats in my head before I convinced myself to pull away. "Chess . . . " My breath was ragged, in a good way.

He rested his forehead against mine, panting. "It's too embarrassing. I'm afraid . . . you're not going to like me anymore if you know everything."

"Then you don't have a lot of faith in me."

He sat back up and closed his eyes. This was the moment before clarity. Finally knowing what it would feel like in my ears as I heard the truth. I imagined this was what sex would be like. Silence, and then sound.

"My dad made me go to boarding school even though I had no interest. Told me he wanted me to have a better education, when really he was just trying to get me away from Wonderland. And because of that, I didn't notice our financial problems until it was too late."

I grabbed his hand and laced my fingers through his.

"It's my fault. The taxes kept piling up, and if he hadn't paid for boarding school . . . " He ran his free hand through his hair. "It sucks because I loved living here and now everything's all screwed up."

"Everything?" I squeezed his hand.

He pulled me to him and stroked my hair. "Well, some good things happened."

We kissed again, this time less hungry, like we were both holding back. And I was, because that wasn't my only question. Still, it was harder to pull away. I was the superhero of restraint.

"Why'd he want you away from Wonderland?" I asked, even though I also desperately wanted to kiss him again.

A grimace tightened his lips. He held my gaze with a new intensity. "The township has a lot of power here. They've hurt tons of people."

"Like with the energy crisis?"

He shook his head. "It was good that the power plant shut down, but that's not what I'm talking about. More like, closing the farms and building houses instead. We're trying to get them to see the error of their ways, to reinstate the things they screwed people over with. But there's also a lot at stake." He trailed his fingers along my arm. Tingles spread under his touch. "My dad lost his job because of them. He needs to get that job back."

I nodded, finally understanding the personal connection here and what he stood to gain from these missions.

"Whitney told me yesterday she wanted to warn people. Does that have anything to do with your dad's job? Since he was part of the activism stuff before?"

"Exactly. He lost his job because they targeted him, so we're trying to make sure it doesn't happen to anyone else." He tipped my chin up to his face. "Okay? So now you know."

He trailed kisses along my jaw line. I closed my eyes. "And the wet hair?" I murmured, not even sure it was loud enough for him to hear.

"That's the embarrassing part," he said into my ear. Chills swept across my body like a tidal wave. He paused there, to kiss me in a crazy-dangerous form of torture. I patted his back as encouragement to continue—whether it was with the conversation or the kisses, I didn't care. "My water got shut off."

"Oh, Chess." I wrapped my arms around him and squeezed. I hadn't realized the extent of his money problems. "You don't have to be embarrassed. I'm not exactly going to make *Forbes*'s wealth list."

"I know. But guys are supposed to impress the girls. Take their girlfriends out on dates. You know, dates that aren't in back seats of cars or in trees. When I say it like that, it sounds so sleazy."

I laughed. "I don't need fancy dinners. The best dates are the missions."

"Even if we have a third wheel now?"

"Wait—" Something he'd said caught up with me. "Did you say girlfriend?"

"You like how I slipped that in there? I thought that was pretty slick."

This time, the kissing was much harder to wriggle out of. "I still have more questions. Why is Kingston doing this stuff?"

"I honestly don't know. They would never tell me. He promised to help me as long as I returned the favor when we were done. I was grateful, so I never pressed the issue." His head snapped toward the window where a few kids straggled up from the track. "We should go."

We scrambled out of the car.

"Does your dad have a new job?"

He squatted to put back the key. "He's not qualified for anything else, so he's working minimum wage. But also, he's lying low. He's paranoid and afraid. Thinks it's his fault that—" He stopped short and turned to me. "Alice, there's something else I've been keeping from you. Whitney doesn't know this. It has to do with why my dad sent me away."

The look on his face seemed more fit for a funeral than a school parking lot.

"How did your parents die?" Chess asked.

"What?" *Where did that come from?* I glanced at the gravel pavement. "Car accident." After three years, I could finally talk about this without bursting into tears. "It wasn't their fault," I added, because I didn't want him thinking my parents were irresponsible. "We're not sure, but we think they swerved to avoid a deer and hit a tree instead."

"They were on their way to a protest, right?" Something about the way he said it sent the hairs on the back of my neck standing.

"I—I don't know." That seemed like it could be true, but it was the first time I'd heard it. I'd been barely thirteen and got spoon-fed information, the kind that was picked over and reduced down to its very essence to help my sensitive little brain cope.

"Are you sure it was a deer they were trying to avoid?"

My throat started to close. I couldn't answer.

"That day, my dad was supposed to go to a protest he was organizing with your parents. They were trying to stop the rezoning of the farmland. But he never got there either. A few township officials showed up at the house before he left, presenting him with a cease-and-desist letter and demanding answers. He surrendered and told them what your parents were planning. And then they were run off the road."

"By a deer?" I wasn't making the connection here.

"There were no witnesses, Alice. And some of the newspaper articles reported tire tracks, possibly from an oncoming car headed in your parents' direction."

I dropped his hand. "Wait." My breath shortened with each inhale, becoming more rapid. "Are you saying my parents were murdered?"

"No." He reached for my hand, but I snapped it away. "I don't know. All I'm saying is, my dad believes they were, that he's responsible. He's racked with guilt, and the township has done everything in its power to screw him over. He sent me away to keep me safe, which means he believes this town is unsafe. And if that's the case, we have to stop it before anyone else gets hurt."

CHAPTER 15

Hearing Chess's confession brought back emotions I'd tried hard to suppress after my parents' death. I attempted to concentrate in my next class, but the words in my textbooks all said the same thing: *My parents might have been murdered.* In the middle of the teacher's lecture, I scraped my chair away from the desk and stumbled to a standing position. I didn't even notice people were staring at me until the teacher cleared her throat and asked where I thought I was going.

Even though the lights were dimmed to movie-theater ambiance, I squinted as if they were too bright, trying to focus on her but only seeing a blurry blob. "Uh, I don't feel well." I didn't wait for approval. I weaved through the classroom, smacking into more than one desk on the way. I staggered into the slanted hall that tipped so much it seemed it might slide right off the face of the earth. I didn't stop moving until my legs carried me out of the building and all the way to the bus stop.

At the library, I pored over newspaper articles about the accident. It was exactly like Chess had said: very little information with vague details. One article speculated on the set of tire tracks left on the road, suggesting the other-car theory and requesting that the drivers of the offending vehicle come forward. When no one did, the paper retracted its statement at the request of—dun-dun-dun—the township, whose expert analyst confirmed that the second set of tires was still my parents' car, spinning out of control. The large-animal theory resurfaced after that.

When the sniffles escaped from my nose at the computer screen, I packed up my things and sat in the cold air outside the library until the wind stung my cheeks and froze my tears.

I wanted to interrogate people, dig out more info, but I didn't know who to confront. At school the next day I asked Whitney if the township would ever resort to murder, but she just said, "This isn't the mafia."

I concluded that Chess had been telling the truth about Whitney's ignorance over this. I decided not to ask Lorina because I figured if she knew about a potential murder plot involving our parents, she wouldn't be working at the township. Maybe that was why they put her—an amateur—in charge of such an important investigation. They thought she could lead them to the ecotage suspect because of her ties to Mom and Dad. Keep your enemies close.

Which left Chess as my only news source. Each time I saw him, I fired off question after question about the accident. He didn't know what to believe since the lack of evidence supported and refuted both theories. I felt like we were arguing about whether God existed or not. Or what exactly was that brown, goopy stuff on the salad bar at school.

"What do you think?" he asked me in between stolen kisses in the school hallway, his body pressing my back into the red lockers. It took me a moment to remember what he'd even asked. Kissing must be one of the causes of amnesia. "Do you think it's true?"

"I think . . . I want it to be false." I didn't want Lorina's employer, possibly even her boss, to be capable of murder.

He clasped his hands in mine. "Then let's agree it's false."

It's false. I repeated the words over and over until they were imprinted on my brain, stamped there so I couldn't deny them anymore.

And that worked. But only ephemerally. Later that night I lay in bed unable to sleep, my head spinning. If my parents had been murdered, I needed to know. They deserved to have the culprit behind bars, not running free, able to do it again. All my other sources for info were dead ends. Except one . . .

I sprang out of bed, my pulse pounding with a new kind of determination. Fear and adrenaline mixed together to create a caffeine cocktail even Starbucks couldn't replicate. My head buzzed as I slid on my trusty black hoodie, courtesy of Whitney. I slipped on black leggings and black ballet flats. I could be simply going to dance class, if it wasn't the middle of the night. I tied my giveaway blonde hair into a tight bun and secured it with a headband. Defense against unwanted flyaways and security-camera identification. Sunglasses completed my disguise.

I took extra care descending the stairs. Once upon a crime I'd gone through Lorina's bag; I'd been an amateur. Now I was practically a veteran at snooping.

A single breath left my mouth as I pulled out my sister's keys, fingers sliding between the metal like toe-dividers at the nail salon. Not even a clink sounded as I stuffed them into the front pocket of my hoodie.

I tugged the door behind me and headed to Town Hall to break and enter.

The plan had seemed utterly attractive while lying in bed. Foolproof, even. Take the keys. Go inside. Find the information to link someone to the crime. Solve the case. What I hadn't factored into everything was guts, which happened to be something I lacked.

I paced in front of Town Hall, my heart pounding as if it was ready to escape my chest and ditch me completely. I paused in front of the rows of white rosebushes lining the entrance and took a deep breath.

You're not breaking and entering, I lied to myself. *You have a key.*

I counted to three and yanked the keys out of my pocket, but my hands were too clammy. The keys leapt out of my fingers and hit the ground with a metallic *clink*.

I should go home and forget about Kingston's stupid-as-hell plan. I tried to move, but my feet wouldn't budge, weighed down by cemented desire. As scared as I was, I wanted to do this. I fumbled for my phone. 3:10 blinked back at me on the LED screen. If I had Chess's phone number, I would call him. Accomplices equaled encouragement.

But it wouldn't have mattered; Chess had refuted Kingston's idea. So had Whitney. If I called her, she'd try to talk me out of this. I knew what a bad idea it was. I'd broken up with my sense of reason when I first followed Whitney through the woods. Might as well descend even farther down the path of wrong and stupid. I let out a crazy laugh that echoed in the silent darkness.

Morality bites.

Before I could stop myself, I flipped through my cell phone until I found Kingston's number. It was absurd that Whitney had made me add my least favorite person's number when I still didn't have my own boyfriend's. Tonight, though, it came in handy.

"What?" he said when he picked up. He didn't sound tired, more like . . . prepared.

"Hey, it's Alice. I have a weird question."

"Wow. Didn't strike me as the booty-call type."

My nerves erupted out of my mouth in a laugh that sounded almost flirty. I covered it up with a cough. He was calling me crazy, and this was the first time he made sense. "I'm outside Town Hall."

"Keys?"

"Yeah." The word came out all choked.

"Be right there."

As soon as I hung up, the gravity of what I'd done hit my stomach like a cartoon anvil. I'd just committed to committing a felony. With my enemy.

Ugh.

To Kingston's credit, he didn't share Whitney's penchant for being late. He arrived in less than five, decked out in the same uniform as me, hoodie tied tightly around his face so only his essential features were visible. A skullcap, complete with an embroidered skull, secured the hoodie in place. He carried a black messenger bag, and brought his face so close to mine I had to turn away. He kept on staring. "Are you a hologram?"

"Yes," I said. "And a robot. I'm a miracle of modern science."

"That's absurd. That kind of technology won't exist for another seventeen years." He counted something on his fingers. "And five days. Now I know you're lying. Which means, you must be Alice."

"That's debatable. I'm starting to think I was changed into someone else in the middle of the night." The real Alice wouldn't do something this stupid.

He nodded. "That's probably true. It happens to me a few days a week."

"I hope you woke up as a superhero tonight." I leaned closer to his messenger bag. "You better not have any cameras in there."

"No cameras." He opened the bag for me to see. Tubes rattled around inside, but nothing as small as a digital camera. He even went the extra mile to show me his empty pockets. So chivalrous.

"How do I know I can trust you?" I asked him.

"You don't, but you called me, which means you thought you could."

I pursed my lips. "I'm not sure I'm thinking clearly tonight."

"Let's just say I need you as much as you need me. Besides, I've got plenty to blackmail you with already." He flashed his teeth. "So why *did* you call me?"

"I need to get inside." I jutted my chin toward the entrance.

"Did you try knocking?" He tapped the air with his knuckle and clucked his tongue for the sound effect.

I ran a hand over my brow. "That wouldn't make sense."

He lifted his finger in an *aha* gesture. "There might be some sense in knocking, if for example I were inside and you weren't. Or you didn't bring the keys."

I jingled my pocket for proof. "Keys, yes. Courage, no."

"Then you could always sit on the steps until tomorrow. Someone's bound to let you in then."

I gave him a dirty look. I knew what he was getting at. Why would I call him when there were other ways to get inside without him? "I need to find evidence about something, and I kind of chickened out when I tried to do it alone."

"And you naturally thought of inviting me? I'm flattered."

"Would you be offended if I said you were my last resort?"

"If I weren't your last resort, I'd think this was a trap." He set down the messenger bag and squatted in front of it, his eyes level with mine. "What kind of evidence?"

I might have been stupid for wanting to break into the town hall, but I wasn't stupid enough to tell Kingston my secrets. "You tell me what you're after first."

"Fair enough. It's probably better if we don't know. This way, we won't get in each other's way." He pulled out a flashlight and twisted the cap. He pointed the beam at my eyes, forcing me to squint. "Though, if you're trying to prove the township has been brainwashing us with subliminal messages, don't waste your time." He turned the flashlight to his own face, scary-story style. "I've recorded and analyzed every school announcement. They're clean."

"Good to know."

He moved the flashlight away from his face. "Where's yours?"

I outstretched my empty palms. "Um, nonexistent."

He smirked and tapped the side of his head with the tip of his flashlight. "Good thing you brought me, then." He handed the flashlight to me and grabbed a second out of his bag.

It was almost sweet that he'd thought of me. Almost. Because really it meant he thought I was too incompetent to do this on my own, which—come to think of it—might have been true. But there was no way I'd ever admit out loud how much I needed him.

Though calling him at three A.M. probably sent the message pretty well.

He glanced back at me as he climbed the steps and offered his hand. I refused to show any more weakness. I forced my legs to submit to my commands while my hands took over nerve duty.

"You aim the flashlight. I'll take care of the cameras." He flashed me a smile more evil than comforting.

"You said you didn't bring a camera!" The flashlight rattled in my hand.

"Not *my* camera. The security ones, dumbass." He extracted a can of black spray paint from his bag and shook it like a maraca. "I thought you were supposed to be smart."

I swallowed hard. "Kingston . . . I don't know."

"You don't know much. And that's a fact." He turned back to me, his eyes sweeping over my rattling hand and defensive posture. "We're not going to get caught." He invaded my personal space, body heat radiating. His voice went soft. "Not with me here, anyway. Chill." He squeezed my shoulder. I flinched and he snapped his hand away.

He pulled on the string of his hoodie, constricting it tighter so only his eyes were visible. Extracting sunglasses from his bag, he concealed those too. "Nerves are for convicts." He reached into my pocket and dug around for my keys.

By the time my reflexes kicked in and I swatted his hand away, he'd yanked the keys free of their vault.

The keys jangled in his hands. "Stay there. Let me get the other cameras first."

Cement surrounded my feet, holding me down in this spot. I didn't even let my chest swell with breath. My pulse slammed into my neck. Paint fumes wafted to my nose, and the steady spraying of the can drowned out the pulsing in my ears. Kingston rushed through the darkened hallways, flashlight pointed forward. He attacked the security cameras with the paint like an Old West battle, spreading art instead of gunfire. So much for slipping in unnoticed.

He disappeared into one of the far rooms for more than five excruciating minutes. Just when I was working up the courage to check what was happening, I heard a loud noise, like computers shutting down, and then the whirring stopped altogether. Kingston strutted back to me, removing his sunglasses.

"What was that?"

He ignored me, pivoting on his heels to face the reception desk. He dragged the spray paint across it, swirling blurry letters on the mahogany wood.

"What are you doing?!" I rushed forward, panic rising.

"Might as well leave them a thanks while I'm here."

I grabbed his arm, interrupting a letter and sending the spray paint onto the top of the desk, blackening some typed papers that were stacked in a neat pile. He shook me off. "The file room's the last door on the left. You can start if you want."

I reached again, but he raised his arm in the air. Horrible déjà vu came over me. Lost games of monkey-in-the-middle, me racing back and forth while the taller girls kept the ball away. I braced my hands against his side and pushed. He didn't even flinch, just wrapped his free hand around my body, pressing me closer to his in a death grip. He actually smelled kind of good, if you ignored the cigarette scent masking the floral aroma. In any other circumstance the gesture might have been romantic, but being enemies and watching him vandalize my sister's workplace kind of put a damper on that. Also, he was Kingston.

"You gotta stop that. This will only take a sec. Shine that over here."

"Right, because holding me hostage is going to get me to obey you." I switched my flashlight off.

He blindly aimed the graffiti. When he finished, he set down the spray paint and turned on his flashlight so I could read. So considerate.

I know what you did.

"What is this, a horror movie?"

"It's only half the message. I hope I can add '*and I can prove it*' later."

"Like you proved all your other conspiracy theories?"

"Correction: I disproved them." He started for the file room.

I didn't point out that they were clearly strange and false to begin with. Probably similar to whatever reason he had for being here tonight. Still, I trotted after him like a puppy dog. The sweat that had been clinging to my body started to freeze, and I knew I wasn't that skilled in the art of staying cool. "What did you do to the heat?"

"Nothing. They must have it on automatic." He yanked open the file-room door.

How did I ever think I could accomplish this alone? I'd have been caught on fifty security cameras and turned on all the lights within the first fifteen seconds.

The file room contained rows of file cabinets protected with locks, but they might as well have been spells because I couldn't crack them. I went around and tugged on each drawer, coming up with nothing but a strained muscle.

"Hey, genius." Kingston jangled Lorina's keys and jammed one into a lock.

It's a sad day when you realize someone like Kingston might be smarter than you.

The drawer slid open with ease. Too much ease. In fact, this whole operation was too easy, thwarted only by my nerves and not, you know, the police. Things were never this easy . . . unless people were overlooking something.

I joined him at the drawer and set my flashlight on top. A beam of light flooded the ceiling and illuminated the room. My fingers bypassed folders with labels that didn't seem helpful. *Echolls case. Catalano file, one of two.*

"You're going too fast," he snapped.

I slowed my stenographer fingers. "It's hard when I don't know what you're looking for." Sleuthing with the enemy? Not the best method for productivity.

He lifted one folder. "Hey, these are dated." He stuffed the folder back into its spot. "June two thousand ten. I don't need this stuff."

I pushed the drawer shut. "Next."

He opened the next drawer and checked a file. "May two thousand ten?" He made a face. "I don't like things that begin with M."

"I agree with you on that." After all, murder began with an M. As did menstrual cramps. "If this is all two thousand ten, then I don't need this entire cabinet."

He slammed it shut. "I knew that cabinet looked suspicious. It was giving me the stink eye." He grabbed my flashlight and brought it over to a cabinet a few down from the first. "What date are you looking for?"

I fiddled with the zipper of my hoodie. "Um . . . like April two thousand twelve. Give or take. You?"

He eyed me. "Now you're the suspicious one."

"Why?"

"Give or take the same date." He broke eye contact and twisted the key in the next drawer. "I'm curious what you're looking for."

"And you weren't before? Told you I had a reason to be in the group." I picked up a file and checked it. "Right cabinet, wrong date."

"I did wonder what could possibly make a squeaky-clean girl like you sneak out in the middle of the night and attempt to enter the ranks of criminals."

Attempt?

He opened the next drawer.

"And I wondered what could make you put someone else before yourself."

"Are you calling me selfish?" He yanked the drawer open hard, and a few files flew to the floor.

"It was the blackmail that clued me in."

"You think I'm selfish. That's . . . " He fanned himself with the files. "Awesome. Quite a compliment, actually. Normally I hear the entire thesaurus worth of synonyms for *loco*. I've been working hard to make people think otherwise."

"Well, there's a fine line between assault and flattery." I bent and scooped up the files, then paused before I stood up. This was weird. Even if Kingston and I had the same goal, we shouldn't be working toward it or acting civil to one another. Even weirder? I was having fun teasing him. I was sure if I got caught they'd skip jail and send me right to the psych ward. Guile, interrupted.

My eyes caught the numbered stickers on the side of the file. "This is it."

"Way ahead of you." Kingston snatched up a large stack of files. He lifted one knee onto a chair and balanced the files on his lap, furiously flipping through them.

I opened the first folder in my hands. My eyes roamed over some sort of soil-analysis report. I placed that folder beneath the others.

Outside the room, something crashed. I jumped, heart going frantic.

Footsteps sounded in the hallway, growing louder as they approached our room.

CHAPTER 16

The footsteps outside triggered fight-or-flight mode. Apparently, I chose the same path as most deer when faced with an oncoming car. Fight. Or more accurately, freeze, since I certainly didn't choose flee. Kingston clicked the flashlight off and tugged me into a standing position. On wobbly legs, I managed to follow him, knocking into a table in the process.

"Shh!" he whispered.

My hip throbbed where I'd smacked it, but I bit my lip to keep from crying out. We squeezed behind a desk and crouched down, pressed between the wall and the chair. My leg muscles strained from the squatting position. I tried to readjust, but Kingston slapped a hand on my shoulder and steadied me. The folders in my hand cut into my skin.

The footsteps in the hallway grew louder.

My body betrayed me, erupting in tiny earthquakes of convulsions when all I wanted was to be taxidermied into this very position, like a trophy moose mounted on the wall. Kingston snaked his arm around me and pulled me to his chest to muffle me. His heart competed with mine for the quickest to have an attack.

The footsteps entered the room.

I sucked in a diver's breath. The blaze in my chest could ignite a whole forest. Now that my eyes had adjusted to the eerie darkness, I could make out the faint outline of shoes on the opposite side of the desk. They paused, one pointed toward us. Kingston squeezed my arm.

My lungs ached and I leaked a trickle of air through my lips, eyes squeezed shut because I knew how this would end. I'd get caught and arrested, and would never be unfashionable again because all I'd ever wear would be an orange jumpsuit like everyone else in jail.

The footsteps pivoted and headed to the open file-cabinet drawer. Papers rustled as whoever it was shuffled through them.

Kingston and I exchanged glances. Someone else arriving at three A.M. on a random day to sift through the same files as us? That couldn't be a coincidence.

The mystery person slammed the drawer shut, making my teeth clatter. Heart racing, breath desperate, I waited once again for my sentence. This time the footsteps grew softer, and then the door to the room banged shut.

I let out a breath and started to rise, but Kingston held me back with a shake of the head.

He flipped open his cell phone and set it on his lap, a makeshift, less-obvious source of light.

"What are you doing?" I whispered.

He texted so I could read: *Shh. Coast = not clear. Not wasting time just in case.*

He opened the top file on his lap and started perusing. My hands were so clammy they could lubricate a desert, but I followed suit, if only to distract myself from the inevitable end to my freedom. Being grounded actually seemed tempting.

The file on my lap was bulky with papers. I slid the top page off and held it up to the light, leaving the rest of the open folder balanced on my lap. It looked like a phone transcript. All the names of the speakers and phone numbers had been blacked out, as well as some of the lines of dialogue. My eyes immediately fell to my parents' names, like a beacon, halfway down the page in the dialogue.

The pages trembled in my shaky hands. Kingston glanced over at me.

First speaker: Lewis and Carol Liddell and Charles Katz. I don't know where they are, but find them and stop them. This can't get out, and if they do this protest . . .

Second speaker: And how do you expect me to do that? If arresting them didn't work, nothing I say will.

First speaker: I'm not asking you to say anything. I'm telling you to do anything.

Kingston snatched the rest of the open folder off my lap, leaving me with the phone transcript in my hand. He stared at the other files in the folder for a second, mouth parted.

"Hey!" I yelled before I remembered I had to be quiet.

He snapped the folder closed, rolled it into a tube, and slid it down his pants.

"Kingston, I need that," I whisper-yelled. I waved the phone transcript at him like it reinforced my claim. I wasn't about to reach down his pants.

"I think the coast's clear." He stood up and pushed himself out from behind the desk.

I scrambled to a standing position and tucked the folders I hadn't looked at yet under my arm. I didn't know what they contained, but they might be useful. Or maybe Kingston had stolen the most useful one of all. He raced toward the door without waiting for me to follow him.

I scurried after him, tripping on my feet to get to him before he bolted with my file. "Wait!"

He wrenched the door open and stopped short right outside it. "Oh, shit."

I stepped outside and my feet came to a dead stop at the sight of what had caused him to freeze.

Chess.

"Alice?" Chess divided his gaze between Kingston and me.

Kingston relaxed out of his rigid position and boasted a smirk as if this showdown could feed his drama fix for at least a week.

I let out a breath I'd been storing since I entered Town Hall. I wasn't going to spend the rest of my junior year in a square cell. I snapped my body into action and raced to Chess, almost knocking him over with the force of my relief. I wrapped my arms around him, so happy to see him in such an unusual place. He hugged me back, but loosely.

He cocked his head. "What's going on here?"

Good thing it was still kind of dark and Chess couldn't see my red cheeks. "I should ask you the same thing," I said, my voice starting out shaky but growing more confident by the end of the sentence. "I thought you said you would never break in here."

Kingston chuckled, enjoying this way too much.

"I wouldn't." He dropped his arms from around me. "The door was open."

"You guys can stick around and fight, but since we didn't actually get caught, I'd like to keep it that way." Kingston hiked down the hall at a fast clip. One that resembled more getaway than departure.

Kingston tossed Lorina's keys behind him. They clattered to the ground. I bent to retrieve them, my hoodie falling into my eyes. My sweaty hand wiped it out of my face.

"I'm not happy you did this," Chess said. "But—"

"I needed evidence. Why are *you* here?" I pumped my arms as I jetted for the exit.

"You didn't let me finish. But you should have told me. I would have come with you. Made sure you didn't get caught." He reached for my hand. I let him take it.

I spun in place to face him. "I wanted to tell you. I wish you'd been here with me." I smiled at him, mostly so I could get one in return. "But I didn't have your phone number." I dropped his hand and headed for the door again. "And you're avoiding my question."

He held the door open for me outside. "I followed Kingston."

The cool air stung my face. A breeze lifted my hoodie and made it sway in the wind. Kingston peeled out of the parking lot.

"If you followed him, why did it take you so long to find us inside?"

Chess shoved his hands in his pockets. "Alice, let's talk about this in the morning. Not when you're angry."

"Fine." I stomped toward Lorina's car. I thought Chess had told me everything when we ditched gym, but clearly there was something else he didn't want me to know. I would have brought him instead of Kingston. We could have been a team.

I wasn't sure who my ally was tonight.

CHAPTER 17

The next morning, Chess met me at my locker. He carried two extra-large coffees, the scent instantly doing wonders for the bags under my eyes. There was too much blood in my caffeine system.

The students passing by looked like they were speeding through the halls while my body was moving in slo-mo.

"I couldn't sleep last night. Before I found you." He held one cup out as a peace offering, along with a sincere smile. "I've been feeling horrible for making you so upset. I was racking my brain to figure out how to make you feel better."

My head pounded with theories and lack of sleep. I grabbed the coffee and brought it to my lips. The liquid coated my throat, hot and painful, a self-inflicted punishment for betraying my sister.

"I went on Twitter to kill time, and suddenly Kingston posted something odd. *The key to the future is in the past.*"

"That sounds like something Whitney would say."

"She's said it before." He sipped his coffee. "When we first started doing this stuff and we tried to figure out a way to get access to the files but couldn't. That's why I got concerned."

"So you went straight to the township. And you live far, so it took you a while." I nodded, understanding.

He looked confused for a second, then nodded, too. "Exactly." He brushed the hair off my forehead. "I'm sorry I wasn't there for you. I know coffee doesn't quite make up for it, but—"

"I found evidence." I pulled the phone transcript out of my pocket and showed it to him.

He scanned the paper. I sipped the coffee, willing it to work faster, like rapid-release Tylenol. It tasted perfect without me telling him how I took it: with a sugar overload to amp the caffeine.

I pointed at a spot on the page. "See, they said to do *anything* to stop them."

He shook his head. "Anything is too broad. They threatened my dad. Took away his job. They did do *anything*, just like the transcript says. There's no reason why *anything* would mean something different for your parents."

"What about the blocked-out text? Isn't that suspicious?" I'd tried everything to read it: holding it up to a window, squinting, praying to a God I didn't believe in. Nothing had stripped the censor bar off the paper.

"Looks to me like they blacked out any identifying information. I mean, even if they only made threats to stop our parents, that's still shady."

"I think there was other evidence, but Kingston took the rest of the files in this folder."

"Why?"

"No idea. He snatched them right off my lap. I went through a few other folders, but nothing was useful. It was all stuff about the water supply and soil samples."

My face must have looked sad because he cupped my chin in his hands. "Hey, we'll find a way to get them back. I'll help you, okay?" His fingers trailed up the side of my jaw.

I closed my eyes and leaned into his touch. "I'd really like that."

He wrapped his arms around me. He smelled so good, like fresh soap. His hair was still a little damp from his stolen morning shower.

"I'm really sorry I told you that," he whispered in my ear. "It was just a theory, and I'd like to think the township isn't capable of something like that." He pulled back to gaze at me. "What happened to us agreeing it was false?" He grinned, and his voice contained a hint of laughter.

"I couldn't exactly shut my mind off."

"I can help with that." He kissed my nose. "You just need a good distraction." He sank his lips into mine until my mind replaced the worries with endorphins.

I knew he was right. Kingston might have had the files I needed to prove or disprove this, or he might have had nothing useful. Murder was a big accusation, one that put the citizens of Wonderland in danger and added us to the top of the hit list. We had to lie low, which meant I had to stop obsessing over the murder, at least until it was safe to gather more info. When Lorina came home with frazzled hair escaping her bun and the news of the break-in, I forced myself to paste a frown on my face and not indulge in interrogating her about who the township suspected of the crime. Best not to make her suspicious. Whenever I regretted that decision and needed a dose of memory loss, Chess was there to help me, with making out for hours after school in his car. I cursed his job whenever it dragged him away from me.

A few days later, I was waiting outside the locker room to meet Chess for gym when Kingston sidled up next to me. "I'm curious," he said. "What did you say to that redhead about destroying her house?"

I rubbed my arms against the chilly breeze. "I didn't say anything."

"Well, she thinks you did it. She was hounding me about what I knew."

I swallowed hard. "What did you tell her?"

"I told her you did it." He smirked.

"WHAT?!" I spun around and headed back to the track. I had to get to Quinn before she spread the rumor.

Kingston huffed alongside me. "Or maybe I said 'didn't'." He panted. "I can't remember. The phrases are so close, it's hard to tell them apart."

Oh God. "If you told her, I'm gonna—"

"Alice, hey." Chess had raced to catch up with us. Kingston pointed a finger gun and walked away.

My arms flailed as I ranted to Chess what Kingston had just told me. Chess grabbed my hand. "Come on, let's go talk to Quinn." We rushed to the track, but when we got there, Di and Dru were waiting right inside the gate, identical scowls on their faces.

"Were you going to tell me?" Di asked.

"Tell *us*," Dru corrected.

"Whatever Kingston told you, I had nothing to do with Quinn's house." I crossed my fingers behind my back and hoped only the good lie young.

They exchanged a glance.

Dru smirked. "We know that. It wasn't you. No how."

Di still wore the scowl. "Contrariwise, we were talking about you dating him." She pointed at my boyfriend for emphasis.

Chess looked about as comfortable as the boy who accidentally walked into our fifth-grade health class when we were learning about menstrual cycles. I mouthed that he should go, and he gladly obliged.

"We had to hear it from Quinn," Dru said.

Di crossed her arms. "Not my best friend!"

"Then you did hear about it from your best friend. Optional S at the end."

Di snapped her head up. "What's that supposed to mean?"

"Di . . . " I focused on the gravel at my feet, then changed my mind and met her eyes so she could see the honesty in them. I didn't include Dru in my statement. "We both know we stopped being best friends a long time ago."

Dru laughed. "I knew you wouldn't be able to explain yourself because you're not yourself!"

"I don't even know who you are anymore." Di spun on her heels, her sandy-colored hair whipping her face. Dru followed after, of course.

Di's words were icicles, but they didn't stab me, just melted away as they plunged into my chest. I'd known for a long time she didn't understand me. We'd both tried to fit the other into a mold: me begging her to be a do-gooder, and her turning my good deed into the latest gossiple. Our sham of a friendship had buckled, too flimsy to stand on its own ever since we'd each silently bartered each other away for someone who got us in a way the other never could.

Throughout class, Chess reassured me that if Di and Dru believed I hadn't damaged Quinn's house, then it meant Quinn thought that, too. Di and Dru's minds were impressionable, filled with tall tales from the gossip queen herself. Still, I would have talked to her in gym if she'd come to class.

Chess calmed me down by squeezing in a few extra kisses after gym, mostly so I could avoid Di and her minion in the locker room. And, okay, because I liked the kissing. The girls must have changed like they were backstage at a runway show, because I didn't see them anywhere.

By the time I threw on my clothes and exited the locker room, I was on the verge of being late to my next class. Whitney would be proud.

My ponytail stopped swinging as I froze in place.

Up ahead, Kingston stood over a girl at her locker, his hands outstretched on either side of her like he was keeping her prisoner. The girl's face was tilted up to him, which suggested she didn't mind in the least. Guess you could teach an old dog new chicks. Red curls spilled out from behind Kingston's body. Quinn.

WTF? What, did she need to resort to extreme measures to get people talking about *her* instead of me? Or maybe Kingston had drugged her into submission.

I stalked over to them. "Tell her I had no part in what happened to her house."

"I'm a little busy here." Kingston met my eyes, then sank his mouth into Quinn's in a showy gesture meant only for his audience of me. I snapped my head away.

I already felt sick about possibly getting caught; I didn't need to see this make-out session to push me into toilet-worshiping territory. I started to turn back.

He broke away from Quinn. She smirked at me like she was hiding a juicy secret.

"Thanks for all your help, Alice," Kingston said. "But I don't need you guys anymore." He set his eyes on me. "I have an army now."

CHAPTER 18

After the hallway incident, I spotted Kingston and Quinn sitting together at lunch, holding hands in the hallway . . . basically, everywhere. What in the world would make Quinn help with his agenda? Or date him?! My best theory so far: his kissing technique contained the power of compulsion. My worst theory: she was just as crazy as him. Each time I caught them, his eyes shifted to mine, as if he wanted to watch my reaction. I countered with my own form of showy PDA with Chess.

As much as I enjoyed the make-out sessions—mine, not Kingston's, just to be clear—my body itched to keep investigating, find out more about the murder, defeat the township. Stop lying low. I experienced all the symptoms of addiction withdrawal: insomnia, paranoia, and preoccupation.

I couldn't even search my sister's bag for answers because Lorina was never at home anymore. She'd started practically living at the office, ever since the break-in occurred.

I was poring over the files one more time, for lack of any better source of information, when my doorbell rang one Saturday afternoon. My parents had always told me not to open the door to strangers, but I needed my rebellion fix. I dashed downstairs, expecting a telemarketer. But Chess stood on the front porch, hands in pockets, next to Whitney. She wore a terrible brunette wig.

"Do your hair in pigtails and put this on." Whitney thrust a baseball cap into my hands as she brushed past me. Embroidered lacy ribbons circled the mirror appliqués against the gaudy pink fabric.

"Are we dressing up as Kingston for Halloween?" I let Chess inside and followed behind.

"Ha ha," she deadpanned. "It's a disguise. You're my little sister. And sorry, but Chess is my boyfriend for the day."

"I haven't agreed to that yet!" Chess kissed me hello, then grabbed my hand and led me down the long hallway. He peered into the rooms of my house as we passed them. "Not until you tell me what we're doing."

"I second that motion," I said. Inside, though, I squealed. Another mission!

"Surprises are best left unspoiled."

"I still think it's too soon." Chess squeezed my hand.

Whitney rolled her eyes. "I told you, it's an emergency."

Despite my excitement over the mission, my lips slipped into a frown. If Whitney had planned this, it couldn't be related to my parents' potential murder. She didn't know about it.

"I'm hoping it involves something with the old nuclear-power plant." Chess let me go ahead of him into the kitchen. "We've left that alone for too long."

"But isn't that a good thing?" I spun around to see Whitney dawdling behind. "I mean, they destroyed the nuclear plant, so it's not doing any harm anymore." Unless you counted the night vision the entire town had had to acquire to adjust to the lack of lights.

Whitney cleared her throat. Chess covered by dropping my hand, wrenching open a cabinet, and studying the contents. "Got anything to eat?"

I wasn't letting him change the subject that easily. "Is there something I should know about the power plant?"

"No," Whitney said. "Because our mission today has nothing to do with that. Your job is to cure Chess's hunger so he stops bitching."

"Tell me what it is, or you drive." Chess pulled the keys out of his pocket and dangled them in front of Whitney's face. "Oh wait, that's right. You can't." He cupped the keys and turned back to the cabinet. I joined him by the counter.

"Hey, I had more important things to do than practice for my driver's test."

"She failed," Chess told me. "Three times!"

I reached into the cabinet, pulled out a can of soup, and held it out for Chess's approval.

"Perfect. Thanks."

I dumped the contents into a pot and set it to boil. If Lorina hadn't packed up the good china and hidden it from me, I would have served it in that. Instead, I had to settle for a cheap bowl, which I set on the counter. Chess and Whitney sat at the table and continued to argue about her annoying love of secrets and riddles. I wanted so badly to impress Chess with my cooking, but canned chicken soup? Not exactly gourmet, the-way-to-a-man's-heart-is-through-his-stomach memorable. I twirled the spice rack and chose a few seasonings to add, hoping it might make the soup more exotic.

I was twisting open the pepper when Chess said after a minute of silence, "Okay, please tell me why we didn't load the car with plants?"

His abrupt question startled me. My hand, slick from the steam, slipped and I dropped the entire contents of pepper into the soup.

"People expect the expected," Whitney said.

I bolted for the silverware drawer and yanked out a spoon.

"These disguises better not be your solution to spying on Kingston." Chess tapped his fingers on the table.

I frantically scooped out as much black pepper as I could before it dissolved. Most dots sailed right off the spoon back into the pot. I transported each spoonful to the sink carefully, like the old egg-on-spoon relay race we used to do in elementary school. The aroma of the pepper seeped into the air. In the middle of carrying my fourth spoonful, I sneezed. The contents went flying, dousing my clean shirt.

I raced to get a paper towel off the counter. Another sneeze forced my eyes shut as I was reaching for it. My arm knocked over the bowl I'd set out and it crashed to the floor, shattering into pieces.

Chess hopped up from the table. "Are you okay?"

I couldn't answer because it was difficult to speak while being attacked by sneezes. I went back over to the cabinet, hoping I could salvage Chess's lunch by starting over. But that was the last can of soup. We weren't exactly stocked for the apocalypse here. Fighting sneezes, I headed back to the soup and continued excavating the pepper.

My nose tingled. I stepped away from the stove and the cause of my newfound allergies before I could taint the soup even more. "I'm sorry. I was trying to make it taste better, but . . . let's just say culinary school is not in my future. Apparently klutziness is."

As if on cue, Chess let out a monstrous sneeze.

I wiped a hand over my sweaty brow. "Maybe I shouldn't go with you guys. I keep messing everything up." Soon I'd need an abacus to tally my mistakes, because I was running out of fingers to count on.

Chess placed his hands on my shoulders. "We're not doing the mission without you."

"But I screwed up your lunch."

"No, you didn't." Whitney pushed herself away from the table. "Do you have any lemon?"

"We have lemonade, does that work?" I asked.

"Yeah." Whitney grabbed it from the fridge and sidestepped the mess on the floor in order to add a cupful to the soup. "That should counteract the pepper."

“I’ll help you clean this.” Chess scooped a few pieces of broken porcelain into his palm.

I bent down next to him and plucked a large piece. “I hope this doesn’t bring me seven years bad luck, like breaking a mirror.”

“Hey, you know what? This is totally good luck!” He grinned. “Like breaking a glass at the end of a Jewish wedding.”

I stood up. “In that case, you should break something, too. We can use all the luck we can get.” I reached into the cabinet and took down all the cheap bowls. “Besides, I never liked these dishes anyway.” I threw a bowl to the floor, making sure it didn’t land anywhere near his legs.

Chess held out his hands and I laid a bowl in them. He did a little twirl, brought his arm behind his back, then slammed the bowl to the ground.

“Fancy! We’re going for style points, huh?” I took a bowl off the stack and brought it to my chest like I was gearing up to throw a bowling ball, then I sprinted forward a few steps, dropped one arm, and let the bowl dangle at my side before I sent it flying toward the wall.

“I give that a nine-point-five.” Chess took another bowl off the stack. “Would have been a ten, but you didn’t stick the landing.”

Whitney casually stood up, left the room, and pulled an umbrella from the holder by the front door. She sat back down at the table and opened the umbrella, all without saying a word.

Chess and I attempted to show each other up with the next four bowls, until the entire kitchen floor was littered with the remains of our war against ugly dinnerware. “Now Lorina will be forced to use the good china!” I said. If I’d learned one thing in the last few weeks, it was that you only got results with extreme measures.

Chess and I got to work scooping up the mess. “Now that recess is over, I found out where Chapera Farms sold the pigs.” Whitney shut the umbrella and headed to check on the soup.

"Where? How?" Chess looked so happy, I thought he might do a Herkie right there in the kitchen. Then he set down the broken pieces he'd been holding and stood up. "Wait, please say they're alive."

"Sorry, only one is. The rest of his friends are bacon."

My stomach dropped.

Chess closed his eyes for a second, burying his face in his hands. "I was afraid of that. We should have made this a priority! Ever since we found out they were shutting down Chapera Farms, too!"

"Chess . . . " Whitney bent down and picked up the broken pieces he had discarded. "There was nothing we could do until we could do something, you know that. It took me forever to track the pigs down. Eat your soup."

"Okay." He carried the pot over to the table and sat down. "Tell me what you know."

Whitney scooped the rest of the broken dishes and threw them out. "The farmer got more money selling him to the university."

"What about another farm?"

She leaned against the counter. "Everyone's scared, Chess. Saving money just in case."

My head volleyed back and forth between the two of them. I felt like I was watching a foreign film without subtitles.

"Why the universi—Oh God." He ate a spoonful and then cringed, swallowing hard.

"Yep, so we've got a rescue mission before he becomes some kid's science project."

"You don't have to eat that." I stepped closer to the stove where they both stood.

"It's really good." Chess forced another scoop into his mouth and gave me a strained smile.

As Chess ate his terrible soup, trying very hard not to make sour faces, and I aged myself down a few years with pigtails, Whitney filled me in on the details. The farm we'd been doing all the protests for hadn't just lost its land. It had lost its animals. The farmers had kept them until the very last moment but eventually couldn't anymore. They sold them to another farm over a hundred miles away. Except that farm suffered the same fate as the first one.

"How'd you find this info out?" Chess washed the pot.

"Everyone has their price," Whitney told him. "Kingston still helps with the missions, even if he doesn't know it." She rubbed her thumb against her index and middle fingers in the universal sign for "money."

It didn't take a valedictorian to know Kingston might not be so gracious to learn that.

On the half-hour drive over, Whitney briefed me on the mission. No fancy flowers; we'd only have our wits to work with. Based on my brilliant break-in attempt the other night, my wits weren't exactly something I was confident in. Especially when the mission relied on, well, me. I wished I'd had the foresight to realize that in the real world I'd need acting more than calculus, back when I loaded my schedule with academics. My guidance counselor had deceived me.

As we stepped onto the grassy quad, buildings made of gray stone tried to appear old and gothic, but their sleek shapes confessed their modernity. Students milled about, and no one paid attention to us. I'd always thought I'd need a fake ID to fit in on a college campus, not pigtails. Who knew invisibility was a perk of childhood?

We waited until a tour group of prospective students headed our way. "Right on time," Whitney said. She and Chess slipped into the middle of the group. I pushed my way to the front of the crowd, secretly praying my acting wasn't as bad as my gardening. Or my cooking.

"This is the science lab," the college-age guide explained, using her arm like a pointer. Not hard to miss, in her hideous orange-and-navy-striped shirt. "It was donated in—"

"What kind of experiments do they do here?" I tried my best to sound enthusiastic and play the part right, even though my voice quivered. I shot a big smile at the tour guide.

"All kinds. As I was saying, this building was donated in—"

"Do they study time travel?"

"Yes, and after this tour I'm going to travel to the future so I can get paid more." The guide waved us around the building and into a field, with several fences confining animals inside.

"This is the animal-science department." She gestured to the pens. "I'm partial to the pigs, but they don't let us tour them anymore." She leaned in conspiratorially. "Swine flu."

I made a big show of laughing at her terrible joke.

The guide led the rest of the tour back to the quad. I hung back so I could tie my shoe, and Whitney bent down to help me. Chess lingered with us.

With our cover established—*What? We were on the tour! Ask the tour guide!*—we slipped out in the opposite direction to rescue a pig from experimentation.

CHAPTER 19

The three of us raced through the field, checking the various pens for pigs. The cold air stung my face, turning my cheeks a rosy pink. Adrenaline kept me warm.

"How will you know which pig it is?" I asked.

"He'll be wearing a 'My name is . . . stolen pig' sign." Chess grinned. "Really, though, I'll know."

We rounded a corner where a whole other set of wooden fences segregated the animals.

"There." Whitney nodded to a fenced-in pen where several pigs fought for prime position at a water bucket. Even in nature, it was cutthroat to get a front-row spot.

We headed that way until a student wearing a college sweatshirt and carrying a feed bucket stepped in our path. His thick eyebrows looked like a crop of their own. "Whoa, where do you think you're going?"

Whitney pushed me forward.

"I . . . uh . . . " Crap, how to distract him? "Wanted to see the other animals."

His eyes swept over me. "Are you part of the tour? You can't be here. Come on, I'll take you back—"

So much for our alibi. He stepped back in the direction we had come from, waving us toward him with both palms like an air traffic controller. Whitney shifted her eyes from the guide to the pen. Then I realized. He was looking at the pen; I had to turn him around. I jogged, circling him until he had no choice but to spin on his heels and face me.

"All I've ever wanted is to feed some animals." I glanced over my shoulder so I didn't accidentally crash into a fence as I walked.

"Maybe you should aim higher with your goals." He tapped his bucket, and a tinny sound reverberated in the air. He stopped short. "Hey, where are your friends?"

They stood against the gate, coaxing pigs toward them with outstretched palms.

He placed two fingers in his mouth and whistled. "Get away!"

Whitney and Chess shuffled their feet and chatted way too animatedly with each other. The noise from the nearby quad drifted in.

The guy shook his head and set down his bucket. He hustled toward them, muttering to himself. I followed, not sure what else to do. Chess raked his hands through his hair and Whitney grabbed the guy's bicep. "So you really take care of all these animals?" She giggled.

He shrugged her off. "I feed them."

"Like a zookeeper. That's amazing. What's your name?" She tugged his arm in a direction away from the farm. "And more importantly, are you single?"

I had to stifle my laugh. Watching Whitney try to play an innocent flirt was like watching an army sergeant take dance lessons.

"I'd rather hear your name."

"Mary Ann," Whitney said out of nowhere. She tried to bat her eyelashes at him, but it looked like she had something stuck in her eye.

"Well, Mary Ann, you need to get out of here before I—"

"The tour!" I yelled. "We have to get back to the tour."

Whitney glared at me because I was clearly ruining her flirting attempt. I guess she hadn't figured out it wasn't working.

"We don't want them to miss us," I said, my voice forceful.

Catching on, Whitney shrugged nonchalantly. As she did, her backpack slipped off one arm and Chess grabbed it.

"Which way did the tour go again?" Whitney asked.

As soon as the student pointed, Whitney sprinted in the opposite direction. She headed for the sheep at the far end of the farm. The zookeeper glanced at us, then at her, and sighed before racing after her. Whitney must have aced her Presidential Fitness test because she reached the sheep before he did. She unhooked the gate.

You could count on sheep to help out with both insomnia and sheepwalking.

Whitney only waited for the first animal to break free before she headed to another part of the farm. The sheep scattered in various directions, some pausing to chew the surrounding grass, while others merged with the crowd of students walking to their next classes. Screams rang out, and a frenzy of frantic running became the latest campus trend.

The zookeeper dove for one of the grazing sheep. It let out a loud noise and escaped to the quad. He rushed after it, yelling dog commands.

Chess opened the pigs' gate and shut it behind him. My fingers clutched the fence so hard, I was afraid I'd break off a chunk of the wood.

"Come here." He patted his knees with his palms.

The pigs stopped and lifted their heads from the water bucket.

"It's okay, I won't hurt you." He took a tentative step forward.

The movement set the pigs on alert. Before he could get close, they squealed and raced around the pen, smacking into the fence with ungraceful, sharp turns.

Sweat gathered on the back of my neck. I checked behind me for Whitney, expecting security to show up any second. Where was she?

Chess dove for one, landing with a splat and missing his target by a good foot. Mud shot up and sprayed all over his face. The pigs traced zigzags in the mud, squealing and snorting.

"Guess I shouldn't have passed on those rodeo lessons at summer camp," Chess said, straining a forced laugh, his brow furrowed in frustration.

"Think of it as a free spa mud treatment."

We had to figure out something quickly before that zookeeper—or security—came back. I glanced around, not even sure what I was looking for. Maybe Whitney. My eyes fell on the silver bucket the zookeeper had set down, glinting in the sun near an adjacent pen. Maybe I could coax the pigs with food.

I ran toward the bucket and snatched it off the ground. The feed inside shifted while I hustled back to the pen. Mud clung to every surface of Chess's body, looking like an art project gone wrong. The whole place smelled like dirty gym shoes.

"Good call," Chess said when he saw me.

I opened the pen and carried the feed over to a long, wooden trough that looked like a planter. Chess took the bucket from my hands and spread it around. Something bumped my knees, knocking my leg into the side.

A pig squeezed into the space next to me and ducked his head into the feed, standing on his hind legs to reach. The rest of the pigs soon followed.

"Take the stuff out of the backpack and put some of the feed into it," Chess said, inching toward the smallest pig with his hands stretched out, ready to grab him.

I picked up the backpack and emptied the contents, staring skeptically at a white . . . baby's bonnet? And a plush, pink blanket. "Hey, what are these for?" I scooped feed into the sack until it felt heavy.

When I approached Chess with the items, a pig writhed in his arms, desperately trying to break free. He held the pig out to me. "Quick—Put the bonnet on her head."

"What?" I'd heard of dressing up dogs, but pigs?

"People might notice us carrying around a pig . . . "

But they might ignore us carrying a baby. Nodding, I approached the pig tentatively. Sweat dripped from my forehead even in the frigid fall air. Her head flailed about. I snapped my hand back.

"Here, hold her."

He laid the pig in my arms. She kicked at my stomach and thrashed around. I gripped her tighter, wrapping my arms through her legs to keep her stable. "How do I calm her down?"

Chess gently stroked her head, stopping her spastic movements. He smiled down at her as he tied the bonnet around her head. "It's okay, Runty," he cooed. "You're safe now." He met my eyes and smiled. "Thanks."

I stared at him, the way he so lovingly cared for the pig. "She's yours. The pig."

Chess's hands froze, mid-tie.

The world started spinning. "And the farm. That was yours, too. The job your dad lost?"

He turned his head away and grabbed the blanket from the ground. "Yeah."

"I thought you told me everything."

"I'm sorry." He wrapped the pig in the blanket like an hors d'oeuvre. "I wanted to tell you. I did. But Whitney said—" He sighed. "I was trying to protect you. The less you knew—"

"Hey!" a voice yelled from a distance.

We both snapped our heads up. If Chess's hands hadn't been there, I would've dropped the pig.

"What are you doing?" A security guard ran toward us.

"Run!" Chess pulled my elbow, leading me out of the pen.

The pigs squealed behind us, charging for the open door. The pig in my arms shifted wildly, opening her mouth in a wide squeal. Chess grabbed her out of my arms, and we kept going. The frigid wind blinded my eyes. We had no idea where Whitney was. I couldn't tell which way was up, which way was down, only that we were stealing a pig from its rightful owner. My criminal record was going to be fuller than my transcript soon.

As I dodged a passing sheep, my feet caught on something, and I careened forward, landing on the ground. Chess stopped running and doubled back for me, shifting the pig to one arm and lending me his other hand. The pig went wild.

"Don't wait for me, just go!" I said.

He waited. With shaking limbs, I managed to push myself off the ground. Once I stood upright, he jogged beside me, slowed by my pace.

I could only hope that security had decided to herd the stray pigs instead of following us.

My feet slapped against something hard and it took me a second to realize the soft padding of the grass was gone. We had reached the parking lot. The car sat there, waiting for us like an obedient puppy tied up outside a store.

"Get my keys. They're in the front pocket."

I hesitated. We hadn't exactly reached the below-the-belt level of hooking up yet, so I felt a little more than awkward digging my hands down his pants. A blast of wind sent my pigtails slapping against my face, and my teeth chattered.

He laughed to himself, then grinned at me. "Man, this is a perfect opportunity for you to make a joke about are those your keys or are you just happy to see me."

I laughed, too, tension easing with our smiles. I stuck my hand inside the scratchy denim, fumbling awkwardly until I gripped the keys. My cheeks heated. I felt disoriented, so busy trying to shake off my fear that I missed the keyhole on two attempts. Once I strapped myself into the passenger seat, Chess set the pig on my lap. "You okay?" he asked, face concerned.

"Yeah." The word came out scratchy. I cleared my throat. "In fact, let's go back for the rest of the animals. My stress levels aren't high enough to cause serious damage yet."

He stroked my cheek. "I really appreciate what you did for me today." He circled to the driver's side and started the car.

"Wait, what about Whitney?" The pig trampled on my lap.

"We have to leave her." He set the gear in reverse.

I brushed sweaty hair out of my face with one palm. "No, she'll get in trouble!"

"It's cool. We all agreed. If one of us gets caught or stuck at the mission . . . we leave them." Before I could argue further, he backed the car out of the parking lot.

I thought of her there, trying to cover for us. I gnawed on my lip. Could she talk her way out of it if she got caught? My guess was police officers wouldn't be so tolerant of her riddles.

The pig continued her desperate escape attempts. I tried to pet her, but I was shaking too much to make contact. "How do I keep her calm?"

"She's just responding to your nerves. If you're calm, she's calm."

I jammed my eyes shut, breathing so hard it came out more like Lamaze than Zen or yoga-soothing. The pig squealed louder, and a panicked eye rolled back to peer at me.

I screamed.

"Here, if I talk, will that help?"

I met his eyes. "Only if you tell me the truth."

He turned to me, his eyes honest. "That one time you asked me to help with the farmers' market? And I told you no?"

"Yeah, that was nonsensical." I stilled my fingers enough to stroke the pig's back through the blanket, trying to calm down both her and myself. Chess swung the wheel onto a deserted road, trees encasing us. We'd taken the highway here, but I guessed now we were going the more inconspicuous way. The road less traveled.

"If a farmers' market gets erected before I get my farm back . . . there won't be any need for a farm in town. They could get produce from however far away, especially if the farmers volunteer—which they would. They need the extra money."

The pig's erratic movements calmed under my hands, and my heartbeat drifted away from my ears.

"The battle for a farmers' market has gone on for years without any progress. But this—what we do—this is making the township pay attention. If I can just get my farm back, it will solve everything. I'll gladly start up a farmers' market myself." He eased on the break to take a sharp turn with less speed. "That's why I didn't tell you. I was afraid you wouldn't agree."

Without a local farm in the area, a farmers' market did seem pointless. It was supposed to benefit the community, sure, but the other point was to preserve farms and save them from fates like Chess's. Now, all the farms were too far away to really provide consistent produce for a market. Still, I could argue that the creation of a farmers' market could reignite the need for a local farm.

Chess's story must have worked, because I calmed down. So calm, in fact, my shoulders relaxed as I sank into the seat. Without realizing it, I must have loosened my grip on the pig.

A split second later, she leapt from my arms and jumped into Chess's lap. He lifted his hands from the wheel, an involuntary reaction to the pig's ramming her snout into his chest. The wheel spun, taking the car with it.

Flashes popped in my mind, not of images, but of the terror my parents must have felt when this happened to them. My heart squeezed and my lips frantically took up religion, forming a desperate prayer.

The scenery blurred by us: the green of the trees, the black interior of the car, the pink of the blanket. Directions switched, disorienting me. My head tingled, and my stomach swirled as violently as the car.

I heard the sounds of the crash before I felt the impact. Something hard knocked the wind out of me, crushing me against the back of the seat. My teeth slammed together. I was being backed into a brick wall, all sides closing in on me and squashing the air from my lungs. Steam billowed somewhere, and an eerie hiss rang out. Everything went white.

CHAPTER 20

Turned out the white wasn't death but the airbag that cushioned my crash. It deflated, and my lungs gasped for all the air they could take. Sounds leaked back into the silence. The pig's squealing drowned out the hissing car. Remind me never to go "parking" with a guy again.

"Alice! Alice! Are you all right?" Chess shook my shoulder.

If he was asking, it meant he was all right, too. I let out a relieved breath and turned my head toward him, all movements slow and exaggerated. I squinted at his blurry form, and my head pounded like construction workers were renovating it. But that was the only thing that ached, a good sign. Optimism tended to be the result of a near-death experience. "Yeah. I feel . . . like I could . . . run a marathon."

Chess laughed. "I guess gym class has really made an impression on you." He propped open his door and slid out. I pushed my own door open, stumbling for a moment like a newborn calf taking her first wobbly steps. The world spun around me even though I stood on solid ground, so I gripped the side of the car and shut my eyes until my equilibrium returned.

The back of the car was wrapped around a tree, smashed like an accordion. The mangled trunk zigzagged open, warped and dented. I shivered, knowing that could have easily been me.

Chess stared at the damage for a moment, then sank to the ground and buried his head into his knees. Dark brown splotches dotted his body. I rushed over to him because it looked like blood, but as I got closer I realized it was mud.

"All those assemblies at school used to warn about drunk driving." I sat down next to him, outstretching my legs. "But they really should have focused on the dangers of getaways while transporting rabid animals."

"It's not funny." His mouth flatlined on his face. I wanted to inspire his trademark smiles again, not erase them from existence.

"I know, but I'm a big advocate of laughter being the best medicine." I placed my hands over his and clasped them in my lap. "We're going to have to try really hard if we want to mend the car that way." I stretched my arms out, flexing my palms to show I was getting ready for an attempt. "I failed my mom today."

He turned to me. "Why?"

"She always told me to remember two things. Wear clean underwear in case you get into a car accident, and always carry mints in case you talk to a cute boy." I curled my legs underneath me. "And, well, I haven't had a chance to do laundry in a while. Underwear fail."

He let out a brief laugh.

I peered through the window at the pig, which had stopped squealing and now stumbled around the mangled cushions. "Is she going to be okay?"

"I think so." He sighed. "I hope so."

I dragged his head to my chest, rubbing his hair with my fingers. "It's okay," I said, knowing it wasn't. His dad didn't have a job. They couldn't pay to fix this. "We're both okay; that's what matters. You don't need a car."

Chess nestled his mouth into the crook of my neck. "That won't fix the real issue."

"I know, but—"

He lifted his head and met my eyes. "Alice, there's something else I haven't told you."

I stopped stroking his hair.

"It's where I live. My car." He broke from my grasp and scrubbed at his face. "Oh God."

My mind provided a movie montage: Chess with wet hair early in the morning, coming out of the gym. Chess asking me to make him lunch. Chess not wanting to give me his phone number . . . because he didn't have a phone. Losing his farm, because of course, if you lose your farm, you lose the farmhouse!

I stared at him, wanting to say something to comfort him, make it all better, but my mouth didn't have access to the right words. Clouds settled inside my brain. Despite every hair standing on end, I knew I had to pretend to be calm, take control. Be what he couldn't be. I slid my arm back around him, his anchor.

"Okay . . . " My voice was scratchy. I swallowed hard and tried again. "Does your dad live in the car? Where is he now?"

"At my aunt's. We can't call him, if that's what you're thinking." Chess hunched over and I rubbed his back. "She lives two hours away, and I don't want to leave."

"But—"

He spoke the next words in a rush, like ripping off a Band-Aid. "Alice, my dad isn't doing anything about the farm, so I have to. And I have to be here to do it. If that means being homeless for a few months, that's a small sacrifice to make."

"Wow, your dad must be the coolest ever if he allows this."

"Only because he has no idea." He twisted his hands in his lap, rubbing at a spot on his wrist where a blue bruise bloomed. "You're not the only loved one I've lied to, if that helps." Two pink dots appeared on his cheeks. "I mean—"

In all my fantasies of a guy telling me he loved me, it usually occurred on a beach at moonlight or in a spaceship with Saturn as our backdrop.

Hey, I said it was a fantasy. But there was one thing fantasies never got right—besides, you know, reality. It didn't matter where we were. All that mattered was how I felt in return. A smoking car could morph into the most romantic scene ever, when it was the best and worst moment of your life. He might have lied to me, but I knew he had his reasons, and I knew that since my first reaction wasn't anger but compassion that I was falling for him.

I tilted his head to mine. His eyes held a question. I answered with a kiss. Slow and gentle, because he was fragile and damaged and I didn't want to break him. He broke away and smiled. "You like how I slipped in that I love you? I thought that was slick."

That seemed to be his trademark move. "You're the master of subtlety."

He raised his eyebrow. "Oh yeah? How's this for subtle. Are you going to say it back?"

I wanted to, but I wanted to find my own way to say it, like he had. Also, I wanted to distract him, and teasing was the perfect way. "Eventually." I struggled to keep from grinning.

He scoffed.

"You're expecting it now. I want to catch you off-guard. Keep you on your toes."

He pouted like a puppy. "But—car accident! You were wrong about laughter. It's love that heals all wounds."

"Is that a bet? I accept." Just for emphasis, I chuckled. "But I might be persuaded to your side once I've heard the truth. All of it."

"Okay. Where to begin?"

"Begin at the beginning and go on till you come to the end: then stop."

He met my eyes. "I knew my dad only sent me to boarding school to keep me safe, get me away from Wonderland." He paused. "And to keep me in the dark about what was going on with the farm, because I didn't discover any of the rezoning stuff until I got home. One day he called me up crying, and told me he had to be out of the house in thirty days. The town put a lien on the farm for unpaid taxes that turned into a foreclosure. He hid it all from me." His voice cracked. "My dad needed my help packing and selling equipment, so we worked it out with the boarding school that I'd transfer to Wonderland for the last month and return to boarding school in the fall as a scholarship student."

He went on to tell me that he had intercepted the letter his dad was sending to Wonderland, explaining Chess would not be returning in the fall. Chess copied the same wording, forged the signature and sent the letter to boarding school instead, plus changed the address of record so all mail went to the Garden Center. He emailed his dad every few days from the school computer lab, since paying for a landline or cell phone was out of the question anyway. "I drove myself to school, supposedly, at the end of the summer. He literally has no idea I'm not there."

"That's crazy," I said, partly in shock, partly in awe that he'd pulled it off.

He shrugged. "We're all mad here. We wouldn't be doing this stuff if we weren't."

"Do Whitney and Kingston know?"

He nodded. "I used to crash with Kingston every night, but ever since their parents caught me and grilled me, I've been too afraid to go back. They threatened to call my dad."

"Then I'm sneaking you into my house tonight." There were worse things to be caught doing, I knew all too well. Getting caught with a boy in my room seemed like a minor infraction.

He opened his mouth to protest, but something in my face must have made him shut it. Or maybe he recognized the make-out potential involved. "Thanks."

"Wait—when you found us at Town Hall that night, you said you saw Kingston online . . . but how?"

He sighed. "That was a half-truth. I really did follow Kingston that night. I had parked my car near his house, but hidden, because I didn't trust him. I woke up at one point and noticed his truck was gone. Went to Town Hall, natch, and saw it parked right in front. I didn't want to break and enter, but I wanted to confront him." He looked at the floor. "I had no idea you were there, too."

I squeezed his hand. "What about your Garden Center job? You've saved up a lot of money. You can afford rent."

"I can't, though, not on minimum wage. And no one will rent to a minor."

I lowered my voice. "I wish you would have told me."

"Hey . . . " His arm curved around my shoulder. "I was going to tell you. But . . . everything was going so well. I didn't want to ruin it." He kissed my forehead. "It was the only good thing I had going."

I stared at the dusty road, trying to process all this in my cotton-stuffed mind. "What about the nuclear-power plant? You guys were acting weird about it at my house."

"Whitney's mad because they turned the land into a parking lot and not another farm." Chess tilted my chin, forcing me to look at him. "You know everything now. So is there anything you feel like saying to me?" He waggled his eyebrows.

It was half a joke, half a serious plea for a declaration. But he wasn't frowning anymore. Maybe we both won that bet.

"Yeah." I leaned in and whispered in his ear. "I really have to use the bathroom."

He closed his eyes and said in a sexy voice, "That's the most romantic thing any girl has ever said to me."

"Wait, I can beat that." I brushed my lips against his ear. "I think I have an ingrown toenail."

He braced his hands on my shoulders and pulled me forward, hovering his lips above mine. "I better kiss you before you say anything sexier."

We distracted ourselves from responsibility with heavy kisses until daylight started to fade and the lower temperature made me shiver against his chest. I pulled out my cell phone.

"Who are you calling?"

I turned my phone on. "We have to call the police."

"We stole from a university." He grabbed the phone from my hands and twirled it between his fingers. "We can't involve them."

"We have no choice. They're going to trace the car back to you. If we call them, we can control what story we tell them."

He thought about that for a second. "Fine, but not until we get the pig somewhere safe."

I brushed my hair out of my eyes. "We'll call someone else first. They'll take the pig, then we'll call the police."

The wind rustled leaves while he considered. "Who?"

I tried Whitney first, but her cell went straight to voicemail. I bit my lip. There was only one person who would understand about the pig, who might help us and keep our secret. "Kingston."

A half-hour later, after Chess had changed into a clean outfit from his "closet" in the trunk, Kingston arrived in his truck. He hopped out and assessed the damage. "Whoa, man. First Whitney, now this."

"Whitney?" Chess tilted his head toward Kingston.

Kingston looked back and forth at us, jingling his keys. "Oh shit. I figured you knew. She got arrested. Looks like time finally caught up to her. I knew he would. He's determined that way."

My chest tightened.

Chess squeezed his eyes shut. “Tell her I’m really sorry.”

“You tell her.” Kingston crossed to the truck and lifted a dog’s cage out of the back. “I don’t talk to her on prime-number days. For her own protection, obviously.”

“A cage?” Chess looked horrified.

“Yeah, I stopped by the pet store.” Kingston set the cage back down. “Whitney fenced off part of the basement this morning. I’m assuming it was for the pig?”

I glanced at Chess. The lifeless color of his skin matched my airbag-enhanced memory of the crash. “Is that okay?” I asked.

Chess blew on his fists to keep them warm. “Yeah, I guess. Since it’s only temporary.”

“You should call the police.” I pushed the cell back into his hands since I wanted a moment alone with Kingston. Chess thanked Kingston, then headed to the road’s edge where we’d learned the cell got the best reception.

Kingston crossed his arms and stood in place. “This was really stupid. You guys got caught, and you were almost killed. If I’d been here . . . ”

“I thought you had an army now? Or is dating Quinn somehow your way of getting back at me for stealing your spot in the group?”

Kingston let out a quick laugh. “I’m not that predictable. Keep thinking that and you’ll be pleasantly surprised.”

“Pleasantly?” I raised my eyebrows.

He pursed his lips. “Well, that’s still open for interpretation.” He sidestepped around me and headed for Chess’s car door.

I smoothed the hair off my face and followed him. “So what’s your personal agenda then, with all these stunts? And why in the world is Quinn helping you?”

“Don’t act so surprised. You’re practically the only girl in school who isn’t in love with me.”

Delusional and crazy, what a combo. "And maybe I just want a girlfriend?"

I so did not believe him. After all, he'd phrased it as a question. "Really? Because you two have so much in common."

"We do have a common goal." He grinned at me.

"Right, I forgot Quinn has been on the front lines of saving the environment."

He smirked as if he found my comment cute. I decided to try another tactic: kill him with kindness. "I'll hold the cage."

"I think you've done enough." He waved his hand at the damaged part of the car.

A million comebacks bubbled in my throat, but I swallowed them down. "Maybe you can convince Quinn to use her student-council powers to help Chess somehow. Raise money to buy another farm?" I knew it sounded implausible, but my rational thinking meter had been crushed in the accident.

He lifted the pig out of the front seat. It thrashed in the air and squealed like a rusty gear. "You can't just buy a farm. You need land for it, permits . . . What do you think we've been trying to do this whole time?" He adjusted the pig to his side and brought his broken watch to his mouth. He whispered to it, then tilted his ear so he could listen. His eyes met mine and he looked surprised, like he'd forgotten where he was.

I shut the door behind him. "Even if we could somehow get him a house, like Habitat for Humanity?"

He snorted. "You really know nothing. At least in the zombie apocalypse you'd be safe. They only eat brains, after all."

I climbed onto the truck bed and looped my fingers through the metal bars of the cage to keep it steady. "Kingston, I don't want to fight with you. We're on the same side."

"Are we?" He eyed me for a long moment. "Seems to me you're siding with Chess and Whitney."

The metal bars cut into my palms as my fists tightened around them. "They're on your side, too."

"No, they're not." He grunted as he lifted the pig onto the truck. "It's all about Chess." Kingston shot a quick glare in his direction. Farther in the distance than he'd stood before, Chess pressed one finger into his open ear and spoke into the phone, his back to us now. "I waited and waited, and look what happened."

Kingston let go of the pig too early, almost like he was throwing her. The pig's eyes widened, and she flung her limbs wildly. Kingston shoved her into the cage. He snapped his hands back, fingers shaking.

"Oh my God! You hurt her!"

"I didn't mean to—I—my hand was all tingly." He glanced up at me, mouth ajar, and I expected anger, but he looked . . . scared. He brought one palm up and dragged it across the side of his face. His voice went soft and he squeezed the tufts of his shirt with white knuckles. "Sometimes . . . I have a problem with my anger."

I nodded. No way was I going to argue with him anymore.

"Don't you see, Alice?" He let go of his shirt, leaving behind star-shaped wrinkles. "My problem *is* as big as Chess's. It needs to be dealt with."

Curiouser and curiouser. I didn't see how one related to the other. "I'll help you." If he was this desperate to get someone on his side, then maybe he really needed it. It might be illegal, but it couldn't be worse than what we'd already been doing. Ideally, anyway.

"That's the problem." He slammed his fist into the metal of the car, rattling it. The pig reacted in familiar terror. Kingston's fist left a dent, and I got a horrible sense of déjà vu. "No one can help me."

CHAPTER 21

In my sixteen years, this was my second encounter with the police. The first had happened when one of them came to tell us about the car accident that killed my parents, and that was an experience best forgotten. After filing a report where we claimed Chess lost control of his car because an animal crossed his path—hey, it was true—the police insisted on calling EMTs and our guardians because we were underage. Both our guardians.

Chess looked horrified as he gave up his dad's number. The EMTs checked our vitals and though we aced the exam, it was standard protocol to send us to the hospital for a more thorough check-up; our guardians would meet us there. Chess gave me a skeptical look, and I tried to beam him the telepathic message, *It's okay, we'll find a way to keep you in Wonderland.* On the bumpy ride over, I couldn't help but rack up all the bills Chess wouldn't be able to afford: ambulance, medical, insurance, tow truck, the ticket for reckless driving, totaled car.

The hospital smelled like antiseptic and staleness mixed with clean linens. Nurses in colorful scrubs poked in and out of the curtained sections. I was numb all over, drained of energy. Even my brain was too tired to come up with loopholes to get him out of here before his dad arrived.

Stomping footsteps made me glance up a second before I spotted Lorina approaching. Her face was as white as the décor. As she got closer, the redness outlining her puffy eyes became visible. "What happened? Are you okay?"

Lorina settled her eyes on Chess's and my interlocked hands swinging between our adjacent cots. She used telepathy to break us apart. I clasped my hands in my lap. Chess sat up and swung his legs over the side of the bed to face my sister.

"I'm all checked out." My voice sounded hoarse, and I wished they'd given me a glass of water and not just a tongue depressor shoved down my throat. "I'm sorry," I added.

The sectioned-off room felt smaller than normal, like it couldn't fit all of us and the heaviness of what had happened.

"The police said—but I want to hear it from you." She put on the brave mom-face I'd always wished she would discard.

Chess stepped in with the dry facts, the ones we'd told the police. "I'm not a bad driver," he insisted. "It wasn't my f—I tried to avoid—" He sighed. "My fast reactions saved us," he said weakly. The unspoken part of his speech rang in my ears. *We were lucky to have survived.*

My parents weren't so fortunate. I pressed my fingers against the wrist of my left hand, and my pulse pounded beneath them. I let out a breath. I really was alive.

Lorina, however, looked like she wanted to die, her face pinched from the story. Redness crept under her eyes, and she fanned her palm in front of her face to prevent more tears. She strode forward and wrapped me in a bear hug.

"I'm glad you're okay," she said into my hair. She let go of me and pulled back to study my face. "What were you doing all the way out here anyway?" They'd brought us to the university hospital.

"Alice came with me to tour the school," Chess said, and I nodded to corroborate.

Lorina sighed. "Alice, you should have told me you were coming here. You want me to trust you, but—" She glanced away from me and set her eyes on Chess. “A university tour?” She pursed her lips. “Were you there when the animals got out?”

Chess and I exchanged glances, which did not go undetected by Lorina. She pushed herself off the bed and crossed her arms. “Some girl—a student at your school, actually—released all the animals. A few are still missing. Pigs and sheep and cows. I was listening to the police scanner at work. Do you know anything about this?”

Blood drained from my face. Good thing I was in a hospital because I might have required a transfusion.

“No.” Chess shook his head a little too vigorously.

“That must have happened after we left,” I tried to keep the hitch out of my voice. “Is this related to your investigation?” I didn’t want to ask, and I especially didn’t want to put the idea in her head, but I had to know.

“We don’t think so. This seems isolated. None of the other incidents involved animals. Still, we’re checking it out.”

Sensation returned to my numb fingers. Okay, so they didn’t suspect us for anything else.

“Alice . . . ” She crouched in front of me, placing her palms on my knees, and whispered in my ear. “The reports state there were two other people with the girl and the descriptions match you two. And you just admitted to being there today.”

The one time I needed to lie more than ever, the words stuck in my throat like peanut butter on the roof of my mouth. They were there, but I couldn’t dislodge them. I glanced over at Chess. He looked like a wax figurine, a lifeless replica of himself.

“That’s what I thought. Alice, what were you thinking—why were you—was this the first time—I don’t even understand.” She jerked away from me and buried her head in her hands. “I’m so disappointed—

God!" She brought her hands down to her sides and balled them into shaky fists. "Let's go."

I hopped off the bed and placed a palm on her shoulder, rising on tiptoes to reach. "Lorina, calm down. I'll explain."

"Fine, explain." She crossed her arms.

A nurse shuffled by, checking the chart hanging off Chess's bed and smiling at us before departing again. In that momentary pause, I saw an opening.

"Not here. Maybe you can sign Chess out, too. His dad's too far away to come get him and he needs a place to crash tonight."

Chess's head snapped up.

"Excuse me?" Lorina backed away and laughed like a crazy person. "The guy almost kills you in an accident—somehow gets you involved with . . . with . . . criminal activities! And you want to bring him home?"

"It's not like that." My voice came out desperate and high-pitched. "I'll tell you everything. He's a good guy. But he . . . doesn't have any place to go. For one night, please! We'll figure something else out tomorrow."

Lorina aimed her eyes at Chess. "Where are your parents? Why are you in Wonderland if you don't live here?"

"He's been living out of his car, it's a long story, it's—"

"It's okay," Chess said, shooting Lorina one of his beaming smiles. She clucked her tongue. "I have an aunt I can stay with. It's really no big deal."

His words hit me hard because I knew how much he didn't want to go to his aunt's, but now that he'd offered in front of Lorina, there was really no way around it. He was already so transparent, like a flickering hologram about to fade away. I tried to soak in all the images of him I could before he disappeared completely.

Lorina nodded once. "Good." She paused and eyed him. "What's your last name again?"

I wondered why she wanted to know. Was she going to turn him in?

Chess didn't say anything, just fiddled with his gown.

"It's not a hard question." Lorina set her wild eyes on me.

If he didn't tell her, she'd only get more suspicious. "It's Katz," I said.

"Katz. Katz. Why does that sound so familiar?" She slung her purse up onto her shoulder.

"Because you've always wanted to own one," I said quickly, in case she made any connections to Chess's farm and her investigation. "Remember that play you once put on to try to convince Mom and Dad, where you had me crawl around on the floor and meow?" Oh God, I should never play poker.

Lorina looked at me like she didn't think that was funny at all. "Let's go." She huffed toward the reception desk. I glanced at her, then back at Chess, and committed what would probably be my last act of defiance for a long time.

"Is your dad even coming?" I placed my hands on his knees.

"He better. But I'm not looking forward to this reunion." He let out a strained laugh.

"Alice," Lorina hissed. She marched back over.

I kept my eyes on Chess and forced brave words out of my mouth. "I think maybe we should . . . take a break." It killed me to say the next words even though they were fake. "From us," I said loudly, for Lorina's benefit. I suspected she might protect me, but she had no loyalty to him. She might be more apt to turn him in if she thought he'd still be a bad influence on me.

Chess's mouth parted in surprise. I added a wink and reassuring smile in case he thought I was serious. I also squeezed his knee for good measure.

Lorina must have heard me because she hung back, arms crossed, and waited.

Chess's eyes flicked to Lorina then back to me. He gave me a brief, knowing look, then donned a stony expression. "Yeah, I thought you might say that. I won't ask for your help anymore."

Ugh. He was trying to protect me, so Lorina would think this was a one-shot deal for me. Couldn't he see I was trying to protect him with this fake breakup? I pleaded with my eyes. "Not that it matters, because it's done," I added.

"Right." He nodded. "As is this." He pointed back and forth between us. "A bit of advice, though," his voice was cold and hard, but his foot slid over to mine, rubbing against it in a subtle way. "Stick with Whitney," he said in a lower voice, for my benefit, not Lorina's. "You shouldn't stop because I'm not there." He glanced up at me and met my eyes. "No wait, you *should* stop. Don't put yourself in danger."

"You just contradicted yourself."

"Like I said, sometimes both paths are right. The way I see it, both directions lead to the same place."

"What does that mean?"

He raised his voice again at Lorina's approach. "It means you're not going to listen to me either way."

"Come on." Lorina tugged on my arm.

I gave him a quivering smile as I rose to a standing position on shaky legs. I followed Lorina to the reception desk, walking backward. My chest rose and fell as Chess grew more and more distant, vanishing slowly until the only thing left of him was his grin. Imprinted on my brain.

CHAPTER 22

As soon as Lorina left for work the next day I hightailed it to Whitney's, despite my firm grounding orders. As each second ticked by without the door opening, I worried Whitney would blame me for her arrest. Plus, I still had to tell her my boyfriend had been forced to go who-knows-where without even an overnight bag or a cell phone and I had no idea when—if ever—I'd see him again. Notify Homeland Security to change the suck levels to red.

The multi-doors opened to loud rock music blaring in the background and Whitney's scowl. "You're as predictable as a chick flick."

I braided my fingers together. "Are you okay?"

"Grounded for a while." A clatter of pots and pans issued from inside, and Whitney snapped her head toward it. "Rain check?"

"I have to talk to you about yesterday. It's important."

Whitney paused, studying me. "Fine. You're a ghost. Don't let my parents see you." She placed a finger to her lips for emphasis. "I'm in enough trouble."

I took baby steps as I followed Whitney through the hallway. The banging sounds increased the farther we went inside her house. With all the noise, I probably didn't need to take such grand procedures to conceal my entrance, but I'd gotten a lot of practice sneaking around lately.

Whitney's hand perched on a door we'd never gone through. When she opened it, I spotted stairs that led to the basement.

The stairwell started out normal. White walls. A wooden railing. Rickety steps. But then, like we'd teleported to a jungle, dracaena trees rose above us, towering over potted plants that created an aisle down the center of the room. Everything smelled fresh and flowery, attacking my nose in the same way Quinn's over-applied perfume did. The lush lime green of the plants turned the area into a monochromatic painting except for the colorful flowers popping up every now and then.

"It's . . . amazing." A soothing melody wafted through the room, classical music. I felt like I'd entered another country. Or planet.

Whitney shrugged, then stalked to the far end of the room. Lamps hung from the ceiling, illuminating some areas with dim light, while shadows darkened others to dungeon levels. White signs were stuck in front of the plants, with their species names and various details scribbled below in her cryptic handwriting. "So what's the self-destructing message?"

While I told her about the hospital and Lorina forcing Chess to go to his aunt's, she showed me where she kept the pig: happy in a back room with an unlimited supply of feed and water. And life. "Chess hasn't contacted me yet. I'm worried." And, oh, I missed him so much. *No, Alice, focus—you have to get him back, not freak out.* "Have you heard from him?"

"Cliffhanger alert. My mom confiscated the computer and cell phone. So you'll have to wait until I get to school tomorrow."

"We have to figure out how to help him."

"We're at half-mast with our members." Whitney lifted a watering can from a shelf and quenched the thirst of a plant that sagged too far toward the ground. "And your sister knows it's us." She set the can back down and stomped away from me without saying another word.

I rushed to catch up. "No, she's only suspicious of us releasing the animals. She hasn't connected anything else."

"She will. As soon as she connects Chess's name to Katz Farms, she'll figure out the motivation, too."

"She hasn't turned us in yet."

"And we shouldn't give her reason to." She led me to the far back corner of the basement, where she pushed aside several plants and revealed another wooden door that had been entirely concealed by leaves. "Trust me, I don't like it either."

Inside, a miniature model of the town rested on top of a long table. Pushpins stuck all around, with strings attached to them like a cat's-cradle game. A place carpeted mostly in green farmlands was dotted with houses and apartment buildings. Each of the buildings was modeled out of clay, artistic and delicate. Sculptures as detailed as Michelangelo's.

She leaned back against the table and crossed her feet at her ankles. "This is where I keep all my plans, past and future."

"What about the one in your room?"

"That's where I keep my notes for current missions, not my plans. Sometimes I put up false information there. And anyway, I paint over it constantly."

She trusted me enough to say this. "So the part about flooding the school to cut off the power supply was fake?"

She smirked. "No, that was real, and apparently Kingston carried it out on his own without informing me."

"What do you mean? He flooded the school a second time?" I ran my fingers over the sharp edges of one of the houses, painted with a red X on top, miniscule trees covering the front like enclosing vines. This must be the house I'd nearly fallen off of.

She opened a file cabinet and extracted a newspaper clipping. "*Town Hall workers are baffled by a break-in last night*, blah blah. Here we go: *At press time, power still wasn't restored and emergency workers are . . .*" She put the clipping back in the cabinet. "Some files also went missing so it had to be Kingston. When you failed at cutting off the power to the school, he must have taken it upon himself to do this instead. It certainly got notice."

Huh. Was that what happened when the heat suddenly shut off? Great, I didn't just burglarize Town Hall and vandalize it; now I was an accomplice to private-property damage. "Why did you want to shut off the power?"

"To remind Town Hall that the plant is still closed, yet nothing's in its place." She waved her hand over a replica of what I assumed was the parking lot that had replaced the power plant. "No new energy solution, no farm."

I fought back a smile. "So this town replica is why you wanted to keep me away from here?"

"That, and Kingston's marijuana closet is a few doors away. Was, I mean."

I perked up. "He got rid of them?"

"No, I did. Early Christmas present."

My body grew hot. "Why?"

"I was arrested. They might link me to the other crimes. Might go all fancy with a search warrant. I saved his butt."

I swallowed hard. "What did he say?"

"He doesn't know yet. That should be fun." She swept her hand over the mini-houses. "Hope you have a photographic memory, because after today I'm making sand art out of these."

I snatched my hand back from the table. "What?"

"I don't need them anymore. I'm done with the missions." She bent beneath the desk and opened a drawer.

My mouth went dry. "What about Chess? He needs us!"

On the table, she fanned out five sets of manila envelopes, each labeled with cryptic phrases. "This isn't a riddle. You have the answers."

"We have to get Chess back. He needs a house. And . . . " I couldn't believe I was about to suggest this. "Kingston needs us, too. I want to help him."

She scooped up the file folders and tore them in half, papers separating like broken hearts. "Kingston seems fully capable of doing things on his own. And Chess, well, he has a house now. Not his own, but . . . " She started to tear the folders into fourths, but I yanked them out of her hands. Shrugging, she plucked a house from her town model and chucked it at the wall, shattering it and everything we had built into pieces.

"Then let's do this my way," I said out of desperation, my voice rushed. "We'll start an eco club at school."

She paused, another miniature house clutched in her fist. "An advertisement in school would be evidence."

"We'll do things that are completely legal, like . . . I don't know. Start a petition or something. Things that even the township can't get us in trouble for." Except for possibly murdering us to shut us up, but I still had hope that speculation was false. The only negative thing a petition might bring was unpopularity, something I'd gladly take over death. Or juvie.

"Petitions are worthless. So is a club with only two members."

"We'll recruit more."

"Have you met the other students at school?"

I let out a huff. "Maybe . . . maybe we don't need anyone else to join." I nodded like my words made sense. "If we make a big campaign to get people involved, it could get notice, even if no one actually signs up."

Whitney set the figurine down. "That's an interesting idea."

"What?" A moment ago she'd hated it. But hey, I wasn't complaining. I surrendered the papers to the table as a peace offering.

"Using the start of an eco club to voice our opinion might work."

The smile wouldn't leave my lips. "We can make signs and stand outside the school and—"

She shook her head. "No, people won't care if we do that. We need to make them pay attention. Intrigue them. Tout this as the coolest new thing to hit the school so everyone wonders why. That would get notice. Maybe if it turned out to be popular, people would actually join."

"How are we going to do that?"

"Leave that part to me. You just set up a table outside the school tomorrow morning. I'll try not to be late."

I couldn't think of anything that would change the students' minds, but I'd be there tomorrow. Even if it didn't work, we still had to try. Doing something open and in public might be the craziest idea of all . . . if it worked.

After Whitney assured me the coast was clear and her parents were safely occupied with some new and highly dangerous art-installation project in the kitchen, I tiptoed back up the stairs but paused by the front door. "Is Kingston home?"

She cocked her head to me. "No idea. He won't let me put a GPS tag on him."

"Can I just check his room real quick? I have to talk to him." Truthfully, I hoped he wasn't home. It would make it easier to snoop. My powers of persuasion weren't nearly as honed as my powers of investigation.

"Why?"

"I want to . . . thank him. For his help with the pig."

"I'll deliver the message."

"It will mean more coming from me."

She studied me for a moment, obviously suspicious. "Fine, but if my parents catch you, I'm claiming you're a burglar."

"Striking while the family's home and wearing jeans is the perfect cover."

Whitney went into the kitchen to distract her parents with loud complaints about her unfair grounding—because wasn't getting arrested punishment enough? I tried not to giggle and instead padded through the foyer and up the stairs.

I pressed my ear against Kingston's door to listen over the loud sounds coming from downstairs. I knocked softly. No answer. I twisted the knob carefully and eased the door open.

Kingston sat cross-legged on his bed, huge earphones covering his ears. His alarm clock looked like it had been smashed in with a hammer. A large manila envelope rested next to him, and he was sliding photographs mounted on black, matte board into it. Other photographs littered his bed. One depicted a rose at the peak of bloom, crushed beneath a sneaker. Next to it, one of a gorgeous sunset taken through a streaky glass window, the vivid colors subdued by fingerprints. His eyes rose to meet mine. My stomach flipped, and I slammed the door shut.

I hustled back down the hallway, heart pounding. I had enough insight to know this wasn't something Kingston would want me seeing. Taking photos of me to use as blackmail? Manly. Taking photos of flowers and sunsets? Lost him a bit of his intimidation cred. The door burst open and Kingston emerged, headphones wrapped around his neck.

"What you saw—" He broke into a coughing fit before he could finish.

"Got into a fight with your alarm clock?"

"It started whispering things to me, mocking me. So I destroyed it." He pounded one of his fists against the other. "Didn't stop the whispering." He waited a few seconds. "Is that all you saw?"

I held up my hands. "Hey, I'm not like you. I don't blackmail people or reveal their secrets."

He stared at me, coughing one last time. "I know."

"But I *will* secretly laugh at you for taking such girly photos."

"You thought they were—" He brought his fists to his temples and punched himself several times. After a moment, he dragged his hands down his face. "Never mind." His fists shook at his sides. "It's not a big deal." He forced his hands open with struggle, keeping his fingers splayed. "Just this thing that probably doesn't even matter."

Except to him, I could see. I bit my lip. Now I felt bad for making fun of him when he was obviously insecure about it. If the situation were reversed, I knew he'd use it against me, but I was glad I held the power for once. Because I knew the best way to get people on your side was through kindness, not force.

"Why'd you come to my room, anyway?"

"Ammunition?" I raised an eyebrow for good damage-control measure.

"Didn't you learn anything from our night together?" He shook his head and clucked his tongue. "You can't walk in and steal the files back. If I wasn't here, you think I'd leave the door unlocked? I already have the voices in my head. I don't want them sneaking into my room, too."

"Huh, and I thought you *could* walk in and steal files. Since that's what we did." I started for the stairs, knowing defeat when I saw it. I'd have to think harder, think like Kingston instead of like Alice.

"Was what you found useful?" he asked, stopping me. He sounded almost curious, concerned.

"Sort of, but I need the rest of what you took." At least I hoped I did. "What about yours?"

"Enough to get me started." The cocky grin on his face returned. "So glad I snatched your folder."

I ground my teeth together. Gah! I hated him. But more than that, I hated when he was almost nice to me. I wished he would stick with one direction. I liked him better when he was an asshole, because at least it made it easier to stick with my hate. I was an idiot for wanting to be civil to him. He'd used me to get inside Town Hall and then he'd stolen what I needed. He might have been crazy, but he knew exactly what he was doing. All the guilt and connection to him I'd felt a second ago shed from my body like a flaky, dried-up second skin.

I stood straighter, shoulders squared in battle mode, wanting to taste power over him. Experience what it felt like to be lord of the sting. "Have you checked your basement closet recently?"

He tilted his head. "How did you—?" Kingston swung his fist at the wall, punching it so hard his hand went right through the plaster. He yanked it out hard, plaster spraying. "If you did anything to—" He sucked in a deep breath that made his nostrils flare. "I need that." He rubbed his hand.

"If the township starts investigating . . . goodbye freedom. Whitney was just protecting you."

He closed his eyes, and his chest expanded and contracted. "She had no right."

"Hey, I hear there's a vacant job at the Garden Center you can take instead of dealing." Of course, my stupid words made me think of Chess. A lump grew in my throat. I hated Kingston for that, too.

"That's not why I needed it." Kingston glanced at the floor. He must have noticed he looked weak because a second later his body went rigid and the venom in his eyes returned. "Just you wait. You'll understand, and then you'll regret what you did."

"I doubt it. I have no room left for any more regrets." I challenged him with my eyes. "But I wish you regretted taking files I might need."

He stared at me, his chest expanding and contracting. I waited for a moment, and that was when I realized the danger of this situation. I was *waiting*. For Kingston. Because I thought he might do the right thing. Do something good. That was the kind of impossible hope that made people give up religion when it didn't pan out, had made *me* give it up, praying for something that could never come true, like my parents coming back from the dead.

I twisted away from him and rushed down the stairs. From the kitchen, Whitney still argued loudly, now complaining about the spiky, execution-style fridge. I burst through the front door into the cold air. The wind stung my face, turning my cheeks an instant pink.

The door opened when I was halfway down the driveway. "Wait! Alice!"

Kingston.

I amped my pace. But my short legs struck again, carrying me at only half the speed Kingston's long ones could take him. He cut me off on the sidewalk and thrust a paper into my hands. "Here."

I snatched the paper away, expecting more blackmail photos. Instead, I skimmed what looked like a forensics report. I paused, glancing up at him. "What's this?"

"It was in the folder. I didn't need it, but . . . maybe you do."

I hugged the paper close to my chest. "Why would you give this to me?" Either they were very cold in hell right now or a miracle had just happened on 34th Street.

"We were even when I helped with the pig. Now we're not. You owe me one." He grinned and then spun on his heels to strut back inside. Of course, Kingston wouldn't do anything without personal advantage to be gained. So much for thinking he might change.

My sweaty palms crinkled the paper. I read quickly, like it might self-destruct in a moment. Blood pounded in my ears as I absorbed it.

It was a forensics report investigating the tire tracks, dated only a few days after my parents' death, though their names didn't appear anywhere on the sheet. My eyes fell to a single line of text in the center of the page. Most of it was boring jargon I could barely understand. But I got the gist of it. Impressions were made of both sets of tire tracks. Expert analysis determined they were from the same car, not two separate cars.

I dropped my hands, sweat beading on my forehead. If this report was true, it meant my parents weren't murdered. The relieved breath I wanted to let out remained stuck in my throat. Something about the report seemed odd. Maybe it was the blacked-out text; why hide if you don't have anything to hide? Though that wasn't exactly abnormal, based on the other files I'd found. I held the paper up to the light, trying to read through the censored lines. Nothing came from that. Except I also couldn't see any watermarks.

When I'd attempted to read the other forensics reports, a faint logo appeared through the paper when held to the light. Also, there was always a raised seal embossed in the top-left corner. This paper didn't have a seal either, though it did have a dark circle where the seal should have been punched in.

It could have been nothing unusual. Or it could have been doctored.

CHAPTER 23

The next morning, I got to school super early. It wasn't like I'd slept the night before. Despite all the new evidence, I was still so far from the truth. But at least I could try to help Chess. Oh, Chess. God, I missed him so much. And now I felt guilty about not saying those words when I had the chance, and keeping him in suspense.

A janitor set up the table and chairs right in front of the school's entrance, and I laid out several clipboards on the surface even though Whitney had told me to leave the details to her. I settled into one of the chairs and scanned my handiwork. Crap, I'd only brought one pen. Abandoning my perch, I raced into the school and dug through my locker until I gathered all the pens I could find. When I came back outside, I saw three people sitting in the chairs. One bent over, with her cheek pressed on the desk. The next had red, curly hair, a tiara on her head. The last wore a top hat.

The formalwear gave more credence to my opinion of them as royal pains in the ass. I stalked over to Kingston and Quinn and slammed the pens onto the table. "Get out."

Di's head bounced, but she didn't look up. The stream of students flowing into the school stopped at my words, heads tilted in our direction. My skin felt prickly, like their eyes were burning each pore. I didn't wear spotlight very well; it washed me out. Quinn, however, lit up from the extra attention.

"I see you've set aside this special time to humiliate yourself in public," Kingston said.

"Oh? I thought you held the keys to that special privilege." I crossed my arms and eyed the occupied chairs. "Move."

"What? No thanks for yesterday?" His face contained a hint of a smile, but Quinn eyed him pointedly. "And it's not humiliation when I don't give a shit." Kingston pursed his lips at me. "Speaking of which, no room for you, Alice."

Di echoed his claim with a snore.

Quinn shook her head. "No room at all." She spun a clipboard and read the mission statement at the top. "Awww, you want to save a farm." She turned it to face forward again. "I think it's cute that you're trying to be the laughingstock of the school."

What would it take to kill a mockinggirl? "I'm not the one who's sitting at the table wearing a ridiculous crown."

"That's because you have no school spirit." Quinn's tiara glinted in the sunlight. I vaguely remembered something about the week leading up to Homecoming being Spirit Week and each day involving a different task, like wearing school colors.

"Now who looks weird?" Kingston said.

I lifted my chin. "Still you. The answer's always you."

Kingston scrubbed his jaw. "They've bottled the answers in a jar, except I poured it out before I could drink it. It might have been poison."

Quinn burst into a fit of giggles. "He's hilarious, isn't he?"

"Time's the hilarious one." Kingston snickered at some joke only he could hear.

She turned to me, ignoring Kingston. "Hat day was my idea." She beamed. "But Kingston started the trend that inspired me." She tapped him on his nose in a sickeningly cute way. Emphasis on *sickeningly.*

I straightened one of the pens. "Seriously, move."

"Pull up a seat then, if you're so determined." Kingston flourished his hand over the table. "Oh wait, there aren't any."

"How kind of you to offer, Kingston. It's not even your table." I leaned in closer, my torso hovering over a clipboard, and lowered my voice. "Come on, you know why I'm doing this."

"You should say what you mean," he said.

"I do!" I pressed my finger to my lip. "At least, I mean what I say—same thing."

"Hardly." Kingston tapped a pen against the table. "That's like saying 'I see what I eat' is the same thing as 'I eat what I see.' " For extra emphasis, he chomped down on the air.

"Or 'I like what I get,'" Quinn said, stroking Kingston's cheek, "is the same as 'I get what I like.'"

"I breathe when I sleep," Di mumbled, possibly talking in her sleep.

"I sleep when I breathe," Dru finished, joining the group, pink cowboy hat tipped on her head. "Why are we reversing phrases? We better not be studying." I'd forgotten how nice it was without her. Di was endurable. Though that might have been because she was only half-present in this conversation.

"It *is* the same thing, with you." Kingston's eyes slipped downward, aiming at the open space created by the neckline of my dangling shirt. We caught ourselves at the same moment, both of us straightening. I felt like I was on display, the stolen glance just another checkmark on the list of things Kingston had tried to take away from me. The real problem was, his track record boasted a winning streak. "I'm not stopping you by sitting here, am I?" He shook his head, clucking his tongue. A gesture too exaggerated to be anything but a cover-up. "You always misread me."

"So are you going to join then?" I challenged with my eyebrows, pushing a clipboard and pen toward him. Kingston held my stare for several seconds. I couldn't tell if he was really considering my idea or challenging me right back. My brave face wavered. The rhythmic footsteps of the students walking up the steps acted like a stopwatch, marking the seconds in our competition. The silent-treatment Olympics.

"Join with you?" he finally said. "Are you saying you like having me as your partner in crime?" He leaned in to whisper. "Literally."

"*Like* wouldn't have been my choice of words. It's too generous."

"You know you miss me," he said, and I let out a high-pitched laugh. He grinned at me. "I mean, you're the one who keeps calling me. There was that time at three A.M." He ticked off his fingers. "That time with the car. And let's not forget when you crept into my bedroom."

"What?!" Quinn's mouth gaped.

My cheeks blazed like a three-alarm fire. "Kingston, you really are crazy if you think that way."

Quinn lifted herself from her chair and dropped into Kingston's lap. She smiled at me. Not a satisfied smile; the kind of smile that made you think she had something up her sleeve. Or, more to the point, that Kingston did. He secured his arms around her, never taking his eyes off me.

"Our first recruits?" Whitney stepped beside me, setting a giant, yellow jug on the table, spigot facing out.

"Once again, you're too late. If you'd been here on time, you'd know we'd never join your pathetic little club." At Quinn's mention of time, Kingston tugged at his watch.

Whitney shrugged. "Why is a raven like a writing desk?"

I steadied my hand on the table so I didn't tip over. I felt woozy all of a sudden. Kingston's retort had reminded me how much I hated him. Which meant, for one brief moment, I had forgotten.

"Even *I* can't decipher that one," Kingston said. "What the hell is that?" He pointed with his chin to the jug.

"Because I'm in a bighearted mood, I'll give you a freebie. A raven is nothing like a writing desk, just like you're nothing like us." Whitney unpacked a bag of seven-ounce cups and set it on the table.

"Am I supposed to be offended?"

"You're supposed to be a human, but sometimes I'm not too sure you qualify," I said.

Whitney had pulled one cup off the stack and inserted it under the spigot. Steaming, green liquid sloshed into the cup. "Mar-tea-ni?" She held it out to Quinn.

Whitney brought the dizzy-liquid to school? I tilted my head and eyed her. She lifted a finger to her lips.

"What *is* that?" Quinn peered into the cup as if it might contain blood.

"Special recipe." Whitney leaned conspiratorially closer to Quinn. "Let's just say the students will be lining up to drink this, and you won't want to be left out."

Quinn started to laugh, but Dru grabbed the cup out of Whitney's hand.

"Might want to hide it from teachers, though," Whitney told her. "Alcohol's not allowed on school premises and all. That's why we're outside." She winked at me.

Alcohol? I pressed my lips together. The liquid I'd had at Whitney's house before hadn't been spiked. New concoction? Or bluff? I silently prayed for the latter; it was less incriminating.

Kingston narrowed his eyes. "There's no alcohol in there. But what *is* in the tea? Better not be from my closet."

"You wouldn't know. You haven't tasted it," Whitney said.

He tried to reach over and grab a cup, but he didn't have enough mobility with Quinn on his lap. He placed his hands on her hips and pushed to get her off him. She grabbed his hands and placed them back around her waist, holding them there with her own. Holding him prisoner.

For some stupid reason, I was fascinated by their partnership. Obviously, Kingston had to be using her. But what did she see in him? He inspired fierce emotions in me, but they usually resulted in wanting to strangle him.

Watching them, my mind conjured the image of Chess, and my throat got tight. I missed him so much. But thinking of him was like Red Bull, reinforcing my mission and reminding me why I couldn't let Kingston screw it up.

"Is it a Long Island iced tea?" Dru swished the cup. "I heard those are good."

"More like . . . Wonderland green tea." Whitney snatched it out of Dru's fingers. "Oh, but we're only giving it out to people who belong to the Eco Club."

"And sign the petition!" I added, grabbing one of the clipboards off the table and holding it out to her.

Quinn shook her head. "Dru, don't."

"Contrariwise," Di mumbled between snores. "Do."

"Eco Club?" Dru asked. "That sounds lame."

"You think this is lame?" Whitney tipped the contents of the cup into her mouth. "School's going to be really fun today. For me." A slow smile spread across her face.

"When's the first meeting?" Dru eyed the cup.

I glanced up to meet Kingston's eyes. He was watching me with a curious expression, not his usual condescending one.

"Monday," I quickly said.

"Okay, I'll check it out." Dru grabbed the clipboard from my hands while Whitney filled a new cup for her.

"Easy as one, two, tea," Whitney whispered under her breath.

Quinn scoffed. "Dru! We have mock trial on Monday!"

"No how. I thought we canceled it because we'll all be burnt from the prank. I mean, look at this one." Dru waved her hand at Di.

"The prank makes me sleepy," Di said. "Sing me a lullaby."

"Twinkle, twinkle little bat. How I wonder where you're at." Dru rushed through the verse quickly, then turned back to Quinn. "And besides, you're sitting here, so what's so bad?"

"We're here to watch them fail!" Quinn said.

"Twinkle, twinkle, twinkle, twinkle," Di repeated in her sleep.

Dru chugged the contents of the cup, tilting her head back far enough to make her cowboy hat fall on the ground. "Wow, that's good. More?"

"Only if you recruit some people." Whitney grabbed Dru's cup and tossed it into a nearby garbage can.

"What prank?" I asked. I remembered Quinn wanting to retaliate against Neverland after they'd "flooded the school."

"Dru . . . " Quinn said through gritted teeth. "Shut. Up."

"Prank?" Whitney filled a cup. "Ah, *this*," she pointed the cup at Kingston's and Quinn's welded bodies, "makes so much sense now."

Dru waved another girl over, using her cowboy hat as a matador flag, attracting the attention of the bulls.

"There is no prank." Kingston managed to free his arms again and maneuver Quinn onto only one leg. Stretching, he leaned over the table and filled himself a cup while Whitney recruited the girl Dru had brought over. He chugged it, then slammed it down on the table. A green mustache dripped from below his nose. "This is the same stuff you always make, Whit."

She flashed a knowing smile. Then I understood. It was all a trick to get the students' attention. A line formed behind Dru, our new spokesperson. Maybe she was good for something. Besides stealing BFFs, that is.

I headed over to the jug and thrust the petition into someone's hands before he could grab a cup.

Quinn tugged on Kingston's shirt. "Let's go, this is backfiring! People are coming over here because of us!" She hopped out of his lap, hand still connected to his shirt.

"Aww, have you been wasting time by helping us out?" I smirked at them.

Quinn scoffed.

"If you knew Time as well as I do," Kingston said, "you wouldn't talk about wasting *it.* You mean *him.*"

"Right, you already told me that." I pushed a petition into someone else's hand.

Kingston rolled his eyes. "And yet you still haven't bothered to befriend Time. If you did, he would always be six P.M., like he is for me."

I hoped I'd never know what Kingston meant, because if I did? I'd probably be enjoying my newfound knowledge strapped to a bed in the psych ward.

Kingston stood up and leaned in toward Quinn, whispering something in her ear. His hand reached up and squeezed hers. A smile broke on her face at whatever he'd said. The moment was almost sweet, even though I was sure he'd probably said something dirty. She dropped his hand, flashed me a quick glare, and then turned back toward the school.

Dru tapped Di frantically on the shoulder. Di lifted her head and squinted at her personality-doppelganger.

I swept my hair back from my face and stalked toward them. "You can't do the prank, Di. Kingston's up to something, I don't know what, but you could get in trouble."

"Like you did?" Dru raised an eyebrow.

"Alice," Di said, rubbing her eyes, "I can't believe anything you say anymore."

Whoa, pulp friction. "I'm just looking out for you."

Di pushed herself away from the table and followed Dru inside without saying another word.

I spun back around in time for Kingston to corner me by the jug. Whitney was busy giving the pitch to a group of girls.

"Take more tea." Kingston pushed a cup in my direction.

This was why he'd hung back? He wanted to get me dizzy? "I've had nothing yet, so I can't take more." I picked up a clipboard and busied myself with it, with no intention of playing his games.

"You mean you can't take *less*," Kingston said. "It's easy to take *more* than nothing."

"I didn't ask your opinion." I held the clipboard in front of my chest like a shield. Anti-enemy protection.

"But you're listening. This isn't going to work, you know." He ripped the petition from my hands and held it out to me. "You're getting them interested now, but once you try to make them work, they'll bail. I doubt anyone will even show up to the meeting."

"We'd like to have you," I said. "We'll help you."

"Like you helped Chess?" He raised an eyebrow.

My stomach sank like an anchor. "I'm trying to fix it. I think this approach might work, out in the open and legal." I gestured at the table. "I'm hoping if we get a club together, we can raise money for Chess and—"

"He doesn't want to be a charity case. I think the whole sleeping-in-his-car thing proved that."

"Why won't you help him? He's your friend. He needs you, too."

"I *am* helping him. Let's see whose method gets more results."

"The prank? Is that your method?"

He set the clipboard back down. "The prank benefits you, too, you know."

I rolled my eyes. "No, thanks. Leave me out of your schemes."

"It doesn't work that way. If you want to know, you better show up at the Homecoming dance."

My mouth went dry. "Why? What are you planning on doing there?" And more importantly, why was Quinn his weapon of class destruction?

"I'd tell you that, but pigs flying isn't in the weather forecast today." He snapped his fingers. "Probably because you set them all free." He started to lope away, then changed his mind and crept into the space between the table and me. "You know," he said, as if he were sizing me up. "I think you underestimate me."

I took a step backward. "That's not possible. You've met my expectations every time."

"You think I'm the bad guy." He stepped forward again.

This was not a tango I wanted to participate in. I turned my head. "I'm going by fact."

"I'm just saying, the dance will be interesting."

I met his eyes. "Kingston, please don't hurt anyone."

He gave me a sad smile. "No one can be hurt worse than me." With that he tromped away, leaving me with more questions and more confusion.

I pasted on a smile as I handed out the clipboard. The pages filled up fast, but I couldn't enjoy it. Not when my mind spun about what Kingston was planning. And stupidly, every time I thought of the dance, I thought of Chess. He hadn't asked me, and now he never would.

Principal Dodgson came running out of the building, hand raised in the air like she was hailing a taxicab. Her red Wonderland cap looked out of place next to the suit. "I've had reports someone's serving alcohol here!" She stopped short when she saw me. "Oh, Alice. I should have known you might be involved."

Well, on the bright side, I probably wouldn't be branded in the yearbook with "Teacher's Pet" in the Senior Superlative section.

Whispers erupted from the line. Whitney didn't miss a beat, filling a cup and handing it to her. "I'm afraid you've been misinformed. No alcohol here. Try it, it's good for you."

Principal Dodgson brought it to her nose, sniffing. "What's in it? Do I need to get a chem teacher to analyze it?"

"Just a mixture of herbs. There's green tea. Echinacea for health. St. John's wort for happiness. Ginkgo for mind clarity. Stuff like that."

"Oh." Principal Dodgson set the cup down without drinking. "Well, either way, I need to shut this operation down. It's disrupting the school day." She shooed away the line. "Alice, you should have asked my permission."

"I know, but after what happened with the paper, I thought—"

"Let me guess. That I wouldn't say yes?" She studied me. "That's true. Not without a teacher sponsor." Principal Dodgson grabbed the yellow jug and carried it inside for further analysis.

I bit my lip. "Kingston's planning something that will go down at the dance," I told Whitney. It had to be bigger than breaking into Town Hall. Why else would he be so secretive?

Whitney shrugged. "I wouldn't worry. He hasn't exactly been the brains behind our other operations. I doubt he'll come up with anything other than a letdown."

That was the thing, though. Maybe Kingston was right. Maybe we were underestimating him.

CHAPTER 24

Lately, Lorina could barely stand to look at me. The house was carpeted with eggshells, and we went out of our way to avoid crushing them. I kept bracing for a harsher punishment besides virtual handcuffs grounding me. But instead she was giving me something worse: nothing. She'd stopped acting like my replacement mother. She'd even stopped acting like my sister. I couldn't deny how much her absence hurt me, more than extra chores or a phone restriction ever could.

I spent the night worming through my sheets, my mind wide-awake while my blankets twisted into shackles around my ankles. I kept trying to figure out what Kingston might be doing with his plan. What a school prank could possibly have to do with the files he'd stolen. Bags puffed out my eyes the next morning. My heart squeezed when I caught my reflection in the mirror and thought, *at least Chess won't see me like this.*

Chess.

Oh, the agony and the ex-tasy. Well, fake ex, anyway, but plenty of agony. I'd emailed him every day so far to tell him I missed him. And to give him daily progress reports on what Whitney and I were up to. I hated to give Chess false hope about our schemes, but I reasoned that it wouldn't be false if it worked. No, *once* it worked. Whitney and I had filled up several pages with signatures, and lots of people claimed to be coming to the first meeting. A small victory, like the eighth of an inch I'd grown last week. Neither whole nor complete, but progress.

Even though refreshing my inbox was my new favorite pastime, Chess never replied. He was probably cut off from all civilization in extreme grounding, but it still sucked not to hear from him. I needed reassurance that he was okay.

That morning, I banged off another email with a full transcript of Kingston's Homecoming threat, in case Chess might be able to analyze his words better than I could. The sting of so much hope and worry forced me to find a distraction before I crumbled to pieces. I entered the kitchen for breakfast and stopped in my tracks upon finding Lorina, her eyes scanning a newspaper. I considered backing away and grabbing breakfast in the form of a Snickers from the vending machine. Instead, I drew a confident breath and strolled toward the counter.

"Um, I have something for you." I pulled my backpack off the counter and removed the petition sheets, each filled with fifty names. With shaky hands, I set the papers next to her bowl of Cheerios.

She kept her eyes fixed on the newspaper, spoon blindly seeking mouth, as if she couldn't look elsewhere or she'd give too much away. "What's this?"

"A petition . . . from the potential Eco Club. They want a farmers' market in the area, one that will get its produce from a local supplier, which means we also need a farm." I tapped my finger on the headline of the petition. I knew most of the people who signed it hadn't actually read the fine print, but still, it could work, right?

"Alice . . . I don't want to hear about you being involved with the environment again. Am I clear?"

Now she looked at me. It was a look that would scare even hardened criminals. I retreated from her until my back hit the counter.

"This was for school."

Her stare burned into me like sunlight through a magnifying glass. I spun around and popped bread into the toaster.

She didn't say anything for an uncomfortable few seconds. I urged the bread to toast faster and hoped she was reading the petition. That she could see each signature was unique, not forged. Then she said, soft and controlled, "Somehow I don't believe you."

"Call the principal and ask!" My toast popped, adding a *ding* sound effect. "This is important to me, Lorina. The town needs a farmers' market. Mom and Dad were—"

"Enough. I don't want to hear it again. And I definitely don't want you hanging around anyone else involved in this stuff."

I grabbed my toast and my glass of orange juice and carried them to the table. Acting like a coward would keep her thinking I had something to hide. "Lorina, listen to me. I've stopped doing the illegal stuff. And most of the others have stopped, too. But . . . " I swallowed hard. I really didn't want to tip her off, but I didn't see any other way I could get permission to keep going. "I'm trying to convince the last person to stop as well. This is the only way to do it."

"Who's the last person? Your friend Chess?" She swirled her coffee mug on the table. "By the way, I remembered why the name Katz sounded so familiar."

I froze with the toast halfway to my mouth. So much for looking secret-free and halo-worthy.

"Mom and Dad used to have a friend with that last name. Did you ever meet him?" There was something odd about the way she was speaking. All monotone, punching each word at me.

" . . . No." I didn't like the direction of this conversation.

"Too bad," she said. "He. Used. To own. A farm."

I figured out what was so odd about the rest of the conversation. She was enunciating each word. Like a code. Whitney's *I'm late* code, to be specific.

Small earthquakes shuddered through me. She'd made the connection with Chess. "He stopped, too."

"Then tell me who's still doing the terrorism, and *I'll* convince them to stop."

Coming from anyone else, that might have been a threat. It might still be. All the faith I'd had in my sister bled out of my body. I studied the table. Now I was the one who couldn't look at her. "I can't do that. Please, Lorina. I need to be the one to do this. You're choosing your job over your sister."

"You have it backwards." She pushed away from the table and tucked the petition sheets under her arm. "Because of my job, you're not on anyone's radar. So it would be best if you helped me keep it that way."

The implied part of her sentence: *at the expense of your friends.*

"I won't turn my friends in." I stared at the light fixture above my head, afraid to look at her. Afraid she'd see right through me.

"Well, then I have no choice but to go ahead with the investigation. I hear the forensics team we hired is coming close to IDing a break-in the other night."

I swallowed hard. The tone of her voice indicated she didn't really need the forensics team. She'd already IDed the suspect: me.

A few nights later, I lay in bed wide-awake despite the clock ticking away the hours. I heard a car pull up outside, and feet shuffle out of it. I didn't think anything of it, until the hushed whispers grew louder and I could decipher actual words.

"Look out! You're splashing paint all over me," a girl's voice said. It sounded so close, right under my window.

"I can't help it," another one said. This voice I recognized: Di's. Which meant the other voice could only be one person. "Stop bumping into my elbow."

I popped out of bed, ripping the covers off. I parted the curtains and peeked outside to see Di glancing around nervously. She clutched a paintbrush in her hand that dripped red paint on the grass.

Dru bent and dipped her paintbrush into a silver bucket on the ground. "You have to move over then." She pushed Di with her butt, rattling my poor rosebush, the one my mom had helped me plant. The plants Whitney had doctored were all thriving now.

"Shut up. Do you want to get kicked out? Because that's what Quinn's threatening if we don't get this done." Di slathered a glob of red paint over one of the roses.

My mom's roses!

Breathing hard, I backed away from the window and tiptoed out of my room in my bare feet. Once outside, I shivered in the frigid air, regretting that I'd worn one of my dad's oversized T-shirts without pajama bottoms.

"What are you doing?" I whisper-yelled, stepping onto the cold grass. I hopped up and down to keep warm. "You're killing the roses!"

The girls froze, eyes wide. Flowers sagged from the heavy weight of the paint. The floral scent I'd loved was replaced by musty chemical fumes. I bit the inside of my cheek to prevent tears. I couldn't let them see they were getting to me.

Dru dropped her paintbrush into the bucket, and a red splash splattered the side of the house.

Di stepped forward, hiding her paintbrush behind her back. "I'm sorry, Alice. I tried to protest, but—"

"We had no choice. No how. If she didn't . . . off with her head." Dru drew her finger across her neck.

"What does that mean?"

Di and Dru exchanged glances. Red paint dripped from the tip of a rose like a crime scene.

A car pulled up, window rolled down. A face poked out, framed in red hair, eyes aimed at Dru and the rosebush a few feet away from me. “You guys are still only here? You’re never going to finish every—what?” She turned to the person in the passenger seat next to her. One guess who that might be. Quinn’s head slowly swiveled back to us, her face grave. “Alice . . . ?”

I stalked toward the car. “Why are they painting my roses red?”

“They’re trying to break free, but you’re not letting them. You tied them down.” Kingston swiveled in the car to face me. “Kind of naughty of you.”

“Yes, yes, it’s practically bondage. Now why are you doing this?”

“What’s that phrase again? Trick or treat?” Kingston said, laughing. “Seems we’re each getting one tonight. Nice nightie.” He grinned. “You know it’s see-through with the headlights?”

“It’s not a nightie. It’s a T-shirt!” I crossed my arms over my chest even though part of me—a very tiny part, and I didn’t mean my boobs—felt a little sexy. It wasn’t an everyday occurrence that a guy found something worth looking at. Still, I knew my cheeks were as red as my poor, vandalized roses.

“Quick, let me see your camera. This is gold!” Quinn reached over to Kingston’s side, but he must have had a good hold on it, because she gave up a second later and harrumphed back into the driver’s seat.

Curiouser and curiouser. Kingston loved to take incriminating photos, so why didn’t he let her snap this one? Too pornographic and not artsy enough as, say, beautiful sunsets? I was grateful, but only for a brief second until I remembered he was behind the destruction of my roses. Trick or treat, indeed.

Trick or treat. If my see-through PJs were the treat . . . then were the painted roses the trick? As in, the prank?

"Girls, move it!" Quinn yelled. She gunned the gas and peeled away, tires screeching. Di and Dru scrambled to pick up the bucket. They ran across my lawn, paint dripping everywhere.

"Di! What's going on?" I stalked toward her.

"Please don't ask me to explain, Alice," Di said.

"Quinn already stopped talking to Amanda when she refused to participate," Dru added.

Di got into her car, fumbling with her seatbelt. Before Dru could even get her door shut, Di eased the car into drive, following in the direction of Quinn. I stood there, stunned.

I'd thought the prank might be against Neverland High. But maybe it was only supposed to be against me.

CHAPTER 25

I stalked into gym, T-shirt thrown on so haphazardly that half of it was tucked into my pants, earning chuckles from the students crowded in the bleachers. That should have been my first clue that fate was messing with me, but I was too single-minded, my eyes trained on only my targets. Quinn, Di, Dru, and Kingston gabbed away in the middle of the bleachers. A crowd of students blocked them in on every side, a little too strategic to be random. No one looked at me as I stopped three levels below them.

"Hey!" I yelled. "Di! Quinn!" I didn't bother with Dru; she had no loyalty to me.

I would have kept yelling, but the teachers blew the whistle to start class and then started a boring explanation of the process for choosing a new gym activity for the rest of the semester. I plopped into the nearest seat and used the opportunity to alter my appearance from mental patient to fashion victim. The mundane activity of untucking my shirt helped me calm down a little. And by *little* I mean enough to prevent me from turning as vile as Kingston and resorting to the blackmail I'd promised him I wouldn't use to get answers.

The seniors chose first, and the boys practically knocked each other over to get a spot in weight training while the girls scanned all the options and then chose croquet, whatever that was. It had to be something that would result in the least amount of sweat.

Kingston bypassed the rest of the junior boys and beelined for the head coach at the far end of the gym. He produced a piece of paper and the coach nodded, then scribbled something on a yellow hall pass. Kingston waved it in the air and blew a kiss in Quinn's direction before exiting the gym.

Another fake doctor's note? Or something else he'd forged to skip class? How did any teachers ever believe him?

I didn't care what activity we did; I only cared about getting answers. It didn't even matter which girl gave them to me.

The three girls rushed straight for the croquet activity when the juniors were called, so I dragged myself over there and squeezed into the space right next to them. It was only on closer inspection that I realized they were all wearing the same outfit: white shirts with numbers in the center and hearts on the sleeves, resembling cards. Like I needed another reason to think they were indentic-dull.

"What the hell were you doing last night?"

Di and Dru looked to their leader for answers. Quinn turned to me, the corners of her lips struggling to stay flat. "I think it's in your best interest to stop talking right now."

There were people who still intimidated me. Kingston, sometimes. And now my sister. Quinn didn't even make the waiting list. "I've been doing a lot of things that aren't in my best interest lately." Talking to her, for example. "So tell me why you painted my—"

"Shut. Up," Quinn said through gritted teeth. "Because let's just say I was scrolling through Kingston's phone the other day and I found some interesting photos on there." She shot me a triumphant smile.

I clamped my mouth shut.

She could mean that maybe Kingston did take a photo of me in the see-through T-shirt. Or she could mean that she saw other photos Kingston had taken, ones that would get me more than a red face if they got out. Not the printed and mounted ones that might give Kingston the flaming cheeks.

The frazzled gym teacher pointed his finger over our heads, mouth moving as he tried to count all of us, then shook it out and started all over again. After the third attempt, he threw his hands in the air and instructed us to go outside.

We stood on the field, cold wind biting at our arms, but nothing felt as icy as the dread in my stomach. Gray skies weighed down the horizon. A pile of mallets lay on the ground next to a bucket filled with colorful balls. The only two guys who had joined were currently sparring with the mallets, using them like lightsabers. Seriously, courting rituals of male teenagers were sometimes as outlandish as the ones in the animal kingdom.

"Okay, well, this is quite a turnout, huh?" Mr. Card, our gym teacher, raked his hand through what was left of his hair, which wasn't much. "And they told me no one would care about British pastimes." He laughed at his own joke, the sound echoing in the empty air. He cleared his throat. "Anyway, I want everyone to pair up and spread out along the soccer field. Get a feel for the mallets and balls today, and I'll go around and mark down your names." He clapped his hands. No one moved. "Okay, go!"

Everyone charged for the equipment, probably eager to get out of there and grab a spot far away from the teacher. I glanced at Quinn, ready to open my mouth, but she took off for the equipment as well. Di and Dru huffed and followed. I had no choice but to chase them. With so many people trying to get to a tiny bucket, the four of us were separated. I had to follow one of them and I made a split decision.

Di was brainwashed; she'd never talk. If I wanted answers, I had to get to Quinn.

She was attempting to push a girl out of the way, claws out. The girl elbowed her hard, and Quinn got pushed out of the pack. I glanced back at Di. She and Dru had already secured mallets from someone who'd grabbed extras. The two of them were trying to find a spot away from the crowd.

"You have to be my partner," I told Quinn. "Di and Dru abandoned you."

"I don't have to do anything."

I took a deep breath. "Quinn, I need to know what Kingston's planning at Homecoming."

That seemed to get her attention, though I wasn't sure why. She stopped fighting against the crowd and turned to me, brow furrowed. "What are you talking about?"

Curiouser and curiouser. So Kingston hadn't yet informed his "girlfriend" of his plan.

"Homecoming? Kingston said he's planning something and I better show up."

"Wait—so he asked you to Homecoming?" A wrinkle bridged the gap between her eyebrows.

I nearly spat out laughing. I was about to say, *no, are you drunk?* But then I saw opportunity in her question, in her confusion. "Why? Did he not ask you?"

A clapping sound startled me. Our gym teacher was striding purposefully toward us. "Do you girls need partners?"

"No." Quinn grabbed my arm. "We're partners."

"Mr. Card, all the mallets are gone!" someone shouted.

The crowd had dwindled now, only a few stragglers remaining. Mr. Card's eyes widened as he glanced at the empty bucket. "Oh dear. Okay, I need you all to separate and join up with another pair just for today, until we get more equipment."

"No!" both Quinn and I said at the same time. For once, we agreed on something. Weird.

"I'm not playing if I'm not her partner." Quinn batted her eyelashes like a pageant contestant trying to woo a judge.

Mr. Card placed his fingers at his temples, eyes closed. "Um, okay, come here." He led us back toward the gym. "I'll try to find something you two can use for today." He disappeared inside.

"Why did you prank me?" I asked, hoping I could get answers out of her before she tried to get them out of me.

She rolled her eyes. "Oh please, don't be so arrogant. We painted *all* the roses red. Though I can't say I'm upset we did yours."

"What does 'all the roses' mean?"

"Exactly what I said. Every rose in town."

I remembered the ring of white roses guarding Town Hall. Lead weighed down my stomach. So Kingston did get them to do an environmental task. Lorina would certainly be checking on it, and most likely she'd think I did it. She'd probably even reason I'd hit my own house to throw her off the scent. Not good. "Why'd you—"

Just then Mr. Card came out clutching two plastic, pink flamingos and green tennis balls. "Be gentle with them." He held the flamingos out to us. "They're decorations for the Homecoming dance."

On a normal day, using flamingos for mallets would have been the craziest thing to happen.

We searched the lawn for a private section, but most of the students had spread out, standing in gossiping twosomes, spending more time chatting than playing. Now I understood the rush for equipment. It wasn't because they were eager to play; it was because they were eager to slack off.

"The roses were the prank? The one on Neverland High?" I dropped a tennis ball on the grass in front of the gym and tilted my flamingo face down, practicing a golf swing without making contact.

"Obviously." Quinn rolled her eyes, then focused on the flamingo in her hands. "But also personal. So did Kingston ask you or not? Because you two looked a little cozy at the table that morning."

"Why do you even like him?" The question flew from my mouth without consulting my brain first. *Lips, you're on my shit list.* "And I don't get the prank. What does it even mean? *Our* color is red."

"Neverland's color is red, too." She lined up her flamingo with exact precision, like it might win her the PGA Tour. "We did their school first, and then Kingston said it was too obvious, that they'd know it was us, so we did the senior lounge here next, to make it look like they retaliated and—"

"You broke into the school?" I didn't want to resort to blackmail, but if she had really seen those pictures on Kingston's phone, then I needed something on her to keep her mouth shut.

"No, I have a key. All the class presidents do. It's one of the perks of being so awesome." She dropped the flamingo and bent over. "I wear it to keep it safe." She scrunched down both socks, revealing only pasty flesh. "Huh, well, it was here last night. I must have forgotten to wear it today. I do that sometimes."

I stared at her ankle, a dull ache pounding in the back of my head. She had used it last night while Kingston was there. And now the key was missing. It didn't take a forensics report to determine this wasn't a coincidence.

I may have stumbled onto that giant clue, but I patted myself on the back for my sleuthing skills. Maybe Kingston wasn't the only one with the CIA in his future. Or, well, he would probably be working against the government.

"Okay, so you did the school." I tried to keep my voice steady. She was talking, and I wanted to keep her doing that. "But why my house?"

"It was only fair." Quinn practiced a swing with the flamingo, air swooshing. "After all, you destroyed my house. I owed you the same courtesy."

I swallowed. "I didn't. I don't know what Kingston said, but—"

She wheeled, her hair whipping her face. "Really? You're going to deny this? I already told you I've seen the evidence."

Gulp. Guess that explained the photos she'd seen.

She pointed the flamingo at me. "Come to think of it, I let you off easy. You still owe me. So tell me about this Homecoming thing with Kingston. Did he ask you or not?"

"He didn't ask me, no. I just got the feeling he was doing the prank then."

Quinn let out a relieved sigh. "Obviously not, since we already did it."

"Right," I said for her benefit. I didn't believe for a second that Kingston's plan ended at painting flowers.

"Why do you even like him?" I asked again. It was so nonsensical; I couldn't comprehend it.

"Because he's cute. And he's really funny, all those things he says."

We were talking about the same Kingston, right?

"And other reasons." She looked away, a smile tugging at her lips. "I've had a crush on him forever," she admitted. "There's just something about him."

Yeah, his crime streak. Or his insanity. Take your pick. I readied a witty quip but let it fade on my tongue. She was right, I had destroyed her house. I should make it right. "Quinn, you need to know." I tapped the tennis ball with my "mallet." "I think Kingston's using you."

She snorted. "Using me how? Because he told me he loved me."

Right, because Kingston saying something like that wouldn't get him farther with her, in secret plans or otherwise. "He has something planned, and it's not good. I think you should break up with him."

"God, I knew it." Quinn whacked the flamingo so hard, she decapitated it. "I knew there was something going on with you two. Did you dump him or something? Is that why he convinced me to get revenge on you?"

So it wasn't her idea? Now *that* was surprising. But not the part about Kingston being behind it. The side we had briefly coexisted on once again separated into opposite battlefields.

Quinn started to march away.

"Wait!" I rushed after her, heart pounding. "The pictures you saw. Please don't say anything!"

She considered this for several seconds. I thought my lungs might explode from withheld breath. "I should probably press charges. But I know you'd do the same to my friends." She huffed. "Stay away from my boyfriend and I'll forget what I saw."

If only it could be that easy. Because something told me that whatever Kingston was planning for Homecoming wouldn't exactly make her fall more in love with him. And if he turned her off, what loyalty did she have for keeping my secret?

CHAPTER 26

Sneaking out the night of the dance should have been easy. Lorina wasn't home. In fact, the last few nights she'd come home after I'd already gone to bed, tiptoeing through the halls with such care and consideration to avoid waking me, it was like she was stealing something. I deserved a far worse punishment than tacit freedom, which was why my stomach spun with guilt as I slipped out the front door. I almost wished she would come home and catch me, because at least then I wouldn't feel like I was backstabbing her. Like I said, sneaking out should have been easy.

The hardest part of all was going through with it.

I arrived at the school parking lot before Whitney. Shocker. Pinks and oranges streaked the sky, slowly rotting into the black of night. I paced by the back row of cars where we'd said we'd meet.

Fifteen minutes late, she tromped into the parking lot. I brushed down my boring, light-blue, go-to A-line dress as she approached. I'd left the house in such a fit of nerves, I'd completely forgotten to wear a jacket and now my hands were numb. Whitney, on the other hand, rocked a puffy, white ski jacket with a pair of dangerous, thigh-high boots and a frilly, white skirt. Angel and devil rolled into one.

"Talked to your sister today," she said. Her white-blonde hair fell in long crinkles down her back. She looked like a black-and-white pencil drawing, the blues of her eyes the only discernible color.

I froze. "You—you talked to my sister?"

She grinned. "Yep, nice little chat. Nice for me, probably crappy for her."

A scream of frustration built in my chest, but I forced it back down. "What did you talk about? When did you talk to her? Where—"

"At least you have the 'who' question answered." Whitney blew out a breath that curled in the frigid air. "She knocked on my door. Apparently, I was the Grand-Prize Winner, suspect number one. I only obliged because I'm a better chess player than Kingston. I can see all his moves before he makes them."

Her words raised the hair on my arms. "Please. You're killing me. I need a little more info than that!" I spoke my next words very clearly, so there would be no room for misinterpreting. "What exactly did you say to my sister?"

"The truth of my whereabouts. When I watched Kingston disappear into Quinn's car the other night, I figured I better secure myself an alibi. Had a little 2 A.M. hankering for some hot chocolate. Too bad I'm such a bad cook and set off the smoke alarm. Firemen had to come." She flicked a leaf off her jacket. "So clearly there was no way I painted all those roses, since I'm on record speaking to the firemen."

I relaxed my posture, rubbing my arms to keep warm. "That's great! You're off the hook."

"For now, yeah."

Still, I knew the investigation wouldn't stop there. Eventually Lorina would run out of roads. And her main one led right back to me.

"But the bastard used my glue outside Town Hall with his stupid message," Whitney said. "So I'm expecting a criminal callback audition."

The breeze picked up pace and sent a shiver through me. "What did the message say?" *And I can prove it*, perhaps? Completing the message he never got to leave during our heist?

She whipped her head toward me. "You don't know? I figured your sister interrogated you, too."

I shook my head. She couldn't have. It's hard to talk to someone when you're giving her the silent treatment.

"He wrote, '*If you continue to cover up the truth, we'll cover up your beautiful town.*'"

Huh. Different than I'd expected. "What does it mean?" I stretched my dress over my legs. It had felt like it fit perfectly when I left the house, but now it seemed too short, whipping around my thighs whenever the wind howled. Between my soaked shirt clinging to my nonexistent curves after the flood and my peep show in front of Kingston's headlights, I'd had enough public displays of indecency for one school year. I didn't need to add a Perez Hilton–esque underwear shot to my legacy. "You know what he's after, right?"

"The only thing I can think is what he's after isn't what he told me. Because even *I* can't decipher this riddle. Maybe he's been keeping things from me." We all were, weren't we? An aggressive breeze made the trees dance in the distance. Even nature was in Homecoming spirit tonight.

My teeth chattered in the cold air. "We should probably go in."

"Yeah, I hope Kingston's here already. He didn't come home after school." She craned her neck. "But I don't see his truck in the parking lot. Wuss has been avoiding me."

As we approached the school, a silhouetted figure came into view, leaning against the side of the building. The outline of messy hair made me think of Chess, sending a sharp ache through my chest. Whitney was fun, but she wasn't exactly my ideal date for a dance.

"Is that Chess?" Whitney squinted into the distance.

I wondered if she had gained a new talent for mind reading. Or maybe we were both having hallucinations.

The figure stepped into the illumination of a streetlamp and my breath caught. It was him!

My legs challenged my heart to a race, and my long hair blew away from my face, making my smile the first thing he would see. My insides danced, swaying harder than the trees or any of the students enjoying the music.

I crashed into him so hard, I knocked the wind out of him with an "Oof." That wasn't all I knocked. He stumbled and we both fell over, crashing into the soft lawn. Our limbs tangled together, everything blurry and spinning, and I wasn't sure if it was the world righting itself or turning upside down.

"Well, hello to you, too," he said.

I lifted my head, realizing I was on top of him, straddling him. Not the worst position to be in. I pushed my tangled hair out of my face. He wore a smile that was definitely brighter than I remembered.

I bent down and kissed him. It was crazy and passionate and definitely not appropriate for school grounds. We kissed like we were trying to make up for the week without each other, and maybe some extra time for good measure. My hands knotted in his hair and when his arms wrapped around me, I didn't want them to ever let go.

"I guess I'll go in and check out the scene," Whitney said.

"Wait," Chess gasped, cutting a kiss short.

I rolled off him and pushed myself into a standing position.

He joined me a second later and slid his arm around me, a much more G-rated form of PDA. "I've already done some recon. Nothing seems out of the ordinary, which is why it's weird. Are you *sure* Kingston said something was happening tonight?"

"You guys are so fucking impatient," a new voice said from behind.

I craned my neck to see Kingston ascending the steps with Quinn on his arm. Her dress fit her so tightly, her boobs were making a bid for freedom over the top. She always defied the rule that redheads couldn't wear red. Instead, she owned it.

"Alice, guess you were wrong, huh?" Quinn shot me a triumphant smile and pulled Kingston closer to her.

No, I wanted to say, *you were the one who thought Kingston was asking me to the dance.* "I'd say that's yet to be determined. Right, Kingston?" I tilted my head. "When does the fun start?"

"A magician never reveals his methods." Kingston wiggled out of Quinn's clutches and flexed his hands. "But you can kiss my hand if you like." He held it out to us. "Trust me on this."

"Um, I'd rather not," Chess said.

"I'm all for not seeing him kiss again for a while." Whitney jerked her thumb in Chess's direction.

"That could be arranged." Kingston adjusted the crown on his head. He wasn't in the running for Homecoming King but that didn't stop him. "After all, Chess doesn't go to this school anymore."

Quinn raised her arm in solidarity, looking at Kingston as she did. "He should be escorted off the grounds!"

I pressed closer to Chess. I'd just gotten him back; I wasn't going to lose him over something so silly.

"Good try, but if he doesn't go here, you don't have the authority to remove him." Whitney's eyes bore into Kingston's.

Quinn pouted and yanked Kingston away from us. He stumbled for a moment but then blindly followed her into the building.

"I better go play private eye and follow them." Whitney took a step toward the school. "Take a moment of privacy, will you?" She opened the door, music blasting until it careened shut, sealing out most of the sound. Just a few stray chords seeped through.

I really wanted to use the privacy time for kissing, but I also had questions. "God, Chess, I was so worried. Are you okay?"

"I'm okay. And very, very punished." He slid his arm out from around me and tilted my body to force me to face him. "Grounded doesn't even cover it. Think Amish. I had to tell my dad everything." He drew his finger across his throat. "Took a lot of begging and bribery to finally get my cousin to lend me her cell so I could check my email."

"I figured. Either you'd been cut off or you believed me when I fake broke up with you."

He laughed. "No, the only thing I believe in is *us*."

A couple of students dressed in outfits more fit for a nightclub than a school dance giggled all the way up to the door, eyeing us with curiosity. He squeezed my waist. Flutters swept through me.

I fake-pursed my lips. "You're just trying to get me to say the phrase I owe you."

"The phrase was definitely not *I owe you*. You messed up one word."

"I owe glue? Because if so, Whitney has some I can lend you."

He shook his head. "That wasn't the word, but it is an interesting idea. If I glue myself to you, my dad can't take me back."

Music blasted when one student held the door for his date and friends, making the melodic beat linger. It was some kind of slow song I'd never heard of, but that was no surprise. Sometimes it seemed like the only music I listened to was the kind forced upon me in elevators.

"Will you, won't you, will you, won't you, will you join the dance? Will you, won't you, will you, won't you, won't you join the dance?"

"As soon as we go in there, we're not going to be alone." Chess leaned into my ear. "I'm sorry, Alice. For not asking you to the dance earlier."

I wrapped my hands around his neck. He smelled so good, like apple pie, a scent I'd never smelled on him before. I nuzzled closer to him. He was right—as soon as we went inside, this moment would be over.

I had imagined us at the dance together, me in a dress that actually fit and didn't come from Baby Gap. Him looking all dapper and clean in a suit. I pictured myself slaving over my hair, trying to coax a curling iron into altering my image. Because I'd want him to tell me I was beautiful. I'd want him to actually think I was. But that wasn't real.

This was.

Him in jeans and his same old striped shirt. My hair as boring as it always was. The two of us outside, making the most of what we had. I rested my head on his chest, and he pulled me closer to him until our bodies sealed together.

He kissed the top of my head. "I missed you."

"I missed you, too."

He smiled and I wanted to freeze it there on his face forever. "And . . . ?" he prompted.

"And I love . . . teasing you," I said, instead of saying what he wanted to hear. He groaned.

We stayed like that, swaying to a stolen song.

"How'd you get away from your dad?" I asked after a verse went by, when I knew I had to snap out of the moment.

"Claimed I was job hunting. I'm guessing I have another hour or two until they figure out I'm still gone."

"Job hunting? On a school day?"

"Yeah, that . . . I kind of quit for good after I left Wonderland. It was the only bargaining chip I had to try to get back here."

That left a bad taste in my mouth, but I didn't want to argue about it now. Chess wasn't a quitter. "How does quitting get you back here?"

"My dad doesn't *want* me to be a high-school dropout, and I told him the only way I'll continue to go to school is at Wonderland High."

But in order for him to have that chance, and not end up in jail if Kingston was planning something huge that drew Lorina's attention, we had to go face the music.

I tugged him toward the dance.

CHAPTER 27

Inside the school, Whitney perked up when we entered, peeling herself off the white, concrete wall. "I was starting to think you guys ran off to elope."

"That would be one way to get my dad off my back." Chess grinned, but I made a face. I was all for marriage, but not until the very, very distant future, like when I could be legally tried as an adult for my crimes plus a few more years.

"What's going on?" I asked.

"Nothing. Kingston took Quinn onto the dance floor," Whitney said. "Which is why I'm out here trying to figure out what the hell he's up to."

I sucked on my lower lip. "Maybe Kingston was bluffing?"

"I don't know. There has to be a reason he's staying with Quinn beyond the prank," Whitney said.

We headed inside the gym where the tropical theme exploded with paper cutouts of palm trees, clouds lining the walls, and flamingos stationed in front of tables. The DJ was infusing Caribbean backbeats into the pop music that blasted from the speakers. Students congregated in groups around the punch bowl, while a few brave ones danced on the floor. Teachers gossiped on the perimeter, looking out of place and uncomfortable.

"See? Disappointing." Whitney wore a grimace.

"Disconcerting is more like it." Chess swept his eyes over the room. "Kingston wouldn't threaten without reason."

I tugged at the fabric of my dress, nervous.

Chess brought his lips close to my ear, his hot breath embossing goosebumps on my neck. "You look beautiful."

My cheeks could have cooked eggs. I loved how he had the ability to absorb my nerves.

A group of girls migrated from the corner, revealing the scene behind them: Quinn and Kingston in an intense shouting match. The girls glanced back in disgust and burst into giggles as they rushed over to another set of friends whose heads all turned in to watch. Oblivious to anything except Kingston, Quinn flailed her arms, face contorted in an epic battle against tears. He was too busy fiddling with his cell phone to pay attention to her. When she tried to reach for him, he stepped away and raised his arms in the universal symbol for "don't touch me."

"Looks like Quinn got her exit papers handed to her," Whitney said.

I snapped my fingers. "Darn, I really thought they would last."

"Why go through the elaborate gesture of showing up at the dance with her only to break up with her immediately?" Chess asked.

Whitney pursed her lips. "To make sure she shows up as well, and isn't, you know, bawling her eyes out at home."

We all pondered that for a moment as Kingston moved over to the snack table and downed a few handfuls of popcorn while Quinn continued to try and break through his barrier. My skin prickled all over. Now there was nothing stopping Quinn from revealing my involvement in vandalizing her house.

I turned to my friends, speaking in a rush, as if we were running out of time. "We know he most likely stole a key from Quinn. Why would he want that?"

"Maybe it's unrelated," Chess said. "Like he wanted to steal test answers or something."

Whitney was already shaking her head. "No, this is related to everything. He wouldn't make sure we were all here if he didn't want us to witness something."

Her words spun in my head and as they did, my ears started ringing. *He wouldn't make sure we were* all *here* . . . But he hadn't made sure of that. He had only made sure *I* would be here. I was the one who got Whitney and Chess involved.

My body felt hot as an impossible thought occurred to me. Nonsensical, even. Kingston abruptly turned and darted out of the dance. Di and Dru and some other girls swooped in to surround Quinn.

"I'll be right back." I turned on my heels and tried to saunter out the door but found it impossible and broke into a run.

Footsteps chased after me. I paused with my hand on the exit door. "I want to talk to Kingston alone."

"Alice, that might be what he wants. He might be setting you up." Chess pushed open the door and grabbed my hand, willing me to let him tag along.

Chess was right; that was what he wanted.

"Kingston! Wait up!" I called after him before he disappeared down a darkened hallway.

He slowed his steps, then stepped back into the light.

"Don't." Chess pulled me back to him.

"Meltdown, melting, molting, mold." Kingston stared at us. "Can't contain it. It will just spill and drench and soak."

"Are we writing poetry now?" Whitney asked, joining the party.

"No. Instructions."

Sounded like witchcraft to me. "Instructions for what? Your plan?"

"Maybe you're just paranoid," Kingston said, smirking. When you had all the answers, you also had the ability to watch people squirm while they tried to figure them out. "Thinking I've got something planned when clearly there's nothing going on."

"Kingston," I said, my voice a little shaky. I cleared my throat. "I'd like to talk to you for a moment."

His eyes flicked to Chess. I dropped my hand from his, crossing it over my chest.

"So talk. They can't hear you anyway." Kingston gestured at the air in front of him. I didn't want to point out that unless Chess and Whitney had shoved earplugs in their ears when I wasn't looking, they could very well hear me. Though I guessed he wasn't talking about *them*.

A group of students breezed into the hallway at that moment. They took one look at Kingston and their smiles disappeared.

"Not here." I flicked my eyes toward the students.

"Fine, come with me." Kingston paused and studied us. "But just you." He was looking at me, but he pointed toward the wall.

Chess gritted his teeth. "Alice, I don't feel comfortable—"

"What do you think I'm going to do, Chess?" Kingston sounded offended. "Kidnap her? Would have been easier without advance warning."

"I think I might be able to get answers," I whispered, trying to keep my voice low enough to prevent Kingston from hearing.

"Fine," Chess said, squeezing my waist. "But if you're not back in five minutes, I'm sending out a search party."

Kingston and I stood there awkwardly for a moment. I didn't want to lead the way because I wanted to watch where he would take me, in case it gave any clues to what he was trying to hide. If he avoided certain parts of the school, I'd check them later.

He rolled his eyes and stalked off. I hustled to keep up. As soon as we rounded the corner, darkness settled over us. My eyes took a while to adjust, and I didn't realize he had stopped until he caught my arm. "Is this private enough for you?" he said, voice low and cautious. He stood so close to me, I could feel the heat emanating from his skin.

"Let's go somewhere with more light." I wasn't scared of him, not anymore, but that didn't mean I wanted to be in a dark hallway with him. "I have an idea," I said. I turned around and went in the direction of the senior lounge. A sliver of light from the next hallway guided my way.

"Hey, wait, you can't go in there!" He grabbed my arm, stubby nails digging into my flesh.

An image of his violent turn of anger while clutching the pig flashed in my mind. I jiggled my arm, trying to break free.

He dropped my wrist and backed away, hands raised in the air in police-style surrender. "I didn't mean to—" The foot of space separating us felt too claustrophobic.

"Why can't we go in there?" I asked, desperate to break the awkward silence. He stood close enough for me to make out his shadowy features through the darkness. He stuffed his hands into his pockets.

We stared at each other for a moment like two animals about to pounce.

"Because . . . we're not seniors."

Right, because rules had always stopped him before. I pushed open the door, flipped on the light, and immediately understood why he didn't want me in here. Why he had stolen Quinn's key.

Taped to the walls were blown-up pictures of Quinn's minions, painting various roses around town. Evidence on display and laid out like a museum exhibit, each photograph perfectly mounted on black posterboard.

"Ever heard of installation art? My stepmom's a big fan. I'm testing out my new skills."

I stomped across the floor to a photo depicting Quinn in a black hoodie, standing at the entrance to Town Hall, wielding a can of spray paint. I tried to rip it off the wall. Only a sliver of paper came away with my hand. Damn it. Whitney's glue again.

"Not so easy, huh?" He shut the door behind him and switched off the light. What you can't see is what you can't get. Darkness turned everything into the same monochromatic hue, colors muted and subdued.

I pressed my hands to my face, shivering despite the school's heat. "Kingston, I'm tired of trying to decipher everything. Please. Tell me what's going on. I want to help you, I do, but not like this. This illegal stuff? It's only hurting people."

"Hey, I'm just letting Quinn and her friends take credit for their brilliant work. Well, and mine."

"Let me see," I whispered.

He flipped on the light again and pointed to the picture of Quinn in the hoodie. "A pretty good reenactment of our break-in, huh? It sucks, doesn't it, when someone does something and no one ever knows about— Stop it!" He smashed his fists into his temples. "Shut up. Shut up. Shut up."

"I didn't say anything."

He whipped his head up. "You can't hear it?" He pondered this for a moment. "Get your ears checked."

I ignored that little outburst. "You know they don't want credit. Neither do you, for all the stuff you did. That's why you're trying to cover it up." I pointed to the same photo.

"Oh, but you're wrong. Credit is exactly what I want. But not for myself."

"What the hell does that mean?" I dragged my fingernail over the paper, attempting to slice it. My Jersey shore–deprived stubs of nails wouldn't get the job done.

"You might as well stop that. It's useless." Kingston walked over and tugged on my elbow—this time gently—trying to pull me away from the window. "I already emailed copies of these to your sister."

The walls inside the room started to close in, spinning until all the photographs—the doctored evidence—blurred in my vision.

"They're going to take the fall for everything, Alice. We'll all get off scot-free." He smiled. An actual proud-and-arrogant smile. Sincere, even. He was a gesture away from patting himself on the back.

I took a step away from him, freeing my elbow, and pressed my palm to the wall to steady myself. "*That's* why you started dating Quinn? To set her and her friends up?" I wanted to throw up. It seemed my insides might actually oblige any second.

"Your sister was onto us. If she pressed charges, we'd all end up in jail or juvie or whatever and none of us would get what we wanted. I did this for *you,* Alice. I saved you. I saved all of us. That counts for something, right?"

He really was crazy. "It's not even going to work!"

The smile disappeared from his face. His eyes went big and puppy-dog, and he watched me from beneath his long eyelashes. Like he truly wanted to be redeemed. Like he really believed he'd done me a big favor and I should run into his arms and hug him. And for a split second, I almost caved. He *had* done me a few favors lately. Picking up the pig to keep our crime a secret. Giving me that paper from the file. But of course, he wouldn't have had to give it to me if he hadn't taken it from me. Everything else fucked-up he did flooded back into me, and here I was, focusing on his warped sense of redemption.

"Alice, your old friends never understood you. Trust me, you should hear some of the things they say about you." He raised his eyebrows, as if that bit of info would make me feel better about this and not, you know, like discarded gym clothes left rotting in a locker. "It was the perfect opportunity to school them. You'd rather take the blame yourself?"

"Someone innocent shouldn't have to take it!" I dropped onto the nearest bench, my legs too shaky to stand up any longer.

"Don't be mad at me. I've made you a present out of everything I said tonight."

"Why did you target my house then? To get back at me? Or . . . something else?" I held my breath, hoping the answer would be the former, even though I already knew it would be the latter. I could see it in his eyes. What Quinn had seemed worried about on the croquet field—she was right. Kingston, for some nonsensical reason . . . *liked* me.

"Two birds. Quinn figured out you were involved with reforesting her house. I overheard her talking about pressing charges, which is when I realized how to fix both things. Convince Quinn to get revenge on you instead of involving the police, and then use that revenge to cover our tracks." He smiled, proud of his genius. "I knew she liked me. Everyone does. Well, almost. So it wasn't that hard to pretend to date her. It was make-believe, like the rest of my life."

"Why did you want me to come to the dance?" I couldn't look at him. "To witness this?"

"That was part of it." He came over to where I was sitting and stood there for an awkward moment before lowering himself onto the seat next to me, head tilted in my direction. I stared straight ahead, at the gallery on the wall. "I thought you'd be impressed by the trouble I went through to clear your name."

I swallowed hard. I knew I should get up and try to stop Lorina, but Kingston was sitting here, talking openly, and I wanted answers. Plus, without the answers, I didn't know how to undo what he'd done without getting Whitney and Chess in trouble. "And the other part?"

Kingston sighed, leaning back. "There is no other part."

"But you just said there was."

"*Was* was the keyword. *Was* means it isn't, and in this case, it ain't. Never was, never will be. If a part is a whole, I only have half."

"You sound like Whitney. Can you repeat that, but in a more straightforward way?"

"You're going to make me say it?"

Clearly, no. He was going to make *me* say it. "I don't understand," I said. "I thought you hated me. But now . . . ?"

"The opposite," he finished. *Wow, Kingston, might want to write down that romantic declaration of feelings and send it into Hallmark.*

My heart beat fast. This was nonsense!

But it also made a lot of sense. It explained why he'd never turned me in when he could have. Why he'd gone to such elaborate lengths to make sure I was never on the security cameras. He kept finding excuses to touch me that night. And that's why he was such a fussy baby whenever I flirted with Chess—he was jealous! He wasn't collecting evidence about me. He was keeping photos of me! Because he wanted to look at them!

"You feel the same way." He placed his hand over mine.

I snapped my hand away. "That's absurd. No, I don't!"

"Then why are you getting all defensive?" He cocked his head toward me.

"God! I'm not!" Okay, that did sound pretty defensive. But I was pretty freaked out right now. It was hard to reason with someone who's delusional. "Let's back up for a sec. Can you please explain?"

"Birds of a feather flock together."

My eyes were filled with questions. "Okay. And . . . ?"

"Must I?" He mumbled something to himself. I asked him to repeat. "Mustard," he said. "Only, wait. Mustard isn't a bird. Don't let anyone tell you otherwise."

"Good point." And the point was: ask him direct questions to get direct answers. "Don't you hate me?"

He sighed. "I really did hate you at first. You had no obligation to keep my secret, whereas the others did. They don't have lips, and that made it easy to trust them."

I assumed the *others* in that sentence were inanimate objects and not his stepsister and best friend.

"I was obsessed with proving you wrong. It was all I could think about. *You* were all I could think about. And then . . . you proved *me* wrong." He gave me a lopsided grin. "You never turned me in. You never breathed a word to anyone, not even your best friend. You always had my back even when I was a jerk to you. And somehow, during all that, my feelings shifted. Man, I was pissed off when I realized." He laughed. "I'm not sure they're real, though. I'm not sure anything is."

"Did you date Quinn to make me jealous?

"Did it work?" His brow lifted.

"You've been spying on me long enough to know the answer to that question."

"Yeah." I could feel his sigh before I saw the heavy dance of his shoulders. "But no. You were with Chess. I was trying to get over you. That didn't work, so I set her up." He squeezed my hand. "I hoped it might impress you?"

Chess. His name sent flutters through my body.

It seemed I'd led Kingston on enough already. I leapt off the bench. "That's crazy. You know that, right? I can't condone that. You can't manipulate people for selfish reasons." I threw my hands up, and he winced at my words. Once, *selfish* had been a compliment to him, for entirely different reasons. "God! You even tried to trick me into coming to the dance with you!"

He stared at his hands in his lap. I'd never seen him like this, so helpless. Like a turtle without his shell. "I screwed up. And I don't have a lot of time left, so I thought this would be faster." He started fiddling with his broken watch.

"What's that supposed to mean? Because Lorina's coming?"

"No, Alice. Because I'm dying."

CHAPTER 28

Well, I didn't see that one coming. "You're dying?" His words echoed and clanged in my brain, blotting out all thought.

He wrung his hands. "I'll tell you but—don't tell anyone, okay? And don't interrupt or anything."

"I won't." I dropped my hands to my sides and waited. When you had that many things thrown at you in the span of five minutes, it tended to overload your system. The decision-making part of my brain needed to reboot. The rest of me could use some defragging. Sadly, IT technicians didn't yet have the technology to repair humans.

Remind me not to let boys who aren't my boyfriend fall for me again until computers became self-aware.

Kingston wouldn't meet my eye. "I used to live with my mom over by Chess's farm, near the nuclear-power plant. Long story short, Mom died of cancer three years ago and I had to go live with my dad, who I barely knew, which was stupid since I'd lived across town my entire life."

"What about Whit—" I clamped my mouth shut, remembering his one request. My brain supplied a replacement word: *last request*. Oh brain, I see you've relinquished your duties for the evening.

He shrugged, as if this was an inconsequential detail. "I'd met her at our parents' wedding a few years ago, but since we went to different elementary schools, I never really knew her until I moved in."

I wanted to sit next to him, but I was afraid to move, afraid even the smallest sound might make his confession snap like a catapult pulled taut.

"Turns out, the cancer was caused by high levels of lead, mercury, and other toxic chemicals that had leaked into our garden, our pipes, stuff like that. My mom and I both ingested tons. I'm sick, too, but I wasn't out there gardening as much as she was."

I gasped as I remembered Chess telling me his mom had also died of cancer. Kingston lived near them.

"But—you don't look sick." *Oops.* I stuffed my knuckles between my teeth to prevent further stupidity. With Kingston vacating his role as my archnemesis, I guessed my mouth was vying for the position.

System failure of the body parts.

"That's because I'm not getting treatment. No chemo, no side effects." He pulled the bag of shiitake mushrooms from his pocket and dangled it in front of me. "Gotta do it the holistic way." I must have had a question in my eyes because he clarified. "Shiitakes have healing benefits."

Oh screw it, he seemed to be answering despite my outbursts. "So what are your symptoms then?" Besides the obvious: insanity.

"My emotions are all out of whack because of the lead poisoning—it affects my nervous system. I can't control my anger. I have learning disabilities. That's why I suck at school. Because of the mercury, I have moments where I'm fine and lucid and then . . . moments where I'm not. I can't control it. It controls me. I hear and see things that aren't there. Sometimes I can't tell what's real or not." His hand flew to his wrist, clasping and unclasping his watch.

We must have been in one of those lucid moments, thankfully. I also understood his preoccupation with time running out and why he wore the broken watch. If he could convince himself that time had stopped, maybe he wouldn't get closer to dying. "Then why aren't you getting treatment?" I resisted the urge to slap some sense into him.

"I'm trying to! That's what these environmental missions are for me." Kingston bolted to his feet and frantically scrubbed his shirt. "Get it off me. Get this damn curse off me!"

And just like that, the lucid moment was gone. Too bad they didn't make Febreze for nonexistent curses.

When he calmed down, I took a tentative step forward, gauging his reaction. "Wait, Whitney and Chess both said Chess's problem was more time-sensitive than yours." I took another step forward, hovering right over him and forcing him to look up at me. "He needs a house, sure, but if you're dying, that seems just a bit more drastic."

"I've been lying to everyone. You know what I miss?" He waited for my answer, but I stayed silent. "Muzzles. I'd like to bring them back. It would solve a lot of things."

"That doesn't really answer my question. And I doubt a muzzle would solve anything."

"Yeah, you're probably right." He swatted at the air. I repeated my question, hoping this time for better results. "I was diagnosed at the same time as my mom," he said, sounding normal. "I'm pretty sure the leak came from the nuclear-power plant, but I can't prove it. Whitney thinks I want revenge on the township only because of my mom, because they covered up the leak and tried to pretend it never happened. She doesn't know I'm sick. I didn't want to worry her. And also, I felt awkward telling my dad. I mean, he never cared for me my whole life and now I have to spring this on him? I know he can't afford the medical bills, so I was trying to take care of it myself."

"The pot." I sat back down on the bench, less than an inch away from him. "That's why you were selling it. To make money." I felt awful that

Whitney had thrown it out, but I also hoped it would force him to get a real, government-approved job.

"Well, that, and it's medicinal. But yeah, I need the township to pay for my medical bills. They did this to me. They owe me."

I placed a comforting hand on his shoulder. "You should have told us. We would have done more to help you."

His arms responded as if I were suggesting something else, twisting around and caging me into a hug. His fingers dug into my back like he couldn't hold on tightly enough. I felt claustrophobic in his prison-bar arms. But I knew he needed comfort.

"I don't want people to know I'm weak." He leaned into my shoulder, breathing hard. He smelled like smoke and peach shampoo. Bitter and sweet at the same time, like the photographs I'd seen him with. A beautiful sunset filtered through a streaky window. A rose squashed of its beauty.

"The photographs in your room . . . "

Suddenly all of his behavior made sense, the way he acted so tough and mean. It was all a cover, a ruse to distract people from what was really going on with him. He'd created an outer shell to disguise his inner weakness, like a mock turtle.

He sighed. "That's a hobby I don't exactly advertise. The photography helps me figure out the difference between what's real and what's not. It's for a contest, cash prize. Probably won't win." He squeezed me tightly, which was my cue to break free. "But I want to win."

"Fingers crossed," I said. I tried to wriggle out of Kingston's grasp, but he held on tightly. My breathing shortened, the panic of being trapped rising up in me. "Get off me!"

He let go, staring at his hands in a startled way, like he hadn't realized they were capable of their actions.

I hopped off the bench and smoothed my skirt down. I needed to sound clinical. Businesslike. I cleared my throat and conjured up the least sexy question I could think of. "Why didn't you get a lawyer—"

"Too expensive. And I don't have enough evidence yet. They destroyed the power plant. They covered their tracks. There's a highway where my house used to be."

"The files from the township. They didn't have evidence?" Well, that certainly backfired. In my attempt to detach from the conversation by way of snore, I became only more intrigued.

"I found something that helps, but it's not enough. It doesn't prove there was a leak at the plant that made me sick."

The door burst open. "Your sister's here," Chess said to me.

"We're. Late," Whitney sang, code punched into the air. She slipped out of the doorway.

CHAPTER 29

We found Lorina standing in the hallway by the admission table, talking to Di and Dru. Tears streamed down Di's face. Dru donned a scowl. They wore dresses that clearly came from Quinn's instructions. Di usually preferred A-line dresses with poofy skirts that hid her curvy hips. Now she'd squeezed herself into a formfitting mini in champagne, a color that washed out her features. Dru wore an equally tragic, lemon-yellow dress in the same style. When Di saw me, she ran forward. "Alice! You have to tell her it was just the prank on Neverland. We didn't do any of that other stuff."

"They didn't." My eyes locked with Lorina's in a staring contest.

"Alice," Kingston warned with gritted teeth.

"I'm really sorry. We should have listened to you!"

"You were right." Dru clenched her fists, gold nails shimmering. "We never should have done the prank."

Di gave me the saddest puppy-dog stare. But apologies weren't exactly sincere when the motivation was to save your butt.

Lorina's eyes darted to my friends before settling on the girls. She forced a smile. "Di and . . . Dru, is it? Would you do me a favor and round up your friends? I'd like to talk to them."

Di paused, eyes wide. But she was always one to follow the rules, any rules, and she obeyed Lorina's as if it were a commandment, taking Dru with her.

As soon as the door swung behind them, Kingston slammed his fist into the wall. "She's lying. I saw them do the prank. I have more proof."

"Alice." Lorina crossed her arms, looking only at me. "I'd like you to explain."

"The world would go around faster if everyone minded their own business," Whitney mumbled under her breath.

"I—" . . . didn't know what to say. My heart beat so loudly it made it difficult to think. The peppy pop music blasting from the gym sounded upbeat and out of place, like wearing pink to a funeral.

"How about I explain for you then? Because I know those girls didn't do it. The roses, yeah, but not everything else. They certainly didn't break into Town Hall, even though someone tried to make it seem like they did. I know about Chess's farm. Whitney's arrest. And I know that Kingston—" She tilted her head to him. "That's your name right?" She paused, waiting for confirmation he wouldn't give. "He was once apprehended near the scene of an environmental crime but then released because of lack of evidence. This is obviously all some big revenge scheme."

"That's what you think?" Chess scrubbed the back of his neck. "I don't want revenge. I want my farmland back."

"And the moral of that is," Whitney said, "the more there is of mine, the less there is of yours."

Lorina opened and closed her mouth like a fish. Then her voice got soft. "That's why you were living out of your car." She paused for a second, contemplating, then came back strong. "And you three?"

"Our parents were murdered," I blurted, to avoid making Kingston reveal his secret. He might have been crazy and had warped ideas about how to save us, but I felt bad for him. His secret weighed on my shoulders because now I felt it was my responsibility to help him somehow, even if it seemed impossible.

How do you stop someone from dying?

Lorina's arms slipped from their tight coil. "What?"

I told her about Chess's theory and the newspaper articles I'd found, rushing the words out so fast, she probably couldn't even make sense of half of them.

"But we don't know if that's true, Alice. It's all speculation." Chess stepped away from me, shaking his head, his face serious.

Whitney pursed her lips. "I can't tell you right now what the moral of that is, but I'll remember in a bit."

"It scared your dad enough to stay away from here." I reached for Chess.

That shut him up.

"And I found some evidence. A phone transcript where two people are talking about stopping Mom and Dad and Chess's dad through whatever means necessary. It seems too coincidental if they died the same day as the phone conversation."

"Where'd you get the transcript?" Lorina placed one hand on her hip.

I probably should have seen that question coming. Way to basically confess, self. Heat prickled at the back of my neck, but I plowed on. The prospect of spending the rest of your senior year in jail made you pretty fearless, or at least pretty desperate. "Also, I found a forensics report that claims only one set of tires was on the road, but there's no seal or watermark and it's supposed to be an official document. I think it was doctored." Not very well, but still.

Next to me, Kingston shifted his weight from one foot to the other. If Lorina could make even him uncomfortable, that didn't bode very well for our chance of success. Mountain climbers buried under an avalanche of snow probably had better survival odds.

"That's all still spec." Lorina dropped into the empty chair. "You're looking for a way to blame the township."

"I know," I said. "But it makes sense with all the evidence. After Mom and Dad died, the township targeted Chess's dad's farm, drove him out of town. They wanted to get rid of them through any means possible, like they said in the transcript."

She shook her head, hands gripping her knees. "Alice." Her eyes glistened with moisture. "I've already buried them. I don't want to unearth this."

I opened my mouth to protest again but then snapped it shut. Now wasn't the time. We had more important things to discuss; for example: where was I sleeping tonight? In a bed or on a wooden bench with a porcelain toilet as my roommate?

Kingston cleared his throat. "Um, you guys?" He pushed himself off the wall. "I think I may have the evidence you need to solve this." He reached into his pants pocket and pulled out a folder full of paper.

Please let this be real evidence and not one of Kingston's conspiracy theories.

"The document you think was doctored?" He lifted a sheet from the folder and dangled it in front of me. Of course, I should have known the best place for Kingston to hide the original file was on himself. I bet he'd been carrying it around this entire time. Even if I had found a way to sneak back into his empty room, I wouldn't have found it. "It was, but only because I gave you a pretty crappy photocopy and kept the real one for myself in case I needed it." He took a few hesitant steps toward Lorina and laid the file on the table in front of her.

A relieved breath escaped my throat, but I sucked it back in because what the hell was Kingston doing? If he debunked my motivation as the reason for the ecotage, she'd have to find something else to go on, something that would implicate the other three people in the hallway.

Kingston removed a second sheet of paper from the folder and held it up for all to see. Criminal show and tell. "I couldn't figure out why a forensics report was in the same folder as a soil-sample evaluation." He smoothed it out and handed it to Lorina. "I thought this was the soil sample I needed but . . . it ended up not being exactly right."

Soil samples? Why did that sound so familiar?

Lorina perused it, mouth open. "All this says is that some land tested positive for radiation and lead. How does that solve anything?"

"Look at the land's coordinates." He turned to us. "It lists it in technical terms. I had to ask the moon for help in figuring it out. Now I'm her slave. Like the tide and PMS." He shrugged. "Small sacrifice."

Lorina gasped. "Katz Farms."

Chess perked up. "Wait, what?"

"Chess," Kingston said. "The township didn't rezone the land and raise your taxes to drive your dad out of town. They did it to cover their own ass. It had nothing to do with your dad at all. They were just trying to keep the citizens safe because the land was contaminated from the nuclear power–plant leak."

I gasped. Chess's mom's cancer. It was all related.

"My dad never mentioned the leak."

"I doubt he knew about it. The township covered it well," Kingston said. "If it was the township's fault, that is. I'm starting to suspect it might have been the plants. A suicide mission."

Chess's hand flew to his chest. "He never had to flee. It's still safe here."

"Though I haven't ruled out aliens from the list," Kingston kept going as if no one else was speaking. "I haven't had a chance to interrogate them because I keep my window shut at night."

Blood pounded in my ears, and the entire world slid beneath me. The forensics report had been accurate. The threatening talk in the phone transcript was only about about getting them to stop protesting the farm shutdown, to prevent anyone from finding out about the leak.

I clutched Chess's arm to steady myself. "Then . . . my parents weren't murdered?"

I closed my eyes and exhaled. It was a relief, but even having a concrete answer wouldn't bring them back. Either way, they were still gone. My chest ached.

Lorina dragged her hands over her face. "I don't know what to do. My boss is going to fire me. He thinks I'm keeping info from him, which I am. If they fire me, someone else will take over, someone who won't be so caring. I will not turn those innocent student-council kids in."

They weren't innocent, but I knew what she meant. They'd only painted roses, a minor infraction compared to, you know, burglarizing a government building.

I tried not to dwell on the fact that it seemed she planned to turn us in to keep her job. And I guessed that meant I'd always hoped she wouldn't. Either that or I never thought she'd figure it all out, which meant I had no faith in her. I was a horrible sister.

I left her side and slumped back against the wall. Chess brushed my cheek with his fingers.

"So tell me." Lorina stood up from the chair. "What should I do instead?"

She wanted permission to take her own sister into custody. I hated that I had put her in such an awful situation. "I'll confess, then," I said at the same time Chess said, "Let me take the fall."

"No." I shook my head. "Absolutely not."

"Chess," Whitney said. "We should do this together."

"I got you all into this mess," he said. "My life's already screwed up. I'm the one who has the least to lose."

I pushed my frazzled hair out of my face. "You're the one with the most to gain if we correct this." I briefly made eye contact with Kingston so he would know I intended to include him in my statement as well.

The door swung open and Quinn stormed out, face as red as her hair and her dress. "Di and Dru told me." She stopped in front of Kingston. "You sent in pictures of me?" She scrunched up her face as if she might be able to fold her tears back inside.

"I also plastered them on the wall of the senior lounge." He grinned at her. "*Now* are you going to accept that I broke up with you?"

Quinn slapped him in the face. The sound echoed in the reverberant hallway, and my teeth clamped down. She kicked off her heels and ran in the direction of the dark hallway.

Kingston rubbed his cheek as he stepped forward and approached Lorina. "I set them up. Tricked them into doing the prank to try to make it seem like they did everything else, too."

Lorina searched me to see if this was the truth or another lie altogether. I wouldn't corroborate. I'd made a promise to protect him and everyone else, and I wouldn't betray them. I'd be no better than a tattletale if I did that.

"I'll take the blame." Kingston lifted his chin. "Alone."

"No!" Whitney and I both yelled at the same time.

"It was always my job to take one for the team and get arrested." Kingston spun around to plead with his eyes. Then it almost seemed like he . . . winked. Or it could have been a trick of the light glinting off his eyes. Whitney straightened up and nodded. So she'd seen it, too.

Did Kingston have a plan? And if so, what could it possibly be?

I prayed silently that his plan didn't involve tricking someone else into the blame. Or getting plants to aid in his escape.

Sharp lines indented Lorina's forehead. I knew she wanted to protect me, but I also knew she wasn't president of Chess's fan club.

"You don't have to do this, King," Chess said.

"Yeah. I do."

"But what about . . . " I didn't know how to phrase it without revealing his secret.

"That's exactly why I should," Kingston said, clearly understanding me. "You guys have your whole lives ahead of you." He removed the watch from his wrist and threw it on the floor. He stomped on it, shattering the glass.

Whitney sucked in a gasp. I wondered if she got his meaning like I did.

Lorina sighed. "The three of you, leave right now and go straight home. Alone." The fact that Chess didn't have a home must have slipped her mind. "Kingston, come with me." Lorina had made the decision for us. Kingston would take the blame, and we'd get off without a scratch. Every muscle in my body tightened.

I stepped forward to go with him, but Chess held me back.

"He'll be okay." Whitney hopped in place. "I think he has a plan."

But all our other plans had backfired. It didn't take a probability mathematician to determine that our odds of succeeding would deter anyone from betting on us. "Can we trust that, though? That his plan will be . . . "

"Crazy? Undoubtedly. But maybe that's what we need to get this to work."

Kingston and Lorina walked out of the school side by side. He didn't have handcuffs on yet, but the way he held his palms out in front of him, it was almost like he was preparing for them.

CHAPTER 30

"Kingston's sick," Whitney said. We stood in the empty hallway, watching the door swing shut as Lorina and Kingston disappeared on the other side of it. "Isn't he?"

"Um." I twisted my hands into knots, sliding my fingers through each other and back again.

"That jerk. If he doesn't die on his own first, I'll kill him for keeping this from me." Whitney grinned, clearly not serious.

"Chess." I swallowed past the lump in my throat. "Your mom's cancer." My eyelids fluttered closed. The next words scraped against my tongue, heavy and painful. "I think it was caused by chemicals leaking into the soil from the power plant. The same thing that happened to Kingston."

The color drained from Chess's face. The truth hung heavy in the air between us. The township might not have killed my parents, but they'd been responsible for his mom's death.

I reached for his hand. "Are you okay?"

"I need a little time to process that info, but I'm glad to know. Thanks." He interlocked his fingers with mine, then squinted at me. "Are *you* okay? You look kind of . . . frazzled."

"I liked it better when you said I looked beautiful," I said.

He stroked the back of my wrist with his thumb. "Always."

He pressed his lips down onto mine, gentle. I sank into his kiss, aggressively, taking it from grandmother-level to not-safe-for-TV.

Whitney groaned. "I'm not usually a rule-follower. But something tells me we shouldn't blatantly ignore Lorina's demand. I'm not really in the mood to deal with a bounty hunter."

I broke away from Chess, and the three of us trudged for the door.

"I can't believe this whole time Kingston has been trying to save us," Whitney said.

"I feel bad for Quinn," Chess added. "Though I think she was pretty naïve not to see he was using her."

Quinn. Kingston may have confessed, but Quinn was the one person outside our circle who knew about my involvement. Who possibly had evidence. She'd promised to keep it a secret if I stayed away from her boyfriend. Now that he'd dumped her . . . would she stay tight-lipped?

A quarry of lead settled into my stomach.

"Quinn knows," I said. "She saw some of Kingston's pictures of us."

We all exchanged glances, then burst into a run that would have made the gym teachers proud.

By the time we got to the lounge, she'd left her mark and disappeared. The walls dripped with red paint blotches, as if she'd taken a bucket and splashed it at the concrete. Still, it had hid the evidence—and vandalized the school even more.

"It's kind of beautiful, in a strange way." Whitney dipped her finger into a glob of paint. "My mom would love it."

"It looks like someone spilled tomato soup." Chess rubbed his stomach. "Now I'm hungry."

"Beau-ootiful Soo-oop!" Whitney sang as she exited. "Soo—oop of the e—e—evening."

In the gym, the music sounded upbeat, while a singer crooned languidly. Some of the couples tried to grind while others pressed together in a romantic waltz.

Quinn stood with her back to us by the refreshment table, red hair flying about and tangling with her waving arms. Principal Dodgson leaned on one hip in front of her, wearing an expression that could kill on contact. A crowd started to gather around them. A knot unwound in my stomach. I rushed toward them, and my friends followed.

"I'm not an environmental freak like Alice," Quinn shouted. "I was framed, I swear. Alice set me up! I have proof she's been out to get me. You have to believe me."

My stomach settled into the floor. Lorina might go out of her way to protect me, but I doubted Principal Dodgson had allegiance to anything besides the flag.

Principal Dodgson glanced up and saw me. "Alice." Her lips stretched into a thin line. "It can't be a coincidence that you're always involved in school vandalism. What is this, strike number three?"

Quinn spun around and glared at me. "Not just school vandalism! She destroyed my house, too."

"I didn't frame Quinn." It wasn't a lie, but it felt false on my lips. I blinked rapidly to keep from giving myself away with a nervous impression. It took me a moment to realize that didn't exactly send the message of nonchalance. *Please let them think I have a bug in my eye.*

"She's the one who flooded the school." Quinn emphasized her words with a finger jabbed at my sternum. "And decoupaged the desks. Dru and Di witnessed the latter."

Oh crap. If there was a time for an Oscar-worthy performance, this was it. "I didn't!" It came out all strangled, at a higher pitch than even Mariah Carey could hit.

Principal Dodgson studied my face, and whatever she saw must have betrayed me because she said, "Alice, I'm afraid I have no choice but to . . . " Her eyes circled to the ceiling as she considered a punishment. "Expel you."

"You can't expel her." Whitney's knees parted in a fighting stance but the delivery of her words was calm and collected, like it was just another sentence and not a life sentence.

Principal Dodgson tapped her fingers to her coral lips. "Actually, you're right. The school board thinks this is a democracy and I'm not sole leader."

My dress clung to me, fabric sticking to my sweaty skin. My armpits chose that moment to broadcast their scent.

"You know, Principal Dodgson," Whitney directed her words at our fearless leader but pointed her face at Quinn "be what you seem to be."

Quinn stomped her foot. "What the hell does that mean?"

Principal Dodgson's head volleyed back and forth between the two girls.

"If you'd like it more simply." Whitney smirked. "Never imagine yourself not to be otherwise than what it might appear to others that what you were or might have been was not otherwise than what you had been would have appeared to them to be otherwise."

Several weeks of being Whitney's friend and I still couldn't speak her language fluently.

"Translation." Chess stepped between Whitney and Quinn. "You don't have proof that Alice did anything, whereas the pictures of you and the roses have already gone viral."

Quinn looked like she wanted to murder Whitney and Chess. "That's where you're wrong." She turned to Principal Dodgson, skirt swishing as she rotated. "I can get proof."

"Fine." Principal Dodgson swiped her hands in the air in a *cease* gesture. "We have a mock-trial program at this school for a reason. We'll let them handle the he said/she said."

I swallowed hard. My peers would be the jury. There were only three people in the whole school who would have my back, and one of them was in jail while another didn't even go here anymore.

Expulsion wouldn't exactly patch things up with Lorina.

I sat downstairs in the dark, curled up in a chair, eyelids drifting downward and threatening to connect. My hand caught stray yawns. The TV turned my face an eerie blue, blasting but still failing to keep me awake.

The sound of keys jingling startled me. Glowing green numbers showed 3:13 A.M., a time I was not normally acquainted with. I hopped off the couch and cut Lorina off by the door. Her hand flew to her chest.

"You scared me." She set her keys down on the table in the foyer. Her hand stayed pressed on top of them for a few seconds. She kept her back to me.

Fear bottled up the words I wanted to ask in my throat, but I dislodged them anyway. "What happened?"

Her breathing grew rapid and more pronounced. I must have fallen asleep at some point because I felt disoriented and it sounded like she was . . . crying.

She turned to me, knocking her keys to the ground with a harsh sound. Tears dripped from her eyes and she struggled to suck in a gasping breath. I wrapped my arms around her. She had to bend at the knees to rest her head on my shoulder. I tried to meet her halfway, balancing unwieldily on tiptoes like an ungraceful ballerina.

"Your friend . . . he's . . . " A sniffle separated each word.

"Is he okay?"

"Dying," she finished. "And . . . Chess. Homeless."

I squeezed her tight, if only to comfort myself. She was crying for my friends? Or because she felt guilty for turning them in?

"You . . . should have . . . told me."

She pulled away from me, shielding her face with her tilted body.

"Um, I have something you should see. I was hoping you could maybe give it to Kingston?" I bit my lip at my absurd request. Asking her to give stolen files back to the same fugitive who'd turned himself in for stealing them. She followed me into the living room where I peeled the folder off the couch. "In the hallway at school, he mentioned he was looking for a file with soil samples and had picked up the wrong one?" I held the folder out to her. "I think this is the one he was looking for."

Her gaze was so intense, I had to look away. She snatched the files from my hands and just as abruptly as she'd started crying, she whirled around and headed upstairs, her gait strong and determined.

I stood there in the hallway, feeling worse than before. I'd stayed up to get peace of mind about Kingston taking the fall. Instead, I ended up with more guilt, more questions. What had happened to make Lorina so upset? And had I just made everything worse?

CHAPTER 31

On Monday morning, purple crescent moons hung below my eyes after two sleepless nights. By the time I'd gotten out of bed Sunday, Lorina was already gone. I'd spent the day dialing and redialing Whitney and Chess with no answer. Their punishments were probably a lot stricter than mine, abandonment. A faint hint of coffee wafted from the kitchen, and fresh water lined the bottom of Lorina's shower—my only clues she'd come home at all Saturday night.

In English, I glanced up to see Whitney hovering over my desk. Her face was porcelain-doll perfect, and I guessed she hadn't lost any sleep over Kingston's decision.

"Heard anything?" The end of my question rose with hope.

"Only the sounds of silence from Kingston's empty room. They haven't formally charged him yet, and they have until today to decide."

If they didn't charge him, did that mean they would charge us? Maybe that was Kingston's plan all along. Name names and receive immunity. Like the witch trials.

That was the problem with trusting an enemy: you could never fully trust his motives.

When I arrived at the mock trial—held in the music room—Quinn Hart was relaxing at the music teacher's desk, leaning all the way back. She shot me a triumphant smile. Nausea swirled in the pit of my stomach. She was probably the star witness, with her photographic evidence against me. Evidence I futilely hoped was peacock bravado and not, you know, real.

Rows of chairs covered each level of three platforms carpeted in gray. Music stands in the back fenced off all of the instruments from the visiting students. Not very courtroom-like.

I tried my best to keep my posture straight and my face blank, like this was just another school assembly. Students stood between the filled seats while some occupied others' laps, all watching me with curious expressions. Do something shocking enough and everyone wants to pay attention to you. But then again, D-list celebrities had already figured out that particular key to popularity long ago. Everyone wanted to watch a fuck-up; it made them feel better about their own mistakes.

"Looks like the queen is on her throne." Whitney rolled her eyes at Quinn.

"What if . . . what if she gets me expelled?" I twisted my hands together.

"An eye for an eye." Whitney grinned.

Principal Dodgson stood by the grand piano next to the teacher's desk tapping her pen impatiently against a notebook. I approached her. "Where should I go?"

"Nowhere yet. We don't have a verdict." She uncapped her pen and scribbled on the page. No ink came out. She lifted the pen and shook it against her ear. Her eyes met Whitney's. "Are you acting as her lawyer? Otherwise, I'm going to have to ask you to take a seat in the—"

"I'm a witness."

I loved the way Whitney spoke with such confidence; it was almost impossible to question her, even when she was making up her own rules.

"Witness?" Principal Dodgson clucked her tongue. "Fine." She dug the pen into the page and etched the name like a bas-relief. "Why don't you sit behind Quinn Hart on the floor and wait for her to call you to the stand?"

"Wait, is she the . . . judge?" The blood drained from my face. I'd always thought school would benefit my future, but I was starting to wonder if maybe they didn't have my best interests at heart.

"I certainly can't be the judge. Mock trial is a student-run organization," Principal Dodgson said, like that made any sense.

"Quinn can't be impartial. She's the one accusing me."

"Well, she's the leader of mock trial." Principal Dodgson smiled and then strode—or perhaps fled—over to Quinn.

If only I were naked; then I could have written this off as a nightmare.

"This is ridiculous!" My voice was so loud most of the students turned to me. I paced a two-foot tread in the carpet. "It's nonsense! I should—"

"Calm down." Whitney lowered herself to the floor behind Quinn's desk and tugged me down with her.

I pressed my back stiff against the wall, using it like a stretcher, anything to keep me supported and steady and not jittery. Tears made a grand attempt to break through my eyes. Awesome. Crybabies only got sympathy when they were still young enough to actually deserve the term.

"This is good," Whitney said. "We can use this to our advantage."

I took a deep breath and decided to trust Whitney. After all, I had no other option right now. At least Quinn's desk kept me hidden from the swelling audience. My future of gliding-through-high-school-undetected was fading under the cold gaze of my classmates.

The last few stragglers came in, struggling to find seats in the crowd. I wished I had brought a paper bag to help control my breathing, or at least some anesthesia to help me get through this with sedation and memory loss. And only a minimal scar. Everything about me felt squeezed into limbo: between freedom and captivity, being with Chess but not being able to be *with* him, staying calm and throwing up.

Principal Dodgson called the room to order by blowing three blasts on a whistle. She unrolled a sheet of crumpled paper and read, "We are gathered here today in the presence of—"

The door to the room swung open and banged against the concrete wall. My already-rattled nerves almost splintered completely.

"Sorry. We're. Late."

The code. I snapped my head up to see Chess striding into the room, craning his neck to locate me. Kingston hung back behind him, hands shoved in pockets and a bowler hat on his head, looking almost meek compared to his usual show of bravado. Either they were both free of their respective jails . . . or they'd mastered the art of escape.

I sat up straighter, a smile so wide it hurt my cheeks.

"Someone, please stand outside the doors and make sure no one else interrupts." Principal Dodgson pointed to a boy close to the door. He scrambled to get up. The commotion triggered an eruption of whispers.

Whitney waved the boys over. Chess stepped over my legs to secure the spot next to me, and Kingston dropped next to Whitney. Quinn stared at Kingston with her mouth parted. For a moment her face stayed suspended like that, like she couldn't decide if she should be seething or excited. Seething won out and her lips descended into a scowl. He blew a kiss at her, and she folded her arms over her chest.

"You're back!" I slid my fingers between Chess's. "Illegally?" It came out harsher than I'd meant, but I was on edge, my toes curled over the side of a cliff. It was a miracle I could even speak at all.

"Long story." Chess squeezed my hand.

I blinked at him, waiting.

"Oh no. I'm keeping you in suspense just like you've been keeping me. At least until after the trial."

I knew he meant me not saying "I love you" back to him. And I would say it, but not when prompted. As Principal Dodgson continued her speech, I sank into Chess, and his hand held onto mine tightly, anchoring me.

"As I was saying, we are gathered here today in the presence of these witnesses to determine whether Alice Liddell committed several crimes against the school."

Quinn cleared her throat. "Alice broke into the teacher's lounge and stole the paper, then snuck back in later and glued sheets to every desk, making it impossible to learn anything important the teachers were saying. That was only a few days before she flooded the school, causing severe damage to both property and your education." She pointed at the audience, her arm sweeping across the room like a bad rendition of "Y.M.C.A." "Consider your verdict."

"Not yet, not yet!" Principal Dodgson flashed the notebook she'd been lugging around. "There's a great deal to come before that."

"Fine, I call the first witness." Quinn opened a folder on her desk.

Whitney pressed her palm against the carpeted floor and pushed herself up.

Before she could take the stand, Quinn sang, "And the first witness is me." Quinn pushed her chair behind her and stood, as if it would make her more authoritative. "Alice has a history of crime. She tried to get the students drunk one morning."

"Scratch that from the record," Principal Dodgson said. "We analyzed the contents, and it was clean."

Quinn tsked angrily. "Okay, but Alice *forced—*" She yelled the word so loudly they could have recorded it in the soundproof studio across town. "—my friends to help with her paper prank, threatening them if they didn't."

Principal Dodgson pursed her lips. "What friends?"

"Dru and Di, but don't worry, they didn't have a hand in decoupaging the school. They managed to escape."

Yeah, only because I took the fall for them when Principal Dodgson showed up. Whitney rolled her eyes as well.

"And—" Quinn rummaged through the papers on the table and yanked one from underneath a pile. "I have proof that she flooded the school!"

Quinn held a photo of me at the dam up to the jury, one of the same ones Kingston had shown me. Hushed whispers filled the room. A dull sense of dread welled up inside me. I doubted crying "Photoshopped!" would suffice, since Quinn could barely even draw a stick figure.

"If that's not enough for you, here's Alice vandalizing my house, proving that she has it in for me. That's motive for framing me with the roses." Quinn held up another photo of me on the roof of her house.

"Bitch," Kingston mumbled under his breath but loud enough for Quinn to hear. She eyed him like she was trying to cast a love spell on him. Or a binding spell. "You stole that off my phone."

She grinned at him. "Guess we both used each other."

"Let me see those." Principal Dodgson yanked the photos out of Quinn's hand.

Chess whispered in my ear, "We won't let you get expelled. School won't be any fun for me without you."

"Likewise," I said.

"Are we speaking in adverbs? Okay, my turn. Moreover, I'm back."

"Back in school?" My heart thudded in my chest, brain too tightly wound to come up with possible explanations for his sudden return. "How?"

Chess gestured with his chin for me to pay attention. What a tease! Principal Dodgson peered at the photo, and all the lines on her face became more defined. "Well, this is certainly more evidence than I expected."

"Off with her head!" Quinn drew her finger across her neck and pointed at me.

"Not yet. Let's hear from Alice."

Quinn dropped back into her seat. "Alice. Now." She twirled her hand in the air. Well, it was more like a stabbing motion.

I scrambled to push myself off the ground and gulped in a long breath of air. Fresh air. Probably the last I'd breathe for a while because the air at my house would be stifling after my expulsion. Kingston's photos certainly ensured that.

"Why'd you flood the school?" Quinn asked me, eyes narrowed to almost the same degree as the venom in her voice. "It was all some giant environmental demonstration, right? Like, say, the ones your parents used to do?" Quinn turned to face the audience. "And I *know* none of us have forgotten her parents' Adam-and-Eve incident," she said, referring to the time they dressed up as the famous duo as part of a protest against the school.

"I didn't flood the school." Lying under fake school oath wasn't any worse than the other crimes I'd committed. I was becoming desensitized to felonies.

"Okay. Tell me, then, why were you all wet right as the flood hit? Why didn't anyone see you fall in?"

Principal Dodgson made a sound like *hmm, this is starting to fit together.*

"I fell in because I slipped. Whitney pulled me out."

"And you were behind the school because . . . ?"

"Um . . . I . . . " I fiddled with my hands in my lap, my heart beating fast. *Brain, you're usually very good about making words come out of my mouth, even when they sound stupid. Why are you failing me now?*

"Stumped you, haven't I?"

"No. I . . . I love Chess." Okay, those were not the words I was looking for. But they'd been on the tip of my tongue for weeks; they were bound to come out sometime. I knew I should probably look at him and smile or something, but I wasn't making great decisions today. As the students in the room snickered, I fumbled for a way to bring it back to the trial. "And I was . . . meeting him behind the school." Sort of true. If by "meeting him" I meant "doing a pledge task as a way to get into his group of eco-vigilantes." They were practically synonyms.

Quinn rolled her eyes. "Oh please. If that were true, he would have pulled you out of the creek like a knight in shining armor. No, you were causing the flood." She stood up and paced the floor in front of the audience like a lawyer about to reveal irrefutable evidence. "Because you were pissed because your friends wouldn't help you paper the school. This was your way to get us back for being good and wholesome. Damage the school enough and you damage our transcripts."

"That doesn't even make sense. It's ridiculous," I spat. "In fact, this whole trial is a sham."

"A sham? The facts are simple: you vandalized the school with the flood and the paper. So you should be punished."

Principal Dodgson chewed on her pen. "I'm afraid the evidence here is hard to deny."

My skin was on fire, and I fanned my hand in front of my face to cool it down.

"Expulsion is the only solution." Quinn slammed her hand onto the desk. "Court's adjourned!"

"Might not want to be so quick on that trigger." Whitney jumped up before the students could start packing their bags. "Because what I'm about to say will change your mind."

CHAPTER 32

"You like how I slipped that in?" I said when I plopped back down next to Chess, putting my all into a smile.

"Yes." He returned the smile. "But also no. Because it wasn't exactly the smartest move as far as testimonies go."

"It was a creative way to say it though, right?"

"And on the bright side, it gave you an alibi." He placed his hand on my knee. That hand was the only thing keeping me from falling apart.

Whitney dropped into the witness seat next to Quinn's desk. "I think you'll see here that only a portion of the creek crosses onto the school's property." Whitney pulled out a crumpled sheet of paper and showed it to the audience. It was a land-survey map with lines detailing property borders. "The part where the dam resides is owned by the township. If the dam was tampered with, I'm afraid it's not under school jurisdiction to prosecute a punishment."

"School property was still damaged," Principal Dodgson argued.

"Well," Whitney said, crossing her legs. "Recently the senior lounge was covered in paint. Since it's still there this morning, I'm guessing you're having difficulty getting it off the windows."

Principal Dodgson's head snapped up. "We can't figure out how to remove it, some kind of glue, and—"

"That seems like damage to school property. Are you going to expel the kids who did that, too? Or the ones who painted the roses surrounding the school red?"

"Objection!" Quinn yelled. "She's leading the witness."

"She *is* the witness," Principal Dodgson reminded her.

"Fine, objection! This has nothing to do with Alice. I move it be stricken from the record."

Principal Dodgson nodded. "Sustained, the prank was done by Neverland High. It has no particular bearing on this case."

Whitney shook her head. "You don't really believe that. And anyway, I know exactly who did it. Quinn Hart, Di Tenniel, Dru Tweedle, and a few others. I have proof, which I'd be happy to show you."

"Already in your inbox, Principal D." Kingston finger-pointed a gun at Whitney like *I got you covered.*

"Okay!" Quinn stood and circled around the desk. "Thanks, Whitney. I think it's time for our next witness!" She glanced desperately around the room. Whitney made no move to get up. "Di and Dru!" Quinn waved at the back of the audience. "You guys are the next witnesses. Go. Go!"

Both girls rose in unison, like they'd practiced this move for a synchronized-swimming competition. They both wore white scarves tied around their necks, and I immediately ached for them. Even I knew scarves like that had disappeared from the fashion radar, thrust back into the realm of been-there-done-that.

"The decoupaged desks." Whitney raised her voice, ignoring Di and Dru's approach to the stand. "Alice couldn't have done it because I know who did."

"Principal Dodgson, if she says me, she's lying. I swear!" Quinn held up her hands in a way that made her look guilty even though she was completely innocent in that crime. "I didn't do anything wrong."

"You did. Unless you consider the paint in the senior lounge to be school-sanctioned. But anyway the decoupage wasn't you; it was me. Only me." Whitney leaned back in her seat, completely relaxed with the prospect of getting in trouble. Di and Dru paused in the middle of the room, probably unsure whether they still needed to claim their fifteen minutes of high-school fame.

The crowd erupted in whispers. Too bad they hadn't dozed off like they did in class, but I guess this trial was intriguing in a half-to-watch kind of way. Water-fountain material for tomorrow.

Principal Dodgson tilted her head. "Whitney, are you confessing to vandalizing the school?"

"I'm telling you the truth. I decoupaged the desks. Quinn and her friends trashed the senior lounge."

"Alice flooded the school," Quinn added. "Let's not forget that."

Principal Dodgson waved Di and Dru forward. They reluctantly climbed the rest of the way to the front, stumbling over seated bodies. "Girls, is this true?"

Whitney strutted back to her seat next to me. She smirked when she sat down. "You're welcome. I highly doubt they're going to expel all the goody-two-shoes losers involved with the prank, especially not someone who kisses as many butts as Quinn."

I wanted to thank her. I wanted to tell her how impressed I was with her. But I knew words couldn't even begin to convey the gratitude I felt. I wrapped my arms around her in a tight hug. She stayed still and rigid for a moment but then returned the hug. A second later she wiggled out of my arms.

"Well, that's one way to make Chess jealous," she said with a smirk. "But I don't swing that way."

"I know."

Chess nudged me with his shoulder. "I'm waiting for you to deny it, too."

"It would explain my silence for so long, wouldn't it?" I joked.

"Dinah?" Principal Dodgson prompted. "Is this true?"

Di lifted her eyes from the floor. "Yes."

"No!" Dru's eyes widened. "No how."

"Di means no," Quinn clarified. "Alice Liddell and Kingston Hatter pulled the prank. No one else, certainly not me. Right, Di? The photos Kingston sent you are fakes."

"Oh," Kingston shouted. "But the red paint splashed all inside your locker is what? Art project gone wrong? Funny thing that you don't even take art."

"It was planted in there." Quinn narrowed her eyes at him. "By you."

Kingston shrugged and winked at the three of us. Well, at least one of Quinn's accusations had turned out to be true.

"Order! Order! Let's get back on track. Di, you said yes. I'd like to hear more."

"If Alice did the flood, she didn't mean any harm by it. She was trying to save the dry field." Di's voice was shaky and quiet, though the whispering crowd was beginning to drown it out. I leaned forward to hear better.

"What her motivations were is unimportant compared to the crime itself."

"I know that," Di said. She turned and met Quinn's eyes. "I'm sorry, Quinn, Dru. I don't feel comfortable lying."

"She means lying for Alice," Dru said. "Alice paid her off to confess."

"Contrariwise, Alice tried to warn me against doing the prank. She was looking out for me." The volume of Di's voice rose an eighth note.

"No how. She wanted you out of the way."

Di ignored her. It was weird to see her be her own person again. "I can't, in good conscience, be responsible for getting someone expelled who doesn't deserve it. She may have done the flood, but I *know* she didn't do any of the painting. We did." She pointed at the other girls as well as Kingston.

The room broke into intense whispers.

"Off with your head! You're done!" Quinn waved her hand at Di dismissively. "You too, Dru."

Dru held up her hands in protest. "But I—"

Di tugged her friend away to the back wall near me. If I hadn't been shocked into silence, I might have hugged Di for helping me out. But then I heard her whisper to Dru that if Kingston really did send the evidence in, they'd be in trouble no matter what. Confessing might get them a lesser sentence. Good thing I hadn't wasted the hug.

"It's always the ones you don't keep in their place that fuck you over," Kingston mumbled.

"Jail. Expulsion," Whitney said. "One more and you've got a nice collection."

"At least we're going down with you?" I attempted to joke, complete with a half-smile. Humor didn't really work to cheer me up, though.

Principal Dodgson clapped her hands to restore order. "I think there's only one option here."

Quinn coughed *expel Alice* under her breath.

"Alice, you're ex—"

I squeezed my eyes shut and flattened Chess's hand in my own with my grasp.

"—extra lucky you're not the only one who damaged this school. And though I would like to cut down on those crowded classrooms, I can't expel this many students."

I loosened my grasp on Chess, then brought my other hand over to pinch the flesh on my wrist. Just to make sure I hadn't imagined it.

"It's only fair that everyone receives the same punishment for the same crime," Principal Dodgson continued. "So, Alice, Quinn, Dinah, Dru, Kingston, Whitney, and anyone else found to be involved in the damage to the school will be suspended for the rest of the week."

A collective groan escaped from the class. Quinn rose from her seat. "What? That's unfair! That's . . . that's . . . nonsense!"

"Would you rather take expulsion?"

Quinn let out a sniffle, then tried to scramble away from the desk in such haste that she tripped over the leg of the chair and crashed to the ground.

A frenzy of packing up bags began. Students herded to the door, a mass of people forming near the exit. The small entryway was unable to funnel so many people at once.

Whitney stood up and put two fingers in her mouth, whistling loudly enough to make everyone stop and look up. "Don't forget, the first Eco Club meeting starts in ten minutes in Mr. Hargreaves's room. If you want details, you better show."

That seemed to get everyone's attention. The talking increased, taking on an excited tone.

"I'm afraid I haven't condoned the organization of such a club," Principal Dodgson said.

"You told us the other day that we had to get a teacher to sponsor it. I did. Mr. Hargreaves."

Principal Dodgson pursed her lips. "Well, I'm going to have a talk with him about the appropriate conduct of such a club."

I tugged on Whitney's pant leg. "What are you doing? We're suspended, remember?"

She grinned. "The way I see it, the suspension starts tomorrow. Might as well use our new flooding-the-school and damaging-the-desks infamy to our advantage."

CHAPTER 33

"Okay . . . so how'd you get back here? And are you really enrolled in Wonderland High?" I may have been suspended for four days, but that didn't mean I couldn't distract myself with excitement over Chess's presence and Kingston's apparent freedom, now that I could fully appreciate it.

Chess interlocked his fingers with mine, letting me pull him into a standing position. "Kingston should explain first, because my explanation won't make sense without his." Chess gestured with his chin to the packed courtroom, everyone still filing out. Most watched us as if we might do something rash and put on a good show. "But maybe we should take this someplace more private first."

The four of us got in line with the rest of the crowd and dodged questions from the reporter-wannabes. As soon as we broke free of the confines of the classroom, Whitney waggled a hand to follow her. We rounded a corner and I slowed my pace, tugging on Chess's sweater. I pushed him into the shadow of a doorway until his back pressed against the wooden door. I aligned my body against his, slipping into the dark recess between the door and the wall, if only to gain a tiny bit of privacy from watchful eyes. I hoped Kingston would have thc self-preservation to turn away. He shouldn't have to see this.

"Are you going for kidnapping? Need a new goal after not getting expelled?"

"Not the worst idea in the world, kidnapping you. But no. Mostly I wanted to do this before I forgot." I cupped my hands behind his neck and pulled him closer to me.

He leaned away and scoffed. "You were afraid you might forget?"

"Well, you did," I said. He raised an eyebrow. "Hey, I said I love you in there. I deserve a kiss. But no, you just wanted to go somewhere private. And not for this reason."

He laughed. It was adorable, almost as attractive as his serial-killer smiles, the ones that immobilized me on attack.

I whispered into his ear, "I don't want to make the same mistake."

He sank his mouth into mine, finishing the kiss we'd started. I didn't want it to end—after all, we had a week of lost time to make up for—but I knew when I pulled away that it wasn't an ending.

"Any other distractions I should know about?" Whitney asked from her perch against a locker when we returned. A giddy smile erupted on my face, making me look like I'd just swallowed a little too much laughing gas at the dentist.

Kingston, on the other hand, studied the floor like he might be able to see a magic eye in the spotted linoleum.

"Okay, King. Spill." Whitney propped one foot against the locker, launching herself off the wall. "I've already deduced from your presence that you haven't been arrested. I'm good at riddles like that."

That made him laugh. "Well, try this one then." Kingston caught up to Whitney in one quick stride. "What's my one superhero talent that got me off scot-free?"

"You pleaded insanity." Whitney stomped off down the hallway, plowing right through other people's paths like they didn't exist. The few students lingering jumped out of the way. I wondered how many of them had gone to the meeting . . . or gone home. A girl from my homeroom traced her eyes over us, cell pressed to her ear, but she'd stopped talking and I could hear the fuzzy mumbling of "Hello? Hello?" on the other end of the line.

My focus shifted back to Kingston, who was scowling. "I couldn't make it that easy on them."

"Snooping?" Whitney guessed.

"Close."

"Blackmail?" I tried.

He grinned, clearly proud of himself. It was kind of weird to be celebrating that.

"You blackmailed the township?" Sweat gathered along the back of my neck. That didn't seem like the safest move. Not when the township had a habit of quickly rezoning or raising taxes to get what they wanted . . . plus, the exceptional talent of covering it all up. They may have let Kingston go free, but only until they could calculate their next chess move.

"I know. I'm badass. You can create a shrine in front of my locker." Kingston snickered. "But seriously, don't use anything with the color yellow. I promised the bees I'd avoid it, and I don't want to piss *them* off."

"That was the *seriously* you meant?" Whitney said. "Not, *seriously* this is why I'm not in jail?"

"The stipulation about the yellow was important, too. But if you must know, I simply explained the situation to Alice's sister and her boss. They made me sick, essentially killed my mom and Chess's mom, and covered it all up. Then I suggested the citizens of Wonderland might be interested in knowing some of the land here is contaminated."

A chill slammed into my body, freezing the sweat that had been collecting on my skin. It hadn't occurred to me that more people might get sick. Specifically, people who used to live on the contaminated farmland and called themselves my boyfriend. "We need to let them know!" Images flashed through my brain of overcrowded hospitals, flummoxed doctors scratching their heads, newspaper obituaries expanding their one-page sections. More teenagers orphaned by the unholy acts of our town officials. "If it's dangerous—"

"It's not," Chess said as we rounded a corner. No one lingered in this hallway, but heavy chatter carried from a classroom in the distance. I studied him, analyzing the calm tone of his voice in my hazy, fear-laden brain. "Not anymore at least. That, apparently, was the main reason they rezoned the land and drove people away, not the leak. As part of the cover-up, but also to get houses off the bad land and protect the citizens. The nuclear-power plant was shut down. There's a parking lot and a highway on the contaminated land instead. That new housing complex is on the only part of the farm that wasn't affected."

Relief seeped out of my mouth in a yoga breath. "But what about you? Are you sick?"

"I went to the doctor today. So far so good." Chess rubbed the stubble of his jaw. "I'll keep getting tested every few months."

My muscles relaxed. He was going to be all right. For now.

Kingston held up a finger. "Hey, we'll get to that in a sec. It's still my turn to show off my brilliance."

"That's it?" Whitney asked, heels clicking like a tap dancer. "You spewed some loose-lipped threats and their knees buckled?"

Kingston ran a hand over the stubble poking out of his scalp. "No, first Alice's sister brought proof that my story was legit and stuck by me." He turned to me. "I guess we really did take the wrong files, right, Alice?"

"Your fault."

"Thanks, by the way. For giving her the right one. It let me up the ante and demand the township pay for my medical bills, too." He flashed all his teeth at us.

Lorina had . . . defended him? Why? My brain frantically calculated complicated algebraic equations, but something wasn't adding up.

"Your sister convinced her boss that it would be cheaper to pay my bills than to go through all the legal stuff. Done and done. Okay, Chess, your turn now."

But Kingston was just one person. If so much land had been compromised, it was possible others had gotten sick, too. Dread settled into my stomach, burrowing a deep hole. They deserved compensation as well.

"Let me guess," Whitney said. "Your dad had U-Haul on speed-dial, waiting for the 'action!' command, and as soon as he found out it was safe in Wonderland, he made the call."

"Not exactly. We're not moved back yet."

We reached Mr. Hargreaves's classroom, chatter spilling and drowning out Chess's voice. We huddled around our quarterback so we could hear the play-by-play better. Kingston stepped closer to Whitney, and I squeezed into the space between him and Chess.

"I mean, this all happened today. He's checking into a motel right now until we find something more permanent. Showering at home, it's a luxury."

I couldn't stop the smile from spreading across my lips. "What about his job?"

Chess started to speak, but his attention was diverted over my shoulder toward the classroom. The three of us spun around to see . . . Lorina poking her head out.

All the happiness I felt dropped to the floor, weighing down my shoulders.

"I thought I heard your voice, Alice." She didn't sound angry with me. She didn't sound happy either. Her stoic face was mannequin-blank.

I dropped Chess's hand and walked toward her, fighting off the panic building inside me. "What are you doing here?"

"Kingston told me you were having a meeting. I figured your Eco Club might be interested in helping with the farmers' market. I could really use it."

I glanced from Kingston to Lorina, mouth parted, brow furrowed. This all must have been some cruel joke.

"I was just about to tell Alice about my dad's new job," Chess said.

"You guys should really go inside," Lorina said. "The crowd's getting restless."

No one moved. We were all waiting for the cliffhanger resolution. "You go, Whitney," I said. "You really should be president of this thing." She deserved it.

"I want a full recap of the rest. I'm talking details here, not just summary." She backed into the classroom.

"I've already heard this, so . . . " Kingston followed her, probably to get away from being the third wheel to Chess and me. Then he poked his head back out. "Wow, either half the school's really into the Going-Green trend or they're hoping this is going to be a press conference Q-and-A with juicy gossip."

I couldn't help grinning, even though I knew the latter was more likely. "Whitney will reel them in!" And hopefully inspire them to actually join the club, instead of use it to find out more details about the school pranks. Once Kingston disappeared inside, I turned to Chess and my sister. "Your dad's new job?"

"He joined enemy ranks."

Lorina pursed her lips. "Don't say it like that. I hired him, and *I'm* not the enemy." Her voice was firm. "I got him a position in the Parks and Rec department. He'll be working with my department—with me—to start a farmers' market. He has contacts with the farmers left in the area, and he'll know what kind of produce to order. I'll make sure the market is safe and operating legally. Plus, having him there will mean I won't work such long hours." She looked pointedly at me. I swallowed hard. I knew my days of easy sneak-outs were over. But at least it seemed like she condoned the Eco Club. I clung to that.

And also, she could ground me at home, but there were plenty of opportunities for kissing at school.

"I don't understand. When did—how—why is there a farmers' market all of a sudden?"

"My boss was impressed with my work. I mean, I solved the case for him *and* kept it quiet from the public. So I showed him your petition. He was . . . surprised by the amount of signatures."

The petition worked! My legs itched to jump up and down, but I restrained myself. Note to self: gloat to Whitney later. Sometimes the right way was the right way. All our illegal efforts backfired—well, except for maybe the breaking-and-entering one, though that wasn't a performance I wanted to repeat—but the one that worked was the one we did without unlawful intent, out in the open, flaunting instead of hiding.

"And, I kind of think he saw the creation of a farmers' market as another way to distract the community, give them what they want so they don't realize what was taken away."

Another way to cover their tracks. I felt sick. "But . . . why would you do that for me?" I didn't deserve it. Not at all.

Chess rubbed my shoulder, trying to comfort me, but what I wanted right now was a hug from my sister. Confirmation that our relationship wasn't as fractured as I thought, that we could still pick up the pieces.

"I had no idea what went on behind the scenes when I took that job. Your friend was homeless because of them." She gestured at Chess. "Your other friend is really sick. And I couldn't, in good conscience, continue working there unless I worked to fix their mistakes. That's why I gave Chess's dad the job, why I helped Kingston. Hopefully the farmers' market will fill a small void in the community."

I broke away from Chess and wrapped my arms around her. "Thank you, Lorina. This means a lot to me." Tears pressed against my eyes. Happy ones. Even if she hadn't done it for me, she had done it for the right reasons, and hey, it was still a victory in my book.

Her arms remained stiff for a second before she folded them around me. They weren't as tight as mine. In time, we'd work on that. "Don't think this means you're off the hook for getting suspended." She let go. "Come on, we should go inside."

Lorina disappeared inside the classroom, but Chess held me back. He leaned down to whisper, "Thanks."

It was a small word. But it meant so much. Thanks for not giving up on him, for helping to make it happen. He wouldn't get his farm back, not on the old land at least. But his dad had a job again, they'd move into a house, and slowly they'd start putting their life back together.

I glanced at him, and he smiled. In the fluorescent lights, magnified by a stray ray of sunlight, his teeth glowed, the only part of him I could see because it was all that mattered. Until I erased that, too, with a kiss. Then he disappeared completely as I closed my eyes. I knew if I opened them and went into the classroom, I'd see dull reality again: the tar highway replacing sprawling farmland; the coughs issuing from Kingston that meant more than just a simple cold; the other faceless Wonderland citizens who might be sick, too; the sister who would never fully trust me again but loved me just the same; the parents who would never see the results of anything they'd produced; and the secrets hidden beneath the careful façade the township projected.

But for now, I allowed myself to believe Wonderland had finally lived up to its name.

About the Author

Rachel Shane studied Creative Writing at Syracuse University and now works in digital publishing in New York City. She lives in New Jersey with her husband, young daughter, and a basement full of books. This is her first novel.

You can find her on the web at *www.rachelshane.com* or on Twitter @RachShane.